RIVAL HEARTS

MAGGIE RAWDON

To my readers who love a good boy.

CONTENT NOTE

A list of content information you may want before reading can be found on my website.

AUTHOR'S NOTE

Rival Hearts has a novella length prequel called *Before the Chaos*. I highly recommend reading it first as it gives you a better understanding of the family rivalry and how Madison and Quentin's relationship first started.

It takes place ten years before *Rival Hearts* when Madison goes to the family mountain home for the summer with her older brother and his two best friends.

1

M adison

I REACH FOR A.J.'s hand, and he takes mine and gives me a soft squeeze as we walk down the red carpet. The photographers shout his last name "Bernard" over and over until he turns and pauses to let them each get a good shot. He pulls me close again, looking over at me and smiling before he lifts my knuckles to his lips and kisses them. Another round of flashes goes off, and I grin brightly at him—the two of us exchanging a knowing look before we turn back one last time.

I can already hear the women in my comments on social media telling me how jealous they are that I'm his girlfriend because A.J. is take-your-breath-away gorgeous. He's six-foot-three, warm brown eyes with flecks of gold, and a smile that stops your heart in its tracks. Follow it up with the dimples and the charm, and the man is very nearly perfect. There's just one problem—he's still madly in love with his ex-wife.

Well, two problems really. The fact that we've been friends since college—the kind of close friendship that makes it impossible to see one another romantically also puts a bit of a damper on things. But it does make me the perfect foil for the gossip machine when I pose as his fake girlfriend.

A.J. takes my hand as we get into the car, helping me inside before he follows, and the driver shuts the door behind us. He glances out the window and then back at me.

"Think they bought it?" He grins.

"I think they ate it up. You dating your coach's daughter? That's all they'll be able to talk about for a while." I smile back at him, grabbing a mini champagne bottle out of the fridge to hand over and then open one of my own.

We clink the glass bottles and each take a sip. It's been a long night at this gala, and we're both exhausted. Pretending to be in a relationship honestly feels harder than being in one. Then again, I've never been married, and it's been a minute since my last real relationship.

"How is Maya?" I ask when I see him slip his phone out of his pocket and check for messages.

"She's good, I think. She doesn't talk much outside the kids. She's dating again, or at least that's what Mia tells me." His brows knit together, and he tucks his phone back into his suit.

Mia's their oldest daughter who's almost as desperate as her father to get their family back together. They filed for divorce last year, and it was finalized just before the big game. His wife definitely had her reasons. A.J.'s relentlessly dedicated to football, has been since college, and pours most hours of his life into some aspect of it. With the building stress of the end of his contract, the push to deliver above and beyond, and bring home a trophy to Chicago—it put a lot of pressure on their marriage. Too much.

"Well hopefully, an added benefit of this arrangement is that it kills the rumor mill."

He nods and takes another sip of his drink, glancing out the window as the world whirs by, and the car carries us out of downtown Chicago.

"Let's hope," he agrees. "I know it's always a risk with your dad. He's a force."

A force was a nice way to say someone with too much power and too many axes to grind. A.J. and I started this fake dating routine when he found out he lost his potential deal to go to Cincinnati. He'd been nervous after the loss and the interceptions in the championship, worried my father's infamous ability to railroad his own quarterbacks might be a problem for him too. He had his agent shopping around for potential new teams for him, and Cincinnati had eagerly reached out to start negotiating.

But then their front office had unceremoniously fired their head coach—A.J.'s biggest fan there—and suddenly any interest in bringing A.J. on evaporated. But not before several of the sports blogs had leaked information about a potential deal. If my father hadn't seen a target on his back before, he definitely did after he heard rumors that A.J. was looking to leave.

"He won't want the appearance of drama. It's one thing to railroad your own quarterback. Worse when it's a repeat offense. But inexcusable when that quarterback's girlfriend is also your daughter. The rumor mill would go wild. He just needs time to settle down after losing, and you'll be back to being his favorite again. He likes you better than his own children anyway." I nudge A.J.'s shoulder playfully.

"I do usually piss him off less." A.J. laughs.

"This is true." Especially true given my older brother Tobias's team just destroyed his to win the league last year, immediately after Tobias had basically told him to go to hell. I'm half-lost in a daydream about all our family drama when A.J. nudges me and brings me back to the present.

"Do you want to grab some dinner?" he offers.

"No. I have to get back and start packing. I fly out for Cincinnati in the morning." I already freelanced for A.J. doing PR work when he needed it, so when a job opened up there, a team my younger brother Easton already played for, I jumped at the chance. I was desperate to find something anyway after everything in Colorado had fallen apart in rapid order this spring. Something to keep me busy and pay the bills, and the PR job in Cincinnati seemed like the best fit.

"Ah yes. I forgot they're already getting you started."

"Yeah, they told me to come in and be ready to hit the ground running."

"Do you know who the quarterback is yet?"

"No, which makes me nervous. I guess they're still finalizing things and don't want to announce it yet."

"Maybe they're just going to hold tight on the second-round draft pick. It'd help them keep the cap low if they wanted to pick up some other guys."

"Let's hope. Managing a young kid out of college with a golden reputation would make my life easier."

"In some ways... in others though. So many of those guys lose their minds when they get the money and all the freedom that comes with it."

"You didn't." A.J. had married Maya shortly after signing his contract.

"Yeah, but I'm special." He flashes a grin that makes his dimples pop. "And then Maya made it impossible for me to even think about women and partying."

"Still does." I point out the obvious, and he gives me a reluctant smile. "What if it doesn't work out for you two? Do you think you'll ever date again?"

"I don't know. Hard to say with everything going on. You ever going to date again or just continue to hope for Xander?"

I give him a look and then shrug. "I'm over it. Mostly. I knew it was never going to happen, but at least as long as he was some single playboy with an inability to commit, I could pretend it was possible, you know?"

Xander Xavier is my older brother Tobias's best friend. I've had a crush on him since the first time I saw him when I was in high school. He recently got engaged to a woman I actually really like, so I've finally moved on to having no crushes and no dating prospects.

"Yeah. Well, I still say you're wasting too much of your time on work. You need your own personal life, instead of always managing everyone else's. Not that we're not grateful for it, but I'd happily be on the other side of the advice-giving dynamic here."

"Oh, I can only imagine the advice you'd give." I smirk at him.

"Hey now, I've got some good advice on occasion."

"That's not about football?" He starts to respond, but I continue on, "Or golf. Or real estate investments. Trust that I'll always come to you for those things."

"Even football? Tobias and Easton are gonna have words with me over that." He laughs.

"Quarterback things at least." I grin.

"Well, just know you have my permission to cheat. Discreetly of course." He winks at me.

"I doubt I'll need it. Frankly, this is going to make my life easier too. There's always some guy who won't take no for an answer. Sees me as some sort of in with my father and this family, and it makes me feel sick every time. With it being East's team, it would be even worse to deal with. So you'll make a nice fake-boyfriend shield against all of that."

"Glad to know I'm needed."

The car pulls up to my place, and I glance up at it. I grab his hand one last time and squeeze.

"Good luck with everything. Anytime you need me—text or

call. My dad gives you shit. You need advice on winning Maya back. I'm here, okay?"

"Same to you. And I'm serious. Maybe stay away from the football players but find yourself some recreational fun. Not all work and no play. You see where that got me."

"I'll do my best." I smile at my old friend, and we exchange a hug before the driver opens the door.

I hurry up to the small studio I've been renting. The few things I own are scattered everywhere. Half in boxes and half out. Three half-packed suitcases line one wall, and toiletries and electronics are scattered over the dining room table. As usual, I'm packing my life back into a few small boxes and my airline luggage allowance to move yet again. But at least this time I'll have Easton and my sister-in-law close at hand, and hopefully, my best friend Bea as soon as she gets back from her research trip. I might not have some great love of my life like A.J. does, but I'll have family and friends while I work on getting through this contract in Cincinnati and figuring out what's next.

2

Quentin

I'M STILL UNPACKING the last of my stuff in the loft I've purchased downtown not far from the stadium. It's the top level of a converted factory, and it feels about as welcoming as this city has been so far. I probably should hire someone to decorate and warm the place up, but I'm hoping to find a house. If I'm here for the next three years, I might as well make them count.

My phone rings, and I see my uncle's name flash across the screen. He's the reason I'm playing for the Queen City Chaos. The previous coach had been fired, he was hired, and now he's set to work, creating the locker room he wants for his vision of this team. I was his first call. It might look like nepotism on the outside, but if you knew my uncle, you'd know it's anything but. For him to call me meant one of two things: no one else wanted to play here, or I was the best person for the job. I'm still figuring out which it is.

"Hey."

"Come over for dinner in an hour." It's never a question with him. Just orders.

"I'm still unpacking." It's a weak protest—one I know he won't respect, but I make it anyway.

"Your cousins are home. You haven't spent time with your family in years. I'll see you in an hour."

There's a pause on the line, both of our wills silently doing battle. It's useless on my part. I agreed to let him have the upper hand when I came here, but it's the thought that counts.

"See you in an hour," I relent.

"Bring some wine. There's a place down the block from you that has a decent selection. I trust you can pick out a good wine."

"A good whiskey. Not a good wine. I'll ask someone there."

"They'll just try to rip you off. Especially if they recognize you."

"I'll take the risk."

"Let's hope we don't all suffer for it," my uncle muses to himself and then disconnects the line.

I'm not exactly looking forward to going out in public around here yet. Up until a few weeks ago, I played quarterback for the biggest rival team this city has ever known. They hate any player who wears the jersey, and they hate the quarterback twice as much. Coming to play here is signing up to be a traitor, and they hate me for that too. I'm fairly certain it's going to be an uphill battle just to not get booed on my first walk onto the field opening day.

But then, I have a glimmer of hope. I can't help the small smile that forms as I think about her—Madison Westfield. I can only assume she hates my guts since we haven't spoken in ten years, but she's made a name for herself in sports PR. She's a miracle worker and a fixer, which is exactly what I need right now. Someone who can take me from most-hated to most-loved in this city. I just worry that when they tell her I'm her new assignment, she's going to resign immediately.

WHEN I GET to my uncle's house, one of the twins answers the door. It's been near-impossible to tell them apart in the past, but they've got enough scars from fights on the ice now that even if their hair wasn't different, I'd still know.

"Hey, Callum." I greet my cousin when he answers.

"Hey." He nods to me, opening the door and letting me in.

"Your dad around?"

"Out on the grill. I can take the wine."

"Thanks." I hand it to him and follow him toward the kitchen. "How's the big leagues treating you?" Callum and Cillian were both drafted to pro hockey teams a few years back, and I haven't seen them since they started playing.

"The big leagues." He smirks and lets out a little laugh. "Not bad. How's coming to your own personal hell treating you?"

"Hot so far."

Cillian's sitting at the counter in the kitchen peeling garlic, and he nods to me, while his sister Winter and her mother, Elaina, are working at the stove. Winter turns around and smiles when she sees me.

"My favorite older cousin!" She closes the distance between us and throws her arms around me.

"I'm your only older cousin."

"And therefore, my favorite." She grins. "How are you? Surviving? Dad was worried they might murder you in the streets once they found out you're here."

"Just a few stab wounds on the way here. Still breathing." I grin back at her.

"I'm glad you came." Elaina smiles at me. She and my uncle David took me in as a teenager when my mom decided the latest guy she was dating promised a better life than the one she had here. She dropped me off at their door and took off for California. After a very short stint living with my grandparents, I was back with them and they were stuck raising a bitter asshole of a teenager at the same time they were raising their own young kids. It'd been trial by fire for all of us, but we managed to come out feeling somewhat like a family in the end. I lean over and hug her, and she kisses my cheek.

"Me too. Smells amazing, whatever it is."

"Fettuccini alfredo. Dave's grilling steaks outside, Winter's working on a salad, and Callum and Cillian are theoretically making garlic bread." Elaina eyes both of them like they're too slow for their own good.

"No Casimir?" I ask; the youngest of the four is the most elusive. He's been playing professional soccer in Europe for the last couple of years but allegedly was back stateside for a short while.

"Not tonight. Hopefully, in town soon. Would love to have all of you under one roof again for a night before the summer's over." Elaina smiles at me.

"Don't get your hopes up too high, Mother. Caz never likes to be pinned down, and I'm sure they're sharpening the pitchforks for Quen as we speak." Winter flashes me another devious smile and then resumes chopping the salad.

"Might need your knife skills on my side. You hire out for private blade work?" I raise a brow at her. Winter's a professional fencer, and while I don't understand a lot about the sport, she has enough medals to make it clear she'd probably be the first person you want on your side if the zombie apocalypse ever came around.

"Very funny, Cousin."

"I thought so." I shrug. "I'd better go see Coach."

"He's in a mood today," Winter warns.

"He's in a mood every day," I answer as I head out the back door.

———

"GET THE WINE?" my uncle asks when I meet him at the grill.

"Yep. Handed it off."

"Good. Good. I just put these on the grill so good timing." He closes the lid, wipes his hands, and then turns to look me over. "It's gonna be a challenge here, you know."

"I know."

"The city doesn't like you. The front office is wary but willing to trust me. Westfield is gonna be a problem, I'm sure."

"Which one?" I laugh unsure if he means my ex the new Chaos PR person or her younger brother who's about to be my new tight end.

"The one you gotta throw the ball to. If she's a problem, you probably won't have a job left when she's done with you."

"Yeah. It's a risk."

"Speaking of, I was in on a meeting with the marketing team, and they want someone on you full time. They want you to do everything in your power to try and charm the locals, and they think she can do it best. That it might even work better with her because of the animosity between our families. At first, I thought it sounded crazy, but I think it might actually make sense—she'll know best why you're hated. But they obviously don't know you two have a history beyond that. I haven't pushed back on the idea because I don't want to give them a reason to worry if we don't have to."

"I haven't talked with her in years. So I don't know how she'll react. I'd guess it's ancient history to her."

"But you? And be honest. I don't need a heart-to-heart here, but I need to know what's going on in your head. What I need to worry about."

"You used her as bait to bring me here, and I came. That should tell you what you need to know."

"Then if she doesn't balk at the idea of babysitting you, you better be on your best behavior."

"And what about you? You think you can coach Westfield's kid without bias?"

"Seems like his kids don't even like him much these days, so I guess we'll see how it goes."

I shake my head, smirking, and he returns it before he checks the steaks again. We stand in silence for a few moments, the sound of the birds and cicadas the only soundtrack before he looks up at me, something serious behind his eyes.

"I couldn't pass up the opportunity here. The ability to fix this place from the ground up. Make a legacy. We might have our own history, but I believe in you. I like your chances here. You do this right, and I think you can get a spot up in Canton."

I nod because I don't have words. It's the nicest thing he's ever said to me, and it comes with a fuckton of pressure behind it. So now I'm really hoping Madison Westfield can work a miracle because I need her in more ways than one. That's if she'll even be on speaking terms with me.

3

M *adison*

I'D COME to the practice field this morning with the best of intentions. I had snacks, forms, and information for my new players in my bag. I came ready to dazzle them all with my ability to find them the best sponsorships for the most money the market could offer. I was all set to meet the new quarterback they drafted just a short while ago and help him learn the ropes here at the Chaos.

With my brother's help and the quarterback's local roots and reputation as a tireless volunteer at youth clinics during the offseason, a charity he's already established that works to rehabilitate injured animals, and a 4.0 grade point average he earned while being one of the top draft picks this year—I'd have him with sponsorship deals lined up around the stadium and every fan wearing his jersey by the home opener.

That was until I found out that he wasn't going to be the

starting quarterback after all. Instead, they'd traded with the Pittsburgh Rivermen for their quarterback. One who came with a reputation for being disinterested in his public image, unfriendly to the media, and without a single charity under his belt despite the fact he's been in the league for just under a decade.

I also happen to know things about him not many other people do, like the fact he loves cookie dough ice cream, and leaves his would-be bride at the makeshift altar in the park without a single word. Not a letter, a telegram, or a carrier pigeon in sight. Just ten long years of silence. Apparently, Quentin Undergrove, my brother's ex-best friend and my former fiancé, is my new PR client, and I *hate* it.

I love a challenge. I spent my years in college with some of the toughest internships in the business. Ones I was able to get thanks to my family name but had built a reputation with on my own hard work. It means that now, before I even turn thirty next year, I'm known for being the woman who can fix things.

I'm the person you call when you have a problem athlete who needs to be sweet-talked, cajoled, and arm twisted into media submission. The one you bring in when things look dire and their personal life highlights on the gossip sites are outplaying their Sunday reels on the football talk shows. I'm the last line of defense against an early and bitter end to an otherwise promising career.

I've never met a client I couldn't save, but it's hard work on my part and the client's. Lots of collaboration and time spent working together. Hours of personalized media training, developing customized plans for a comeback, and my very own day-to-day hands on image and media curation. These are the things that get me contracts like I currently have with the Chaos.

And now all of those hours, all of those dedicated days of my time that involve in-depth research into a person's likes, habits, family life, and extracurriculars are supposed to be spent on my ex. A man I'd love to bury six feet under. A man whose personal life I actively avoid. A man who ripped out my heart, tore it to shreds, and made it nearly impossible for me to date or trust another guy for years. I wasn't sure I could do it.

My younger brother and the tight end for the Chaos, Easton Westfield, stands at my side as I watch Quentin throw with his quarterback coach. He's wholly unaware I'm on the field and I have no idea how he'll react to my presence here—if anyone has bothered to warn him who his new PR person is. That he'll have two Westfields to contend with. They wouldn't know our personal history, but everyone in this league knows about the animosity between our families.

"I'm sure it'll be a bitter pill for both of us to swallow," I mutter as I stare at Quentin, annoyed that he looks as good as he ever has.

"I can't believe they didn't give us a heads up," Easton grumbles.

"You know how it is when they do trade deals like this. All hush hush until it's done."

"You'd think we'd at least get a warning before he shows up on my field."

"I'm guessing Coach Undergrove knew how unpopular it would be. It's their field now. You're going to have to play by their rules."

"This team and this city love me and hate them. We'll see whose rules we play by."

Coach Undergrove was Quentin's uncle and also the new head coach for the Chaos. Easton had already been wary of that change. He'd been close with the former coach. Was looking forward to my friend A.J. being at the helm. He'd been convinced when we'd talked that this would finally be Chaos's year to go all the way.

At least until he was utterly blindsided by this—our father's nemesis being the man who decides his fate on a weekly, if not daily, basis.

"I could insist I can't work with him. That our family loyalties run too deep to make it tenable."

"Don't test your new coach. He knows you're here. I'm sure he's planning for the inevitable clash. Or at least I hope he is. He should be, or he needs his own new PR team."

"Are you going to be okay working with him? I know you needed this job after Colorado."

"I'll be fine. I've survived worse than him. Besides, it was so long ago I barely remember it." It's a lie. I remember everything and it's the last thing I need when I'm already suffering recent heartbreak over our business and investor problems.

I'd had huge plans this past winter. I was going to start my own PR firm and resort. My best friend and I had property all picked out, several investors lined up to make it happen, and a promising list of potential clients who were excited to see how we could change their careers for the better. All of it had disappeared almost overnight when we found issues with drought and wildfires were regular occurrences, and the disaster insurance and backup water solutions were all prohibitively expensive and nearly impossible to pull off.

My dreams were crushed and I'd been desperate to find somewhere soft to land. So when the position here with my brother's team had opened up and one of my best friends from college was looking at taking over as quarterback, I'd rushed to sign the contract. Even after A.J.'s position here fell through, I was planning to make the best of it. I'd happily gotten on the plane just a couple of days ago blissfully unaware of my fate. The one that involved the gorgeous, infuriating, and despicable man across the field who's just realized I'm standing here with my brother and his friends.

4

uentin

I'M STARING across the sideline as I watch Madison talking to a couple of the other guys on the team. She's laughing hard, and it's obvious she already has a rapport with them from being here before with her brother. I'm just struck by how she looks even more gorgeous than I remember her—all curves and long blonde hair. Her bright blue-green eyes and smile make my heart kick in my chest just looking at her. Even when they're not turned on me.

Madison is the kind who walks into a room, and everyone stares. She could have been a model if she wanted. Could have lived an easy life as a trophy wife, and half the football players in this league would fucking trip over themselves to be Mr. Madison Westfield. I've been holding my breath over the years, expecting an engagement announcement between her and someone I lined up across the field from, just praying it wouldn't be someone on my team or one of my former friends.

But instead, she's working PR for not great money, and she's still not married, even if she isn't exactly single. Her new relationship with A.J. Bernard has the shittiest timing, coming right before I finally get to see her again. A chance I've been waiting years for.

I suppose that's cosmic payback for taking the guy's job here. I couldn't even hate him for dating her. Bernard is a good guy, a great fucking football player, and generally well-liked by anyone who knows him—including the media. So any hope that he's going to fuck up is probably out the window. If I want her, I'm going to have to win her fair and square. Or at least, I'm going to try.

"You can look at her all you want. But if you touch her, I'll fucking break every bone in your throwing arm." I don't even have to look to know who it is. He sounds and looks enough like his brother, Tobias, that Easton Westfield reminds me of my old best friend.

"I thought you Westfields were the nonviolent sort." I give him a sidelong glance.

"I'm sure you're smart enough to stay away from her, and it won't come to that."

"I think you're going to be disappointed."

"I hope not."

"Guess we'll see."

"I'd love to see you off this team. You don't deserve the position here. Whoever thought you were better than Bernard in the front office is a fucking idiot."

"*Westfield*, hit the fucking showers, and then see me when you're done," my uncle's voice booms from behind us, dragging the attention of most of the field to where we're standing.

Easton turns to look at him, a sneer marring his face, and they have a silent but brutal, face-off before Easton heads for the locker room. My uncle's gaze falls on me next, his voice low enough that only I can hear it when he speaks.

"Don't antagonize him. When I throw him off this team, I want it to be of his own making."

I clench my jaw and nod. Fairly certain I'm going to be doing that a lot to make my way through these first few months.

"Go get some more throws in." He nods to the field.

We're only doing OTAs right now. Easy stuff to try and get everyone into a rhythm. All the new guys like me, meeting some of the vets. But the tension here is already cranked up. Because I'm an outsider, an interloper from Pittsburgh, a rival division team, who almost nobody here wants. Add to the fact that my uncle and I are coming onto a team that a Westfield has played his whole career with, and it's a recipe for disaster. I'm probably asking to be destroyed by wanting his sister to be my PR savior. When I look for her again, she's gone, and I jog out to get some reps in.

I'm the last one down to the locker room when we finish for the day, wandering in after I had a chat with the quarterback coach long after everyone else already hit the showers and went home. I've just rounded the corner when I see her standing there, arms crossed leaning against the cinderblock wall. She looks pissed—and she's obviously lying in wait for me.

"Need something?" I ask, realizing too late that in all the times I hoped to see her again, I hadn't prepared what I'd say to her when I had the chance.

"Why are you here?"

"Here?" I point to the door to the locker room. "Mostly planning to shower, get changed, and get some dinner."

"Don't be a smartass. I mean why are you in Cincinnati? Why did you come to the Chaos?"

"To play football."

She's not amused with the answer, and she pushes off the wall. She closes the distance between us, and her eyes lock on me, never wavering. The blue-green depths threatening to drown me already. In the heels she has on today, she's only a few inches shorter than me, and when her chin tilts up and her eyes narrow, it feels like if I make the wrong move, she'll tear my heart straight out of my chest.

"Leave Easton alone. You want to come for anyone else in this family, fair enough. But he's never bothered you."

"I'm not the one running my mouth about the front office."

"Because you started shit. Everyone knows Easton is the fucking kindest guy out there."

"I think you need to talk to your brother about that. Address your concerns with him."

"I'm addressing my concerns with you. Leave *my family* alone."

I take a step closer to her, smirking when I do it because as pissed off as she is with me, I see the slightest flutter of her lashes, a small bob of her throat when she swallows.

"Or what, Madness?"

"I'll give you a reason to call me that name." She brushes past me, and I turn to watch her walk away, the click of her heels on the concrete echoing in the empty hall as she leaves.

5

M adison

I'VE NEVER BEEN SO close to throttling someone as I am Quentin Undergrove right now. I'm used to clients who are pains in the ass. I've had my fair share of dustups with coaches, management, and players who can't seem to handle easy-to-grasp concepts like "don't be a dick to your teammates." But when I have to balance defending my baby brother, a new job, and confronting an ex—it's been a long day, and I'm ready for comfy clothes, a glass of wine, and some time curled up binge-reading my latest book series. As I grab my things out of the office, the head of the Chaos marketing department pops her head in, and I can tell from the look on her face, I'm not getting away just yet.

"Could we chat for a moment?"

"Sure."

She closes the door behind her and motions for me to sit as she takes a seat in the chair on the other side of my desk.

"As you know there have been some pretty big changes since we initially brought you on. One of them being the quarterback position."

"Yes." I nod when she pauses.

"He's as much of a risk as he is an asset to the organization. I don't think I need to tell you that."

In more ways than one, I know exactly how much of a balance between risk and asset Undergrove is. But we don't need to be airing my dirty laundry here today.

"I'm aware he has some messy off-field history, and of course, Cincinnati fans aren't thrilled to have what Pittsburgh thought would be their franchise quarterback playing here. It's awkward at best."

"Potentially threatening to the brand at worst. The reaction on social media has been worse than we predicted. His devil-may-care attitude isn't playing well with fans who were excited for our drafted quarterback or those that were hoping for someone more like... well more like Bernard." She gives me a tight-lipped, awkward smile, and I nod because we're talking about my supposed boyfriend. I can't say too much.

"A.J. did seem like he would have been a better fit, regarding temperament, for the team. But I assume management has good reasons for their decision."

"They do, and of course, Coach Undergrove was part of that decision-making process as well." Her way of saying nepotism was involved without saying it. I nod again.

"So, with all of that, we need someone focused on Quentin full time. Rehabbing his image, making sure he's involved in things in the city—charities, groups, events, local businesses. It all has to be part of the campaign to show he's invested here. He also really needs to overhaul his social media. It's certainly the kind of content that played well with a rougher team, one with more edge that plays the kind of football his former team enjoyed. And definitely plays well with his female fans. But we need him to appeal to families. To season ticket holders. We want people buying Undergrove jerseys and rooting for him in the stands. The team has invested a lot of money, and it's imperative this first year is a productive one. On all fronts." She gives me a meaningful look.

"I understand. Is there some way I can help with that?" Just saying the words puts a bitter taste in my mouth—saving the man who broke my heart and now seems to want to bait my brother into trouble he's never had before.

"Yes. That's why I'm down here. The more we talked about it, we really feel like he needs someone full time. Someone who can monitor and run his social media, keep his social calendar, make sure he makes it to events—on time and looking like he's excited to be there, helps connect him to organizations and people in the city."

"He needs a babysitter," I say flatly.

"Essentially. Of course, we'll paint it like you're just an assistant trying to help make his life easier and pave a path forward for him here. We don't want him to feel like he's being smothered. Those guys never handle that well." The bitter taste in my mouth worsens.

"I see."

"We think you're the right person for the job. You've handled difficult personalities before, and you come from a family who's been through their fair share of challenges in the last year. So you're well-versed in the game. I know it'll be a challenge given the tense nature of the relationship between your two families, but I wonder if we might not be able to smooth that out a bit in the process. Maybe the two of you finding common ground to work together would be an asset to other people in your family."

So news of Easton's trouble has already spread, and I'm

being called to bring all the boys and their tempers to heel. Lovely.

"I understand."

"Are you up for it? We can give you additional resources if you need them. Possibly even an assistant if he proves to be a lot of trouble."

"I do have a close associate I normally work with when I have particularly difficult clients. Beatrix Xavier. She has a similar record to mine—and she's familiar with Undergrove and his former team in Pittsburgh."

"I'll see what I can do."

"Thank you. And I'm looking forward to the challenge." It's a lie. But I need this job, and I don't want my brother's career going down in flames because of Undergrove. So I'll have to find a way to look forward to it.

WHEN I FINALLY GET TO my rental car I want to cry. One of the tires is flatter than flat. Practically pancaked to the ground. East is long gone after I told him to get home and take my sister-in-law, Wren, to dinner to forget about today. So now I'm stuck trying to find the right number for the rental company to have someone out here to fix it. I feel a swell of panic in my gut. It's just another straw on a rapidly growing pile. Between watching my brother get lectured by Coach Undergrove and dealing with Quentin's attitude, I'm questioning why I came here at all. Why I ever thought this was a good place to be.

I open the door and collapse in the driver's seat, kicking off my heels temporarily and dangling my feet out the door. It'll get too hot if I close it and there's no sense in wasting gas trying to run the air conditioning.

Everything gets profoundly worse only a few moments later

when I see Quentin come out of the same exit I did, freshly showered, and heading for his car. I'm praying he doesn't look this way and see my predicament, but I have zero luck today. Absolutely none at all because he looks directly at me and almost immediately clocks the issue with the car, turns on his heel, and marches straight for me.

"Flat tire?" he asks as if it isn't obvious.

"Yes. I'm calling the rental company to see if they can come out to fix it. I'm just on hold."

His brow raises. "Pop the trunk."

"What?"

"Pop the trunk. I'll see if there's a spare."

"I'm sure there's a spare."

"You need the spare on if you want to drive out of here."

"I'm aware."

"So let's see if you've got a jack to get the job done. If not, I've got one in mine."

"I've never changed a tire in my life."

"I assumed. Which is why I'm doing it."

"You are not changing my tire."

"Why not?"

"About a million reasons, starting with the fact that you shouldn't be risking injury to your hands and ending with the fact that we just had an argument."

"You mostly argued with yourself there. I did very little talking." He has the audacity to smirk.

"Nevertheless. There was a heated argument."

"That? A heated argument?" He glances back in the direction we both came from like he's revisiting events. "I don't think so. That was just foreplay. I figured you were gonna bite a few times before you settle down." His eyes run over me with amusement.

"You—" I struggle to find the right words.

"Excuse me." He leans forward, his arm brushing against my bare leg as he pulls the trunk lever, and I hear it click. His eyes slide to the side, self-assurance sparkling in them, and then he walks around to the back of the car. Meanwhile, my heart is pounding in my chest and goosebumps spread in the wake of his touch. I do not need goosebumps from Quentin Undergrove right now—or ever—but especially right now when I'm trying to prove I can handle him.

"You've got a jack and a spare. If you want to hop out, I can get this done pretty quick."

"I'm calling the rental company," I insist, but I'm still on hold, listening to music, occasionally interrupted by a robotic voice that tells me reps are helping other people but will be with me any moment. They needed to choose this moment. Hurry the hell up.

I get out of the car though, less to let him jack it up and more to tell him to put the things back in the trunk. But when I reach him, he levels me with an incredulous look.

"You could do that, or I could just show you, and we could get it done without you sitting around and waiting for them in a parking lot for a couple of hours. Pretty sure half your problem right now is that you're hangry, and I'd hate to see what you do to them if you go even longer without dinner."

"You're rude. Do you know you're rude?"

"So I've heard. Do you know you're stubborn?"

"I'm very aware."

"Glad we've got that covered. Now..." He pulls the tire out from under the floorboard of the back of the SUV and grabs the jack. "Let's get this done."

"If you get hurt and they blame me that you broke a nail on your throwing hand, what then?"

"You want to do it?"

"I told you. I don't know how."

"I'm surprised Tobias or Easton never showed you how. Your dad I get. I doubt he ever does anything he doesn't have to."

"I'm sure my brothers know how to change a tire. They just didn't have the opportunity to teach me."

"How is Tobias anyway? Still hating my guts?" He positions the jack and starts to crank it up while I cross my arms over my chest and try not to stress about the potential danger this poses.

"He never mentions you. He's engaged. So is Xander. Rather ironic that you're the last man standing, honestly." I say the last bit out of habit. A stream of thought I shouldn't have shared because now there's an elephant here with us. Quentin's eyes flash up to mine for a moment before he feels the same awkwardness I do.

"Xander too, huh? How long did you cry over that one?" He doesn't look at me, but I see the furrow of his brow in profile.

"There might have been some Nutella and ice cream involved."

"His future wife doesn't have a protection order out against you?"

"Very funny. Harper's lovely. I'm invited to the wedding actually. And I'm going to be a bridesmaid for Scarlett. She's Tobias's future wife." I don't know why I'm divulging all these details. Mostly I guess so we don't have to talk about our own failed wedding attempt.

"Invited to the wedding? She's living dangerously. Better have someone there to stop you when they ask if anyone has any objections." He pulls another one of the lug nuts off and adds it to the growing pile.

"He's utterly obsessed with her and has been for years. I could crawl naked into his bed, and he wouldn't notice me."

He stands suddenly, a move that brings him dangerously close to me since I'd been leaning over slightly to watch him work. His eyes catch on my face, studying me like he can read every thought I'm having about him. He smells good. Like fresh soap and cologne with just that little bit of him at the end. I didn't realize how much I miss it until it's right there, impossible to ignore.

His voice is rough when he speaks again. "I've got to get a tool out of my truck. This one is stuck."

I blink and take a step back, nodding silently before he moves past me. I bite my lip and take a deep breath, closing my eyes and cursing myself for being so easily swayed by his presence. I've got to get it together. He's a client. I'm his PR rep now. The past is the past.

When he gets back, he's quiet, working silently to finish while I watch. I've got nothing to say in return because I don't trust myself not to say anything damning. Something that will give away the fact that, after all these years, I still find him attractive.

"All right. That should get her back to the rental place. I'll follow you."

"Follow me?"

"Just in case. Plus, if they don't have another car you can use, I can give you a ride back home."

I feel a little well of panic at the idea of getting in Quentin's car. It's stupid. We're going to be spending a ton of time around each other, and I might as well get used to it sooner rather than later. I just expected I'd have a little more time to adjust to being in this kind of proximity to him. Give me a moment or two to prepare. But I can survive the short drive to Easton's. It won't be that far.

"You want to get dinner somewhere after? I'm starving."

Well, shit. I have no easy reason to say no. The man just did me a favor. I've got no one else in town and no car, so I'd just be ordering something to the house anyway. If I say no it's going to sound like I'm scared to be alone with him or still harboring a grudge, both of which will make me look unprofessional considering being alone together is going to be happening a lot in the very near future. So for the sake of not losing face, I say yes.

But it's more time with him when I'm unprepared and that seems like a dangerous prospect.

uentin

"So when does Tobias get married?" I ask when we've peeled through all the usual niceties of the weather and water cooler discussions about work.

"They're still working out a date. His fiancée wants to take time planning it, and he just wants her to have the ring on her finger. It's kind of adorable honestly, to see him fall like that. I mean... you know how he was." She's managed to relax enough that she's stopped talking to me like I'm a complete stranger.

"Yeah. I gotta say, that doesn't sound like the Tobias I knew, but then, that was a long time ago." I stumble ahead even though I know I'm falling forward into a whole sea of awkwardness by mentioning the past and her brother given that our relationship is what ended my friendship with him. So I change the subject to something even more awkward. "And you and A.J.?"

"Me and A.J.?" She laughs nervously.

"When are the two of you walking down the aisle?" Inquiring minds want to know.

"Uh. I don't know. He'd have to propose first, and it's very new."

"Harder on you both now that he's not here, I imagine."

"It's not easy."

"He's all right with you working with me though?"

"Of course, why wouldn't he be?"

"I took his job." I had his girl. I'm not going to touch that though. At least not yet.

"He knows how this world works. We knew it was a possibility when we found out Coach Nelson was fired. Your uncle moves in and brings you on board. Not exactly shocking."

"A little shocking for this team to bring me on. But I guess that's why you're here."

"We just have to work on your image. We'll get it figured out. They'll all love you by the time I'm done."

"Not gonna try to secretly sabotage me? Open your boyfriend's spot back up here?"

"No. I'm perfectly capable of doing my job professionally, but if you'd rather have someone else on the team, I'm more than happy to step aside and work on other aspects of PR. This wasn't my choice."

"I want you."

Her eyes flick up to mine, and I realize the way I just phrased that.

"You're good at your job. I know that."

"How would you know that?"

I guess this isn't a good time to say that I'm stalkerish enough to have followed her a bit. At least the bits that make it into the public eye, or when I've crossed paths with people who have worked with her.

"I've played with a couple of guys you've worked with. You

and Bea. You two have a reputation. I'm surprised she's not here."

"She's coming. We've got another project we're working on, and she's doing some research on that right now, but my boss implied it was a possibility. If it is, I'm planning to bring her. I didn't know you knew her that well." She eyes me carefully.

"She dated one of the guys I used to play with for a while. Saw her sometimes at the parties. Went out to dinner a couple of times with them."

"Oh yeah. I guess I knew that. Her and Rob. She didn't mention you went out together though, so I didn't think about it."

"Probably not memorable enough to mention." I shrug. I can't imagine Bea would want to bring my name up with the woman who hates me. Especially if she was going on double dates with me and other women.

"Are you dating anyone now?" she asks as she goes to take a sip of her drink.

"No."

"I haven't had time to create a dossier on you yet." Answers my question about whether or not she follows news about me.

"Should I be worried?"

"I think I ask you that question. Especially if there's no girl-friend at your age. Am I just going to find a long list of women ten years younger than you who you've been 'spotted out with'?" Her brow goes high.

"I don't look myself up or watch my press, so I don't know."

"But the lack of an emphatic *no* means it's possible."

"I've dated around here and there in the past."

"No steady girlfriend? No marriages or kids?"

"No."

She grimaces.

"What's that for?"

"Peter Pan syndrome."

"What?"

"Nothing. It'll just make it more challenging but nothing we can't overcome. Do you have a therapist?"

"A therapist? No. Am I going to need one after this?" I try to joke.

"I think they're good for guys like you. With the image problems. Usually, there are some underlying causes you could be working on. Plus, it's good if you're the type who gets the yips."

"Don't say that word."

"The fact that you're scared of the word tells me you need a therapist. I'll ask around and get some names."

I feel like I'm being hit by one pass rusher after another with every sentence deeper we get into this conversation.

"I feel like maybe you should do your research first. I'm really not that bad."

"Good. Then the therapist will put you on maintenance sessions quickly, and it'll be more time we can spend at fundraisers and community projects. Maybe even get you some wholesome sponsorships instead of whatever you have going on now."

"Fuck me," I mutter.

"What?"

"You're like being hit by a fucking tornado."

"Do you want this or not? Because this is just the start. I'll have a long list for us to work on. I'll get started on it tonight, and we can get working on it immediately. No use in wasting time."

"I want it." Mostly I want her, but I didn't realize exactly how much torture I was signing up for to get the chance. One that seems increasingly slim given the icy reception.

"Okay good. We should probably find you someone to date then too."

"What?" I nearly choke on the sip of the drink I just took.

"It doesn't have to be serious. But if you're deep into that whole bachelor thing... it's not going to work here like it did before. People here want their franchise quarterback. Someone invested in the community and the team. Better if he has a wife who can help run the charities and kids in the local school district."

"You remember I'm a quarterback and not trying to be a senator, right? I know you got Xander and me confused there for a while."

"There's no confusing the two of you." She levels me with a look that's devoid of all humor.

"Sorry. I forgot he's a sensitive subject for you right now. In mourning and all."

She ignores me and charges on.

"Speaking of sensitive subjects. Any women likely to show up with stories to tell or surprise sons you don't know about?"

I cough again. "Are you serious?"

"I need to know where all the skeletons are buried if we're going to do this right. Surprises won't help either of us. If I know, we can plan for it."

"I thought we were going out to dinner to catch up."

"Isn't that what we're doing?"

"I don't recall asking you about skeletons buried in your closet and secret children."

"Easy. I have neither. You did ask me if I was getting married to my boyfriend, which isn't a very nice thing to ask a woman about to hit thirty. Our mothers ask that enough."

"I didn't mean it like that... I just meant, your brothers getting married before you is not what I pictured."

The look she gives me next lets me know I'm jumping from one icy puddle into another. Possibly a lake this time.

"You're bad at this. I see why you're single now. We'll have to work on that."

"I didn't mean it like that. I just meant I thought you'd get married a lot younger. Have kids."

It was definitely a lake, with a hole underneath it. One I was digging fast.

"Yes well, as we've already established, Xander didn't come through like I hoped, and I have terrible taste in men outside of that." She stabs a cherry tomato on her salad, and it might as well be my heart with the way it feels to hear her say it. But then I perk up. Because if you're in a happy relationship you don't normally describe your taste in men as terrible.

"Minus A.J.?"

I see the slightest flutter of her lashes.

"Yes, of course. Minus him. He's amazing, and I adore him."

And that's a lie. Because I know what Madison sounds like when she's in love, and that's not it.

"Well... I'm glad to hear it. Hopefully, he's not too hurt by you being so sad over Xander. I hope he's not the rebound."

"He is not the rebound."

He's definitely the rebound. At best. At worst, he's a toy she's playing with because she's twenty-nine, and I'd guess her parents are hearing that clock tick louder than ever now that Tobias is doing the unthinkable. Probably already lining up prospects and shoving them her way in hopes her father can get half a football team's worth of grandchildren out of his kids. Secure his legacy for the entire century. It was all he really cared about at the end of the day.

"Back to the subject at hand. Have you done PR relationships before?"

"No." I frown.

"Are you open to it?"

"Not really."

"You should consider it. The right pairing? It could help your image." She flicks a glance at me before she takes another bite.

"I don't think I have time for PR relationships."

"You should make time for whatever makes you a success

here. Part of that is having the fans on your side. And right now, they're not loving the decision. They all had hopes about who their next QB would be, and not many of them wanted to see him come off the team this city hates the most."

"I'm aware."

"Okay. I'm at least going to talk to some of my connections. See if there are any movie stars or singers who might be interested in dirtying up their image a little." She pulls her phone out of her purse. "Which reminds me, how bad are your feeds?"

"How bad?" I frown again.

"Lots of thirst traps and pictures of you working out? Or some of you and your family? Maybe a few of you doing some local charity work back in your former city?"

"There's a few in there from events."

"So thirst traps and gym photos then." She sighs. "That's okay. We'll be working on cleaning that up."

"I have some sponsorships that require it."

"The thirst traps or the gym photos?

"The gym."

"Mmm. We'll get you some new ones. I doubt those are very lucrative anyway."

"I don't want to do sponsorships for things I don't use or don't do."

"Noted. I'll need a list of your hobbies then."

"Jesus."

"What?"

"This feels like the most aggressive online dating questionnaire I've ever experienced in my life."

She smiles. "Do a lot of online dating do you?"

"No, but you know what I mean."

"Good. That would just create more headaches. If these are your public profiles, God knows what you'd put on one of those." She flashes a smirk, and I shake my head.

"I remember when you were nice."

"Nice doesn't save your career. Just count yourself lucky fate put me on your side."

"Oh, I am."

So fucking lucky. This woman's going to be mine again, whatever it takes. If she wants me to complete a list, jump through flaming hoops, and march to the beat of her drum— I'm doing all of it. No matter how much it hurts.

7

M adison

WHEN I OPEN the door to the guest cottage, I take one step in before I stop dead in my tracks. The dining room table, kitchen counter, coffee table, and pie safe are all covered in flowers. Huge all-white bouquets, one with roses, another with lilies, another with mums and gladioli. The whole cottage smells like a greenhouse, and there's a black envelope with silver writing set on the dining room table. My name is written on it in silver ink, so I pick it up. I pull the card out, and I don't immediately recognize the writing, but it's short.

"Condolences on the loss of the love of your life. Thought the flowers and ice cream might help get you through it. And who knows, maybe he'll get divorced someday. Love, Quentin."

I blink and read over the note again. I'm still processing it when there's a knock at the door. When I answer, it's a delivery guy with Wren standing just behind him, her face twisted with an amused grin.

"Delivery for Madison Westfield?" the delivery guy asks.

"That's me."

He holds up a giant insulated cooler. "Would you like me to put it inside?"

"What is it?"

"Ice cream."

"Um... I can take it. Do you need the cooler back?"

"No. You get it for free when you order a dozen."

I blink again and Wren's grin spreads even further, her hand going to her mouth to stifle a laugh while her eyes dance with amusement.

"Well, thank you. Can I tip you?"

"No. He covered it. Have a nice day!" he calls and then hurries off.

Wren's stifled grin floods out until she's full-on giggling at my side as she follows me in. I open the cooler and find twelve different pints of ice cream, plus what claims to be a limited-edition bowl and spoon.

"The driver came up to the house first. Just like the florist. This time I saw your car was here, so I couldn't wait to see your reaction."

"This is..."

"Sweet?" Wren raises a brow.

"Ridiculous. He's taunting me you know?"

"Taunting you how? I wondered what it was for since it wasn't your birthday or anything that I know of. It's not, right? I know pregnancy brain is getting to me, but I was pretty sure of that."

"No. You're good." I start slowly unloading the pints of ice cream from the cooler onto the counter and then into the freezer. It's at least empty enough that these might fit. "It's that he and I were talking. He asked about Tobias, and I mentioned that he's getting married and so is Xander. He knew that I had a crush on Xander. It's how we ended up together all those years ago. He sent a condolence card along with all the flowers."

"Oh... he's obsessed with you then."

"He's not obsessed with me. His family and mine hate each other. Have since the dawn of time. Or at least since his uncle and my dad played. Our run-in didn't help."

"Your run-in?" She raises an eyebrow.

"I might have been engaged to him for a nanosecond."

"Engaged?" Wren's voice goes up half an octave with the question.

"Literally for half a second like ten years ago. I thought we were in love, and my dad lost his shit when he found us in bed together."

"Kenneth found you in bed together?" Wren's eyes go wide.

"Yep. Not long after I lost my virginity to Quentin."

"Oh my god. That sounds like hell."

"It was. I still have nightmares about it, to be honest. Tobias lost his shit too, but no one beats my dad on that front."

"Mmm well, that's true."

"So I rebelled, clung to Quentin. Told him we should get married, and I'd sell everything. We'd live off the money, and I'd help fund his last college year, so he could try to go back and get off the bench."

"Oh. You *were* in love..." Wren's known me long enough to know I'm not a romantic. Not counting my outsized crush on Xander, I was exceedingly practical about all the men I dated. They were subjected to background checks, social profile investigations, put through the wringer, and any guy who showed any ounce of frivolity got the axe fast. I needed someone driven, focused, practical. I'd even take another workaholic like me. We could spend our scheduled free weekends together and otherwise do our own thing. Romance and wild ideas about running away and making do with whatever was on hand were fanciful nonsense that I don't entertain anymore. So it's probably a bit of a shock to hear I was once young, wide-eyed, and very stupid when it came to Quentin.

"Not love when he ghosts you without another word, is it?"

"Oh. Ouch."

"Yep."

"When's the last time you two talked?"

"Before I became his full-time babysitter? Not since he abandoned me. Easton didn't fill you in?"

"He said he'd let you tell me. Said he wasn't there when it all went down and only has some details through Tobias."

"Ah. Well... that's the gist of it."

"Okay... but explain how you got together when you were in love with Xander?"

"Not in love with exactly, just... crushing on. Maybe a little in love with? Ugh. I don't know. Xander just was always this perfect guy in my mind, you know?"

"I mean... I get it. I've met him. Seen how he is with Harper. I can see how someone like that would be a good match for you." She smiles as she helps me put the last of the ice cream away. "Also, are you going to share these with your pregnant sister? Because I feel like that would only be fair."

"Yes. I will share with you. You want some now?"

"I mean... I was eyeing that double chocolate pretty hard."

"All yours." I hand her the pint and a spoon from out of the drawer.

"Have I mentioned how much I love you and how you're one of the best parts of this family?"

"Once or twice." I grin at her.

I move some of the flowers out of the way, so we can sit at the table and then go back for my ice cream. Might as well enjoy it if I have to.

"So... Xander leads to Quentin how?" She waves her spoon in my direction as I sit down with a pint of cookie dough.

"So... there was limited space at the mountain house that summer. They didn't think Quentin was coming, and I had bunk beds in my room. So I offered to let him sleep in there."

"Ohhhh." She grins, and I raise an eyebrow. "What? Listen. Your brother is the hottest guy on earth as far as I'm concerned, but I've seen Quentin. All those tattoos. The chip-on-the-shoulder thing. All the brooding he always seems to be doing on the sidelines. I can see it."

She laughs, and I shake my head.

"Well... we're stuck together, and I was a huge oversharer back then. I asked his advice on Xander, and he gave me some practical feedback."

"Practical feedback, huh? Is that what we're calling it?"

"Ha! He basically told me he didn't think I had a chance and asked me why I wanted him in the first place. And I mean, I wanted Xander, but I also knew it was pretty hopeless that Xander would want me—a college girl—when he was heading off to play pro ball, and I was going off on a gap-year trip. So I just figured I might be able to get him to take my V-card before I went on my trip. Get it out of the way. Seemed like a good plan at the time, you know?"

"Makes sense. Very practical."

Wren was practical too. Part of the reason she almost didn't end up with my brother. So she at least understands the way my mind works.

"I got into a discussion with Quentin about my reasoning, and he was giving me a hard time about not being focused on the right things and just very... I don't know. Sweet about it all, I guess?" I scrunch my nose up as I remember the Quentin I'd known that summer. He was different than the brooding guy everyone else knew. More relaxed. More open. Incredibly sweet and so patient with me.

"Sweet, huh?" Wren echoes my thoughts.

"Yes. We were alone together and one night, one thing led

to another and..." I shrug.

"And? That's it? That's all I get?"

"And... he was very sweet. Very attentive. Frankly, it was a mistake that I fucked him first because other guys were not nearly as attentive or thoughtful after him. Felt like I'd been ripped off, to be honest."

"Oof. That sucks. I had the opposite. A lot of selfish jerks who I'd gotten used to before your brother. Then he was so sweet, I could barely believe it. Figured it was just part of his charm act."

"Right. I wasn't sure what to make of Quentin either." I take another bite of ice cream off the spoon as I look around at the flowers. "Then or now, to be honest. I feel like I'm in over my head with him."

"Because you still have feelings for him too?"

"No. He's attractive. Very attractive. But all of that was years ago. I've changed. Grown up. I don't need a train wreck in my life."

"Well, it seems like you've got one whether you want it or not. It's going to be an uphill battle to get him to stay in shape." She smiles at the flowers. "And he has a pretty impressive charm offensive too."

"Charm." I huff. "More like rudeness. I mean, say I was really bothered about the Xander thing. All of this would just be salt in the wound."

"Yes well, I think that's what he's trying to figure out."

"Plus, I have a boyfriend."

"Ah yes. How is A.J. doing? Still missing his ex-wife?" Wren knows this whole bit with A.J. is fake. She and Bea have to or they'd both think I was crazy and try to talk me out of it. Because the man is very obviously still in love with his ex-wife. Any woman really dating him could only have hopes of being a rebound, and even then, it'd be disappointing.

"Yes."

"I'm sure she hates your guts."

"If she does, she hasn't said. But that is rather the point. Or part of it anyway." I'm hoping that a bonus of our fake dating will be his ex-wife realizing what she could be losing.

"Has your dad said anything?"

"He's made remarks in passing. He's not happy about it. But not enough to start anything—which again, is the point. I mean, A.J. was his golden child before the championship game. Could do no wrong. He might have been excited about it in a different timeline."

"But then he lost, and then he went looking for a job elsewhere."

"Yes, well... We're hoping he gets over that last part."

"And if he doesn't?"

"He'll never fire his daughter's boyfriend. The sports media world would have a field day. They already think Dad's unhinged for constantly getting perfectly good quarterbacks fired. If they layer on family drama on top of that? It's the one thing he can't stand. He still wants to murder Tobias for the sex tape and the fact that he came out engaged to someone else after it."

"I do appreciate that the two of you make everything Easton does look tame by comparison." Wren grins at me, and we both laugh.

"Well, I think a lot of that is your doing. I think he would have been worse than Tobias if it wasn't for you. If you've got any tips, I'd love to know."

"Unfortunately, my tips only work if the guy in question happens to be in love with you. And you say Quentin's not, so..." She gives me the side-eye and then puts the lid back on her empty pint.

"He's not. I'm just an impediment. He wants me out of the way and not to have to do any of this reform stuff. Which is why I'm going to make the list even longer now."

Wren shakes her head, smiling as she disposes of the container and puts the spoon in the sink.

"Well, I'm interested to see which one of you wins out."

"Oh. It'll be me. We already know he runs at the first sign of trouble." I grin, putting my spoon in the sink next to hers.

"One last thing."

"Anything for my favorite sister."

"Your only."

"For now."

"Yes, and I think I'm going to have stiff competition from Scarlett."

"Good thing you're the 'only' while you need something."

"The opening of West Field... Do you think you could get Quentin to come?"

I grit my teeth. "I think that'll be a hard sell given the way the two of them have clashed so far this week. Do you really think East wants him there?"

"Oh, I'd guess not. But for one, it would help for the two of them to show a united front even if they're not feeling it, and for two, Quentin is the novelty. People will turn out to see him. People will definitely turn out to see both of them."

"I'll float the idea and see if he's up for it. I have to hold his feet to a lot of fires, so I'm going to have to see how well he plays first."

"Well, I'll keep my fingers crossed he survives you. Or doesn't if he won't learn to treat East with some respect. You'll let me know which fate I should be rooting for?"

"Absolutely."

Wren turns to look at me before she walks out the door. "And take care of you, yeah? It can't be easy to have to work with someone professionally like that. Especially not this closely. I don't want to see you get hurt in the process."

"I'll be careful. If there's one thing I've learned from him, it's that."

8

Quentin

"WANT to grab a drink and some food?" Cooper Rawlings pauses by my locker after we wrap up some class time with the coaches.

"Are you sure that won't get you in trouble with Westfield?" I glance up to make sure he's not watching us now.

"I'm sure. And if it does, I'll just tell him I'm doing my little brother a solid, and he'll forgive me." Rawlings smirks a little before it fades into a question again.

I played with Cooper's younger brother and Bea's ex-boyfriend, Rob Rawlings, in Pittsburgh, and we were pretty good friends, even off the field. Cooper has a reputation for being a little gruff, not too dissimilar from mine, and I guess if I'm going to make a friend on this team it might as well be him.

"As long as it won't get you in trouble."

"Nah. There's a place I like just down a couple of blocks.

Give me your number. I'll text you the address and meet you over there."

WHILE WE WAIT for our food, a photo comes through of a half dozen flower arrangements and I smirk.

MADNESS:

Really?

Not to your liking? I can send more tomorrow.

I'm not in mourning.

I'm sure his future wife will be happy to know.

You're rude. What if I was actually really crushed about Xander?

I thought we cured you of that.

I thought so too, but then Xander made for a very good shoulder to cry on. Lots of muscles, tattoos... you know—all the things I like.

My stomach turns at the thought of her with Xander. I hadn't considered it in all these years, that after I left, she might have gone after what she wanted all along.

"You all right there? You look like you saw a ghost." Cooper raises a brow at me and glances down at my phone.

"Westfield's sister, busting my balls."

"The two of you paired off seems like a recipe for disaster. Especially the way you and East were on the field the other day."

"Lot of bad blood between our families over the years."

"I'm normally not one for drama, but I feel like if it's gonna affect my team I need to know." He sits back and lays one arm over the back of the booth behind him.

"Coach Undergrove and Coach Westfield were friends in college. Got drafted to rival teams. My uncle took him out in a hip-drop tackle. Fucked him up good and ended his career. Westfield hated him after that. When my uncle started coaching, they ended up on the same team for a while. He started a campaign against my uncle until he got him fired and ran him out of the place."

"And that's the reason for the bad blood between you and East?"

"East and I don't have anything really. His brother and I do though. We were good friends for a long time until we weren't."

"You played on the same side of the ball and played together in college, right? Played you once if I remember right."

"Yeah."

"So if not football, then what? You two don't strike me as the type to fight over a woman."

I make a face, and his eyebrow rises in response. "It was a woman?"

"Sort of."

"Not the sister. Tell me it's not the sister."

I shrug and take a sip of my beer.

"Oh fuck." He shakes his head. "That's even worse than I thought. East never gets riled up about anything. I wondered what could have him so on edge about you. But he doesn't want you near his sister. Now it's all making sense."

"Keep it between us, yeah? It was a long fucking time ago, and I don't want to dredge it up. Besides, I really do need her help setting shit straight around here." I feel anxious that he knows, but then again, East might tell them all anyway. Let them all know they can't trust their sisters around me.

"Your secret's safe with me. To be fair, I get it. She's gorgeous. Not my type exactly, but I get it. If the right woman came along, I might risk it all too."

"Your daughter's mom wasn't the right one?"

"Nah. Not really. She's a good person, but much happier with her current partner and their life. Thankful that right now we live in the same city, and I get to have my daughter every other week and be involved in her life."

"Even during the season?"

"Yeah... I'll have to figure something out then but right now it's working all right."

I nod and the waitress chooses that moment to bring out food, setting it out in front of us and asking if we want another round of drinks. She gives me a bit of a cold shoulder, keeping her eyes focused on Cooper the entire time and smiling like he's the best thing ever. I'm beginning to think it's going to be a trend here.

"So you think you're going to be able to work with her?"

"Madison? Yeah. I have to. She's apparently a miracle worker on the PR front, and I'm going to need it given the restaurant staff even seem to hate me."

Cooper laughs. "Yeah, you're not her favorite that's for sure. But give them a chance to see you out on the field in the uniform. They might change their minds."

"I guess we'll see."

9

M adison

ONCE WE GET Bea settled into her hotel, we head out to my favorite new local place—a taco and tequila bar—and settle into a booth. My best friend and fellow PR expert, Beatrix Xavier—Bea for short—has just returned from trying to hunt down a new place for us to start our new business. We want to offer a one-stop resort where celebrities and athletes could escape from the grind and get away while also having PR staff to help them work through any problems. It'd primarily be for clients in a PR crisis. A way to put a pause on their problems and get the mental rest they need while still formulating a plan for how to fix things.

Bea and I had a place all picked out in Colorado, a few towns over on the other side of the mountain from where my parents have a house. It was gorgeous and the acreage was perfect. But it had quickly turned into a nightmare when one of the owners kept hiking the price, and talks with the locals revealed the well on the property was regularly going dry in the summers and the last two forest fires had gotten dangerously close to town. We needed investors to help fund the property and both of them had turned down going any further when they heard the news.

Instead, we set our sights on somewhere closer to the east coast. It'd give us access to a lot more teams and there were plenty of gorgeous places all up and down the Appalachian Mountains.

"So... how did the hunt go?"

"It went okay. I found a place or two, but the real estate agent said that the properties are moving fast right now. That we have to be able to act pretty quickly if we want to get one. And they mostly want cash buyers because of that."

"Ugh."

"Yep. The properties were beautiful though. I definitely think the plan could work once you're done with your contract here."

"Still a long way to go before that's over. The season hasn't even started yet."

"Maybe they'll let you go early for good behavior?" She muses.

"On his part or mine?"

"Both."

"Somehow I doubt that."

"Has he been difficult?"

"Yes. Well, no not really. He's been agreeable, but he's also being a pain in my ass at the same time."

"How so?"

"Well, for starters he sent me a dozen bouquets in honor of your brother getting married." I blush slightly when I admit it to her. I've always felt a little odd about having a crush on Xander since Bea and I got close, but she'll find out about the stunt one way or another, and I'd rather her hear it from me.

Bea laughs but her brows knit together. "How does that work?"

"Mourning flowers and a condolence card for my loss. Oh! And he sent a dozen pints of ice cream."

"Ohhh..." Bea laughs harder, and her brown eyes dance with amusement. "I mean, that's kind of clever honestly."

"You would take his side."

"I think even Xander would find that funny."

"Don't you dare tell him! It's so embarrassing. I didn't even want to tell you, but I'm so irritated. Wren said the same thing."

"That it was clever?"

"Well, that and she thinks he's still got a thing for me."

"He got you literally hundreds of flowers and ice cream. He has a thing for you." Bea gives me a deadpan look, and I shift slightly under her gaze.

"Well, he had his chance. Years ago, and he didn't just blow it. He destroyed it. Obliterated it. So I don't know why he's bothering, other than he wants to start a fight. Or undermine me. Maybe he thinks if I develop another schoolgirl crush on him, he can have his way."

"I mean, as far as he's concerned, you're in a relationship, right? So he should keep his distance."

"He knew I liked your brother and didn't keep his distance."

"Well. That is unfortunate. I wouldn't have minded having you for a sister."

"Right? It would have worked out so perfectly. So you see now why we have to hate him."

Bea shakes her head and laughs.

"All right. I'll try to hate him while making the public love him. This is already starting out complicated."

"Which is why I've called in special ops." I grin at her.

"Well, reporting for duty."

"Thank you. Truly. I appreciate you coming here."

"I'm happy to help, and I'm honestly kind of excited. It'll be a fun challenge while we get things figured out."

"Yes. Fun. That's the word."

I wasn't sure what to call this. A challenge doesn't quite cover the nuance of the craggy mountain of potential problems we have on our hands. But maybe a little less daunting now that I had my best friend at my side.

10

Madison

"DID YOU LOOK OVER THE LIST?" I tap the stylus against the tablet I have in my hand as I sit on one of the barstools at his kitchen island.

"Can I get you a drink?"

"Not this early in the day."

"I meant like a lemonade or Coke or something." He gives me a look like I'm too highly strung, and frankly, I probably am. I probably need the drink.

"A lemonade."

"Mint lemonade okay?"

It's my turn to raise my eyebrow.

"It's a new thing I've been into. It's good. You might like it if you try it..." He pulls out a glass without waiting for confirmation and pours two of them, scooting one across the counter to me.

"The list?" I ask before I take a sip. And he's right, it is good. Oddly refreshing, and I might have to make some to keep in the cottage. Not that I'll be asking him for recipes.

"It's good, right?"

"Yes."

He smirks and has some himself before he finally answers me.

"Yes, I looked at the list. Some of it didn't make sense to me, but I assume it will."

"Do you have any questions? Objections?"

"No. If that's what you think needs to be done, I trust you."

I eye him carefully. I have a hard time believing he really wants to play nice on this, so I decide to push some boundaries from the start.

"So you're willing to go out to dinner with someone I set you up with this week?"

His brows knit together, but he shrugs before he sets his glass alongside the sink.

"If I must."

"Somewhere nice. Pull out her chair. Charm her. Buy an expensive bottle of wine."

"Should I take notes?"

"Do you need to? Given your age and the fact that you're still single, I have concerns about whether or not you know how to date a woman."

"I've dated plenty."

"Longer than a couple of months?"

He makes a face and shrugs noncommittally.

"Nothing in my research says they've been long term."

"You're researching my dating life now?"

"I need to find out if there are problems. I don't like surprises when I'm working with someone, and you seemed uncomfortable talking about it the other night, so I was looking to see what was publicly available."

"I see." He looks me over again. "My turn then—our text conversation the other day. Did you?"

"Did I what?"

"End up with Xander after all?"

"That's none of your business."

"I'm answering all of your questions."

"You're the client."

"And you were almost my wife."

"Keyword being *almost*."

"You wouldn't want to know if your best friend went after the person you almost married?"

"He didn't 'go after me.' He was just trying to comfort me."

"I'm sure he was very comforting." Quentin's jaw ticks and his eyes darken.

"Are you seriously jealous over something that happened years ago?" My heart rate is speeding up right alongside this hurtling trainwreck of a conversation, bringing back memories I try to block out.

"Nah. Just deciding how we're going to work that out on the field next time I see him."

"You won't be working anything out. He'll crush you and then you'll be fined for fucking up over personal issues."

"He'll crush me—seriously? You think your society boy could take me in a fair fight?"

I can't believe this conversation has gotten us here this fast.

"Do you hear yourself?"

"You're the one who decided to let me know you fucked one of my best friends."

"I didn't fuck him," I say exasperated.

"Why imply it?"

"Why get me dozens of flowers and a condolence card?"

"To try to ease the tension. You were so worked up just letting me change your tire. You barely relaxed at the restaurant. I just wanted you to smile." I flash him a look, but my will to fight is fading as I realize he probably did have good intentions. The guy I knew before he walked out on me always did.

"I said the Xander thing because I just wanted to make it clear that I've been over you for a long time. I didn't want this to be weird with you thinking I'm still harboring a crush on you or something. I have to be able to do my job."

"Whatever happened or happens between us personally doesn't change anything about our working dynamic. I won't compromise your job."

"Good. Then can we get back to the list?"

"Sure."

I roll my shoulders and bring my tablet back up, trying to refocus even though it's difficult. We've stepped into the minefield, and I can't imagine this is going to be the only time. But I have to keep us on track. His job depends on it and so does mine. At least until Bea and I can figure out our Plan B, we're stuck with each other, and keeping things professional is the only way out.

"Okay. So the main goals are that you make some friends on this team, you show the locals you're happy to be here and that you're falling in love with this city, and that you have a softer side people just haven't seen yet. If we can make it look like this city is bringing that softer side of you out, all the better."

"Right." He nods agreeably, the tension in the room thankfully lowering.

"So the next thing would be to give me access to your social media." I look up to watch his reaction.

I'm used to guys squirming when I get to this part. They don't want me seeing all the DMs they get. All the women's DMs they've slid into when they've gotten a little too drunk and decided their celebrity is enough to back up a 2 a.m. "U up?" text. They all want to pretend they're not that guy.

So I'm surprised when he doesn't bat an eyelash. He slides his phone to me instead, turning it to face me as it lights up.

"Passcode is 1003," he says. "I don't know if I remember all my passwords to my accounts. I've got them down somewhere though. I can get them to you by tomorrow."

"How would you feel about being logged out of your accounts on your phone and us getting one that I have control over?"

He raises a brow at that.

"It would take managing your socials off your plate. I could be in charge of all the content and answer any questions and DMs for you."

"Make sure I don't get too many from women, is what you mean."

"Not exclusively, but that too." I enter the passcode, and his phone unlocks. The background is a generic screensaver just like the lock screen was. "Probably want to update this to something more Chaos-y. Make yourself seem nice and festive." I grin at him. Although it makes me a little sad that he doesn't have something more personal there.

"Yeah. I've been meaning to do that." He shrugs, his eyes sliding to the side almost like he's hiding something, but I don't know what it would be.

"On the DMs... and controlling the socials. I've just seen one too many careers derailed or wrecked completely by a late-night thoughtless tweet or a one-drink-too-many DM to a model you think is hot. I'd rather stay ahead of that."

"I don't typically have a problem with either of those things, but point taken."

"Am I going to find anything in your DMs I don't want to see?" I flip open his inbox and see what looks like a bunch of inane conversations about football and one or two group texts that look like they involve his cousins.

"Like what?"

"Dick pics. Inappropriate conversations."

"Fuck no. I'm not fucking stupid." He freezes up when he

realizes what he's said. His ex-best friend and my older brother has just come off a sex-tape scandal from a woman who leaked it from her phone. "I didn't mean... I shouldn't say that it's stupid. I just... it's not my particular kink. To have pictures and recordings and things. No shade for anyone who's into that sort of thing. I just... couldn't handle someone seeing my girl like that."

"What Tobias did was careless. He should have been more cautious with his pastimes and who he enjoyed them with. She could have been a little less cruel. Room for improvement all around. Any kinks I should be worried about?"

Quentin's eyes flash up to mine and then away. He looks flustered for a moment.

"No. Or at least I don't think so." He gathers himself again, and I see the smirk form when he does. "Do you want a list? You seem to like them a lot. That your kink?"

"Cute." I shake my head.

"You asked."

"In a professional capacity. If you go to sex clubs or have exhibitionist tendencies, it's helpful to know those things up front, so I can plan for them." I see his eyes glitter with amusement. "Not like that. In a 'we have a statement prepared in the event that becomes public knowledge' way."

The amusement in his eyes dies a little, and he shifts in his seat.

"I don't have anything like that."

"Men your age who have never been married usually have hobbies. Again, I'm just asking."

"Are you, or are you asking why I've never been married? You can just ask that."

I hold my tongue. I want to say something snarky. Not as a PR person to her client, but as the woman who nearly married him. I can't though. Not if I want him to take this seriously.

"I don't need to know why you're not married specifically. I just want you to be honest with me. I don't want any history to make that difficult for you. If you'd rather talk about these things with Bea instead of me, we can do that. It's just important you warn us if there's something we'd be better off knowing in advance. I signed a stack of NDA paperwork when I came on for the Chaos. Your secrets are safe with me."

"I don't have anything to hide. You're the closest thing to a secret I have and, given the list of people who know about our engagement, I don't think we have to worry about it getting out."

"Noted." I scribble something onto my list and swipe to the next page. He doesn't seem satisfied with that answer though, so I look up to see him watching me. "Something else?"

"Is that going to cause a problem? Our past?"

"It's ancient history. We were kids."

"I mean if it gets out."

Oh. *Right.*

"I don't see why it would."

"Because you have a high-profile boyfriend. One who was supposed to be here instead of me. Now you're here and he's not, and we're going to have to be working together every day."

"Like you said, I don't anticipate it getting out into the world, but I think it's manageable if it does. It was a long time ago."

"Does he know?"

"Who?"

"Does A.J. know about us? About our history?"

"Not details. But enough to know there was one."

"Huh." A smug look warms his face, and I don't like it.

"What?"

"Just interesting you wouldn't tell him. Worried he'll be jealous?"

I raise a brow at him. "Not in the least."

"I see," he says, with more conviction this time, and again—

I don't like it. I'm not about to be baited into something with him though. One heated exchange was enough for the day.

"I'll email you as the list expands. I think we have a good start here though. Do you have any questions?"

"A few, but they can wait." The tone in his voice and the way he smiles lets me know I'm going to have a lot to handle when it comes to him. Maybe more than I can handle if I'm not careful. But something about the challenge of that honestly makes me excited for this job.

11

Quentin

"I REALLY DON'T SEE why you need me for this." Madison gives me a sideways look as she slides into the passenger seat. She's returned her rental car and has been showing up in a car that I assume belongs to her brother on the days she's needed one, so I offered to drive us. I parked at the far side of the driveway though considering it's Easton's house, and I don't have a death wish today.

"Where I live and the house is part of the image, right? So I figure I'd better get your opinion."

"I mean if you're not going on one of those celebrity home shows, I think you're fine."

"Fine. I just need someone's opinion. Someone who knows me."

"This is why you need a girlfriend."

"Yes, well... In the meantime, I have you." I grin at her.

"Besides aren't you looking for somewhere to live yourself? Can't imagine that cottage is all that comfortable."

"I actually like it. I don't know about long term. Might have to start looking but not for a house. If anything, an apartment, but I hate to sign a lease and then have to pay to get out of it."

"Planning on cutting out early?" I feel my gut turn a little at the thought of her disappearing when we've barely gotten started.

"No, but we have an uphill battle. If they don't think you're coming around fast enough, I imagine I'll get fired pretty unceremoniously."

"Did they tell you that?" I frown.

"No, of course not."

"Well... we'll just have to convince them things are working."

"I think that's kind of up to public perception. So far it hasn't changed much."

"We've barely started."

"We need to hurry our pace. That's why I agreed to come today. Figured I'd get some candid shots of you house hunting that you can post to your stories on socials. Let people know you're trying to make a home here."

"All right. What else?"

"Probably make some more social content. I'm figuring we can pick up some local food favorites and take photos. Maybe have a picnic at a local park. Some views from your place—you do have a nice view of the city."

"Advertise where I live so people can come and kill me for being a traitor from their most hated team."

"I mean... they'll figure it out pretty quickly anyway with you living in the city like that. They'll see you coming and going enough. If you wanted it to be a secret lair, you should have picked something outside the city."

"Which is what we're going to look at today."

"Retreating already?" I see her smirk out of the corner of my eye.

"No. Just trying to make sure there is a retreat if I need it."

"I suppose that's smart. Some ancient haunted mansion on a hill to keep them all away?"

"Funny. It's the real estate agent my uncle used. His house is nice, so hopefully, she comes through for me too. I didn't give her a lot of direction yet. She said she had some ideas in mind for me and would show me around. So we're meeting her at the real estate office."

"All right. Oh! And Bea found someone to set you up with. Do you have time tomorrow night?"

"Tomorrow—already?"

"The faster, the better."

"Is this just a blind date, or do I get to know anything about her?"

"She runs a couple of local charities, sits on a few boards in the city. She's about your age. She's pretty—looks like she might fit your type other than being a little bit older than you normally go for. I think it's a pretty good match."

"She knows it's just a setup, though, right?"

"She knows we're your PR team, yes."

"That's not what I asked."

"I might have fibbed a little. We found her on socials, and I might have liked some of her content with your profile."

"What?" I risk a glance at her as I turn to pull into the real estate office parking lot.

"She knows we're meddling of course, but no one wants to feel like a pawn. I told her that you thought she was beautiful, and you were interested in getting to know her better."

I put the car in park and finally turn to give Madison a look.

"Let me see."

"You don't trust me now?"

"I just want to know what content you liked of hers."

She hands me her phone, the one she uses for my content, and helps me navigate to her profile picture.

"So I'm liking her drinking wine with her girlfriends and her in a bikini by the pool?"

"The photo of her drinking wine is her at her book club, and the bikini by the pool is her on vacation, but in the caption, she talks about all the money they raised for the local no-kill shelter and the number of animals that they're giving a second chance."

"That's not why she's going to think I liked it."

"Well no, but you'll surprise her with your hidden depths on the date. Also... like you wouldn't have liked the bikini photo?"

"She's... fine. I guess. Not really my thing."

"Because she's your own age?"

"No." I don't know how to tell Madison that I compare everyone to her, and no one, I mean *no one*, comes remotely close.

"Mhmm." She shakes her head at me, undoing her seatbelt and gathering her purse. "That seemed to be your type. Young and... well I don't want to insult women. For all I know they were wildly intelligent."

"I don't date seriously, so it doesn't really matter if they're my type or if they're intelligent."

"Isn't that lonely?"

"Sometimes."

I look up and the real estate agent is already standing outside, patiently looking at my truck, so I don't have the chance to elaborate further. I hand the phone back to Madison and get out of the truck.

"Quentin?" The real estate agent grins, holding her hand out.

"That's me."

"So excited to meet you. I've heard lots of great things from your uncle, and I've got some great properties lined up that I think you'll like."

"Looking forward to it."

Madison has rounded the truck and is standing at my side. The real estate agent is clearly surprised by her presence but recovers quickly and extends her hand.

"Are you the wife? I'm sorry his uncle didn't mention you! I feel so rude."

"Oh no. Not the wife just the—"

"Friend." I cut her off before she can say who she really is. I don't want the awkwardness of bringing my PR person along with me to look at houses. "Maybe wife someday if I can find the right house and ring." I flash a grin at the real estate agent, but I can feel Madison's surprised glare boring into the side of my head.

"Oh, how sweet. Well, my car is this way if you want to ride with me. Or would you rather follow?"

"We can follow you," Madison answers for me this time.

"Okay perfect. Here's the first couple of listings if you want to look over them in the car on the way over." She hands them to Madison, and we both nod before we get back in the truck.

12

M adison

QUENTIN'S TASTES have changed dramatically over the years, or I never knew them that well in the first place. That or not one was communicated to the real estate agent because the first place she takes us to is a garish gold-plated nightmare of a home that looks like it was built in the late '90s.

"Now... It needs a lot of work. A lot of updating so just try to focus on the space and not the interior. I know you'll want to change that to suit your tastes, but the property is large, very private, and in a good school district." She flashes a smile at me with that last tidbit of info, and I cringe inwardly a little. I'm not going to contradict Quentin publicly if he wants to pretend we're dating to the real estate agent. But the idea of shopping for homes with him, being in this space, and helping him pick something feels so much more intimate than just flipping through his socials or picking fake girlfriends for him.

Quentin disappears down a hallway of the house while the agent putters about the front hall looking at her phone and allowing us to take our time. I make my way after him, noting the stark contrast of the baseboards and the walls, the blue fluffy carpeting, and the years of wear on the tile in the bathroom as I pass by it. When I find him, he's in the master bedroom staring out the window of a door that leads to the back deck.

"That seems unsafe," I note.

"It has a lock." He points to it, but it seems flimsy, and there's no deadbolt. "Besides I'm not worried."

"You're not worried. But I assume the house is because you have future plans for a wife and kids, right? When you're on the road, and she's home alone and hears a noise outside that door in the middle of the night, it won't matter that you're not worried."

Quentin tilts his head in acknowledgment of my point.

"See, this is why I brought you along."

"Is this really your style? It's very... nineties. For how good some of the music and movies were in that era, none of that seemed to translate into good architecture."

"Does it usually?" he muses, his lips twisting a little with it.

"I'd argue it does. At least some of the time. Even if it's not always my taste."

"What's your taste?"

I shrug. He knows what my taste is. Or he knew. But it's been a long time since we discussed it. I shouldn't feel sore over the fact that he doesn't remember. Or maybe he just thinks it's changed over the years. We both have.

"Not this. The layout's oversized and awkward. Lots of rooms and spaces that have no purpose other than maybe for something decorative, and you can only have so many pianos and oversized vases. Then the bathrooms are so tiny and the tile is bad."

"The tile can be replaced."

"You'd have to gut this place. Tear out the carpet in every room and repaint every wall. Why not just build something new with a floorplan you like at that point?"

"The good schools?" he questions with a shrug.

"I'm sure you could find property in a good school district. It just might take some time." I ignore the obvious implication. The idea of him having children with someone else isn't something I really want to spend time thinking about.

"What do we think?" The real estate agent asks like she can hear my thoughts.

"It's okay." Quentin shrugs and then she looks to me.

"It seems like it needs a lot of work. Like there'd be extensive months of contractors and decision-making."

"All right. On to the next one then? The next one's a much newer property. More turnkey. No one's ever lived in it as the previous owner started building and then had a transfer to a new job."

"Sounds good." Quentin nods, and we follow her out of the house and to the next property.

The next one is beautiful. Everything has been hand-selected, and the work on the house looks like it was done with attention to detail. It's huge and open, filled with light pouring in from the windows, and the use of space is at least better than the last place.

"All right. Have at it. What's wrong with this one?"

"Nothing's wrong with this one. It would be good. Plenty of room for you and eventual kids. An office and an extra media room in the meantime. Might be able to turn this into a gaming room," I say as I turn around in one of the extra bedrooms."

"But?"

"But nothing." I shrug. It still wouldn't be my choice, and I'm surprised it's his.

"Nah, you gotta be honest with me here. I need you to tell me what's wrong with it that I can't see."

"Well for one, there aren't his and hers closets." I'm reaching for reasons, but they're not necessarily unfounded either.

"That a necessity? I couldn't share a closet with my wife?"

"I mean you could. But why would you? You have the money; you could give her something custom. Shelves for all her shoes and handbags. Space for her clothes that are dry-clean only to hang. Plenty of drawer space. Maybe even a nice little couch or ottoman in the room. And you could have your own. Hang up all your workout clothes, your suits, all your sneakers—and you could have a place to have your outfit for game day ready and waiting when you roll out of bed in the morning." I try to paint a picture as his eyes get wider.

"That's specific."

"Again… it's your house. Just making some suggestions." It's my turn to shrug. "And the bathroom too. That shower?" I wave in the general direction of the small, enclosed space. "No. You could have one that's huge. Have a nice bench inside. You could even get one that's big enough to put the tub inside it. Make sure it has a nice window with plenty of light."

"Light's important in a shower?"

"I mean your wife is going to have to spend time in here. A lot of the maintenance work happens in the shower." I flash him a smile, and he returns it. "Plus, don't you want the shower to be big enough for two?" A memory of the two of us that summer comes back to me, and I turn away from him, so he can't see it on my face.

"You make good points."

"That's why you brought me—apparently."

"Anything else?"

"We didn't even look at the kitchen yet, but make sure you have plenty of pantry space with an extra fridge. Nothing is more annoying than not having space for the food when you have a party. You being the quarterback means you'll have to host them."

"I didn't in Pittsburgh."

"Because you were the single guy. You're going to change that, right?"

"If I can help it."

"Then my point stands." I shrug, but my stomach tumbles at his admission of wanting to be with someone.

"All right. A big pantry it is then."

We walk through the rest of the house and see the yard before we go to two more houses, one of which is on a private lake, and I watch his eyes light up the same way East's do at having his own recreational space.

"Is this important to you?" I point to the lake as we stand at the edge of it.

"Yeah. I mean. I didn't even think about it. I've always lived in the city but having some place to roam seems nice."

"East loves his. Goes for a walk or a jog around the property most mornings. I've gone with him a couple of times. It's nice. If it's something you want, you should make sure you tell her that. So she can try to find you something that fits all the things you want."

"I feel like that might be difficult."

"It might take a little longer than usual, but she seems eager to help you find something you'll love. And there's no Mrs. Undergrove yet so no rush to have it now. Besides, you like the loft right now, don't you?"

"Right." He nods, his eyes studying me carefully.

"All right then. It's settled. You've got your list now for the realtor." I grin, trying to keep the conversation light and my head from going into a spiral about watching Quentin walk down the aisle and buy a house with someone.

"Thanks for your help today. I appreciate it. You made good

points about a lot of stuff I wouldn't have thought of if it wasn't for you."

"That's what I'm here for."

I need to get this guy on a date. Even if it is a fake one. Something to help me confront the reality that he's off-limits for me. Anything that keeps me from wondering what it would look like if we bought a place together. Where we might live and raise kids. Because that's a wildly dangerous imaginative path I can't afford to be wandering down, even figuratively speaking.

13

M adison

I STARE AT MY PHONE, willing some sort of message to pop through and let me know how things went tonight. Quentin had his date with the local woman Bea set him up with. They went to dinner, and it's already nine o'clock, and I still haven't heard a word. It has me starting to wonder if dinner turned into drinks at someone's place, and the little swell of anxiety I have over that doesn't bode well for me.

Suddenly the phone rings though and it's Quentin's name flashing across the screen. I stare at it for a moment. I was expecting a text, not a call, but I answer it anyway.

"Hello?"

"Will your brother kill me if I park in his driveway?"

"What?"

"Will Easton lose his shit if I park out here?"

"Out where? Here?" I walk to the window and look out of it,

watching as Quentin gets out of his truck and starts down the driveway toward the cottage.

"Yes, I'm here."

"What are you doing here? You're supposed to be on a date."

"It ended early."

"Early? It's late."

"She was late. It ended early. I wanted the dessert for two, she didn't. So I'm here now." I see him smiling to himself as he keeps walking.

"I don't understand what that has to do with me?"

"Someone has to share the dessert with me."

A moment later there's a knock on my door, and I let him in, looking at him skeptically.

"You lied to me." He raises his brow at me, and a stormy look forms.

"Lied to you how?"

"She definitely didn't know we were being set up to fake date. She thought it was a real date."

"I mean, it was supposed to be a blind date. I told you that I told her you liked her and were interested."

"In fake dating her, not in real dating her."

"Oh my god. Please tell me you didn't tell her that."

"She asked me how things were going with adjusting to being here, and I explained that I'm trying hard to fit in. The team and my PR person are helping and made a little joke about how she would know that. She was like 'what do you mean?' And I said, 'Well, us being set up like this.' She looked hurt and asked if I was interested in her or not. I panicked and just said I was thrilled to meet someone new in the city."

"Thrilled to meet someone new in the city?" I take the bag from him and set it on the table, pulling out the container.

"I don't know. I was trying to think of a euphemism for being set up by your PR agent."

"She's not a celebrity, Quentin. She's just a local with a lot of connections. She doesn't have a PR agent. You were supposed to treat her like a person."

"I did. I took her somewhere nice. I pulled out her chair. I ordered the wine. All the things you said."

"But apparently, you don't know how to talk to women. No wonder you're single." I set two forks out on the table.

"I know how to talk to women. I just don't know how to talk to weird professional setup situationships."

"You guys didn't even make it to situationship status it sounds like." I laugh to myself.

"Oh no, she still asked me to go back to her place for dessert, and when I declined, that's when I got left alone. Hence you eating it with me."

"Not up for going back to her place?" I ask, even though I know I shouldn't.

"Nah."

"She's pretty though."

"She is. It takes a lot more than pretty to hold my interest."

"Surprising."

"Why? Did you expect me to be an easy fuck?"

"I didn't expect your standards to be quite so high."

"Ouch."

"I'm just saying…"

"Just because you seduced me easily doesn't make me easy." He grins at me, and it makes something flip in my stomach.

"I did not seduce you!"

"Oh, you did. You knew what you were doing."

"What are you talking about?"

"Wearing those skimpy outfits to bed and taking your bra off in front of me."

"You said that kind of stuff didn't work."

"No, I told you that stuff didn't work on guys like Xander, but it would absolutely work on a guy like me. And then you used that knowledge to your advantage."

"Oh please. That's just what I had with me in my suitcase. I wasn't expecting us to be sharing a room."

"Hard to believe. Especially when you were all 'Oh no, whatever will Xander like in bed? If only I had someone to teach me.'" He presses a hand to his brow like he's in distress and then grins wickedly.

"I was looking for honest answers. It's not like I could go to my brother for that kind of thing."

"Yeah. I guess admitting you were trying to seduce both his friends under his nose would have been a bit much for him to take."

"Oh my god. I was not. I wanted Xander. Things with you just got... out of hand."

"That's one way to put it." He grins before he eats another bite of the cake— one that's shockingly good—and I feel a little guilty that I'm getting it instead of its intended recipient.

I gasp dramatically and point my fork at him. "You seduced me. All the muscles and tattoos and gravelly voice stuff."

"Gravelly voice stuff?" He looks at me amused.

"I was minding my business watching a movie when you were all 'do you touch yourself?'"

"You were watching the movie. I was watching you. And you were sexy as fuck and begging for help to lose your virginity. I just thought you could at least have a good experience with it."

"And your ego!" I shake my head.

"Don't recall any complaints out on the deck that one night."

I blush hard when I remember that incident. He made me come so hard and so loudly that we were nearly killed by a mountain lion, but I'm not sure I would have cared at the time.

"Like I said about things getting out of hand." I stand and take the empty container and the forks, putting the container back into the bag and putting it in the trash before I slide the spoons into the dishwasher. When I go to turn around, he's there, and I take a step backward until I feel my butt hit the counter.

He leans around me to grab a paper towel and wipes his hands, but his eyes rake down over my body. I've never wanted anyone the way I want Quentin. Just one look from him and my entire body snaps to attention—years of separation and dozens of nights of heartbreak don't seem to matter when he looks at me like that.

"Do you ever still think about it? That summer?" he asks.

"Sometimes." I shrug, trying to be noncommittal.

His hands slide onto the counter on either side of me, and he leans down. I close my eyes because I can't look at him. I'm trying to think unsexy things. Find my spine and remember all the reasons I hate him. But right now, I'm just glad he didn't go home with her. Happy he had dessert with me. That he's smiling at me. Thinking about me.

"And is it still my voice you hear talking you through it?"

"Yes." The word's out before I can stop it.

Shit. Fuck. Damn.

"I mean... it was back then. Not now." I clear my throat and try to stand a little taller, the heat burning its way up my cheeks and down my neck until I can even see the flush spreading over my chest.

"Definitely not now." I can hear the amusement in his voice, and when I look up, his eyes are burning with the kind of intensity I haven't seen in someone in years. The kind that's going to take me under. I have to regain control here, or this is going to spiral out.

"We should talk about what other things we can work on with the list. What else you might be able to do this week. Try to set you up on a different date."

His eyes search mine for a moment, but he doesn't say anything.

"The list is important," I reiterate.

"I like your list, Madness." Hearing him call me the nick-name he used to that summer does something for me that it shouldn't. "I'll jump through all the hoops you want me to." He closes the distance between us, so close his lips are at my ear, and his body ghosts over mine. "But you should know I have ulterior motives. There's only one thing I want."

"I want A.J." It comes out high-pitched and shaky. It's the biggest lie I've ever told in my life, and he knows it judging by the self-assured smile that follows.

"Yeah, you thought you wanted Xander too, and we both know how that turned out."

14

Q uentin

"ALL RIGHT." Madison busts through my front door like a hurricane, her arms full of bags from various stores, a camera bag and her purse slung over her shoulder as she makes her way to the dining room table. "We've got a lot to get through today. Lots of candid photos to take, and I already ran around this morning picking a bunch of stuff up to help us set the scene."

"Good morning to you too."

"It's almost afternoon."

"Good afternoon then?" I blink as she unloads the bags onto the table.

"Did you pick out some outfits like I told you to? I imagine it's going to take a few hours. We can get lunch delivered if you haven't eaten."

"Have you eaten?"

"At five when I got up. Not since. Plenty of caffeine though."

"I can tell."

She whips around to look at me then, giving me a warning look. Apparently, she's not to be crossed today. Noted.

"Let me see what you picked out."

"Let's order some food first?" I phrase it as a question rather than a statement because I feel like I might get stabbed if I try to tell her what to do right now, but it's very obvious the woman needs something more than the liter of coffee she's probably had today. She tilts her head back and forth considering it.

"I should have just eaten something on the way over. It was stupid."

"I haven't eaten either, so it's not a problem. I'm hungry. Do you know what you want?"

"I don't know. Whatever you want is fine."

"That's not fair, you gotta at least give me a hint. Or we're going to be one of those couples who argue for an hour before we just settle for the first thing we suggested anyway."

"We are not a couple." She huffs.

"Burgers? Pizza? Ice cream?"

She flashes me a look, but she cracks a small smile. "I think I've had enough ice cream lately. Although the key lime was so good. That and the coconut chip. Hard to decide which one I like better. Ugh. I am hungry if I'm rambling about ice cream flavors before noon."

"All right. No ice cream for now. There's a burger place close by that's pretty good. And there's a brewery that has wings and sandwiches downstairs. Beer is pretty damn good too."

"No beer before we get all this done." Another warning look.

"Yes, boss. Burgers? Wings?"

She rolls her eyes and shakes her head at the "boss" comment.

"You pick. I'll eat either."

"On it." I nod and start rooting through the junk drawer for the takeout menus.

LUNCH BARELY SLOWS HER DOWN; she spends most of it on her phone flipping through the calendar she's created for me and texting with Bea about some project they're working on.

When we finish, she's up on her feet, cleaning up the trash and the table.

"Here..." She pushes a stack of sweats and T-shirts toward me. "One of the sponsorships is for these loungewear outfits. They want candids of you around your house in them. I need to get them done this week so their PR person can okay them, and then we can post them in a few weeks."

I hold a T-shirt up and eye it skeptically when I see how tiny it looks.

"These look small."

"There are a couple of sizes there you can try on. Also... they're supposed to be fitted. Your body is what's going to sell them."

"My body, eh?"

"Not like you don't know how to make a thirst trap given your social media posts. I'm sure that was part of the draw for the company. Not letting all those muscles and tattoos go to waste. Go get changed." Her eyes flash over my chest and arms before she shoos me away, and I hurry off to get changed.

Some days, like today, I wonder if sleeping with her might not be the secret to getting back in her good graces. It was one of the things she liked best about me, and I can't imagine it would hurt my chances. Especially if her boyfriend is always going to be out of town. Must get a little lonely. The kind an ex-fiancé might know exactly how to cure.

When I get back into the living room though, she's all business. Setting up a little scene in the corner with my leather chair and a side table. She's staging it in front of the huge warehouse windows, testing her work by framing it with her work phone. I hear a message ping and when she opens it her brows go sky high.

"That where you want me?" I ask as I walk up to her, peeking over her shoulder to see an image of a topless woman. She startles at the sound of my voice.

"Jesus! You scared me." She glares at me.

"What are you up to?" I give her a playful grin.

"Stupidly opening your DMs. Your inbox is a minefield of hate mail and tits right now." She swipes the delete button on the message. She's even less amused when I laugh.

"Sorry. That's a pretty accurate description though, I guess. Did you need to delete that though? I might have wanted to chat with her."

"You're not chatting with women who send you unsolicited nudes." She straightens my shirt, playing with the edge of the sleeve and then running her hands around the back like she's a tailor testing the fit of it for herself. I'm just enjoying the way it feels to have her touch me again. We could do this all day if she wanted to do that.

"Who says it was unsolicited?" I just want to see if I can get a rise out of her.

"It better be. If you're soliciting nudes, we're about to have a whole other conversation."

"I'm kidding, of course."

Her eyes narrow. "You better be. Just because you rejected the first woman I picked for you doesn't mean it's over by the way. We're finding you someone."

"I don't really think I need a matchmaker. I can find my own dates."

"You really can't. I've seen the women in your DMs and the ones you've been photographed out with. If you want to do that in private, fine. Be discreet. But if you're going to have a public relationship, and I recommend it, it needs to be with someone who will match you. Someone serious and driven. Someone who has clout in this city. Even better if she doesn't see it coming and is shocked when she falls for you because she wasn't the kind to date a football player. Infinitely better if she's the kind they could see you walking down the aisle with. Everything about your image has to be carefully curated right now."

"All of that sounds sickening."

"Thank you. I'm glad to hear what I do for a living sickens you." She steps back and gives me a deadpan look.

"I didn't mean it that way. I just mean... I want to be who I am."

"I'm trying to show people who you are. You're smart, driven, clever, and funny. You're the kind of guy who changes someone's tire for them when they're broken down on the side of the road, and who buys a woman twelve dozen flowers and ice cream to help her get over the guy who broke her heart. You care about people. You want to be part of the community here. It's not just a job for you. Your family's here now, and you want this place to be a real home. You want to make people proud. Show them you're invested. Right?" She rattles the list off as she puts me in position in the chair and pulls her phone out. She's clueless that everything she's saying makes me feel seen. That she knows my joke about Xander was really as much an apology for what I did as anything. Because this girl knows me. Ten years have gone by, and she still knows every detail of my soul. When she finally looks up, I have to close my mouth and remind myself to blink.

"Right," I agree. I don't have more words right now.

"Okay. Let me show them that." She crouches down and

angles the phone. "But right now, I want them to see the way your biceps look in this shirt, so can you kind of casually flex?"

A laugh tumbles out of me before I can stop it, and she gives me a perplexed look.

"Nothing. Sorry. I'll try to *casually* flex."

"Good. Because we've got about a hundred of these to take."

15

M adison

WE MANAGE to get through most of the casual photos I want to take, but nothing's quite working for the final one. A local coffee shop who wants to marry the bad-boy-athlete look with something a little more philosophical. As I root through his closet, looking for a sweater or a button-down for him to wear, I pick up a pile of shirts from the top shelf. There's a pile of books nestled behind them, and the movement knocks them loose, and one tumbles to the ground.

It's a well-worn copy of something, whatever it is. The cover's half torn off, and I pick it up gingerly to not make it worse. I never took Quentin as much of a reader. Not that he didn't read. He was smart as hell, just not the kind of guy to have a library to himself or keep books stashed away in his closet.

I look up at where the book fell from and see three more

books. Which is when I see the spines and the name of the author. My absolute favorite. My heart flutters in my chest, and I turn the book over in my hand to get a better look at the spine. *Sense & Sensibility* is in bold lettering, and I bite my lower lip. The other books are Austen too. *Pride and Prejudice*, *Emma*, and *Persuasion* are all neatly stacked. I run my fingers over the spines.

"They made me feel close to you." His voice startles me, and I take a step back, holding the book that fell behind my back like I've been caught red-handed. His brow raises in response.

"Close to me?" I ask, my voice hoarse.

"That summer. You told me they were your favorites. That you reread them all every few months. I wanted to know what they were about. I'd only read a summary to pass a test once. So I got copies for myself. I started rereading them every year, figuring at some point, on a long enough timeline, we might be reading the same book at the same time. Maybe even the same page. It made it feel like you weren't so far away after all. Especially as time went on."

I stare at him wide-eyed. My heart is in my throat; it's keeping me from being able to speak. Not that my brain is giving me many words in the moment.

"I probably shouldn't have told you that... But you're smart. I know you wouldn't believe me if I told you they had nothing to do with you. Given how much you like them." He shrugs and takes the book in my hand and puts it back on the shelf.

"I can't believe you remember."

"I remember everything," he says softly, grabbing the clothes I laid out on the bed. "We should get the rest of this done, so you can get home."

WHEN I STAND AGAIN, I have to roll my shoulders and tilt my neck back and forth. Everything has already started to get a little sore from crawling and standing in every position imaginable to help him get these photos and videos done for his socials.

"Stiff?" he asks from behind me as he turns to the room.

"A little. I think we got a lot of good content though." I flip through the series of photos on the phone.

"Here..." I can feel him step closer to me, closing the distance between us down to inches, and he sets his drink down. His hands are on my shoulders a moment later, and he's gently massaging the muscles.

"Oh. That feels amazing." I sigh, leaning into him before I even realize what I'm doing.

"I got you, Madness. Can't have you getting injured working with me."

"Ha." I tilt my head, so he has better access to my right shoulder. "Might have to get one of those neck rollers or a massage gun."

"Might." He brushes my hair to one side, and his thumb slides down the length of my spine. I can feel his breath against the back of my neck, and I'm wrapped in his cologne. It's the same one he's always worn, and it feels like I could close my eyes and be nineteen again. Another sigh comes out of me before I can stop it—one that sounds like a soft moan—and I bite my lower lip when I feel his hands stutter in their motion.

He clears his throat and then gently brushes my hair to the other side, taking up the same pattern there. His fingers knead the muscles in a simple rhythm, but one that has me practically melting. My eyes close, and I focus on how relaxed I feel. Letting it bring back wave after wave of memories of what it felt like falling for him all those years ago. How easy it felt to be around him. How right his touch always felt on my body.

"You've got a lot of tension in your neck."

"I have a lot of stress."

"Oh yeah? Day job that hard?"

"When the day job is also a night job and an every-waking-moment job, and sometimes even an in-my-dreams job, yes."

"Dreaming about me?" I hear the self-satisfied tone in his voice.

"Panicked half-awake dreams about you doing something that gets me fired."

"I wouldn't let them fire you. I'd quit if they tried."

"Then they might fire both of us."

We laugh and then he pulls a little closer to me. His arm wrapping around the front of my chest from one shoulder to the other as he pulls me tight against him. I can feel the warmth of his body seeping into mine. His fingertips play over the curve of my shoulder.

"I had a dream the other night." His voice is just above a whisper. "About that summer."

"Oh?" It's not even a word really, more of a sound.

"That first time you let me touch you. The sounds you made. So fucking sexy. I never knew how sexy a woman could sound until then."

My heart beats faster in my chest, and I feel the flush come to my cheeks.

"Well, I was awkward and new to all of that. But you're very familiar with it now if your DMs are any example." I try to make a joke to deflect because I can't handle talking about then. But he doesn't laugh.

"I can't stop thinking about it."

"Given the number of DMs you get, I'm not surprised." I continue trying to change the subject.

"I mean that summer." He ignores my attempts and blusters ahead.

"Quen..." I say softly. "This isn't... Us going down memory lane—we can't."

His lips come close to my ear. "Why not?"

"You're a client. I have a boyfriend. Do you want a list?"

"Just a simple question."

"That doesn't have a simple answer."

His other hand falls to my hip, and he walks backward, pulling me with him and then pulling us both down onto the couch. I land in his lap, and I don't fight it. I should. But the more time I spend around him, the more trouble I have keeping the distance between us.

"Then give me the complicated one." His fingers slide over my shoulders, and he starts to work my muscles again. I lean into it, and the way it's undoing all the knots has me thoroughly distracted. I try to focus—remember all the reasons I can't fall for his charm again.

"It was a long time ago, Quentin. We were both different people then."

"Do you regret it?"

"No. You were good to me. Too good honestly. Set some very unrealistic expectations for me and the next few guys I dated." I laugh nervously, and I hear the faint rumble of his laugh follow.

"Good. I'm glad."

"Do you regret it? It cost you Tobias and Xander, and I know how close you were. I've never stopped feeling guilty for that."

"I miss them sometimes. Still feel it when I play against them and see them on the sidelines. But even if I had another chance, I'd still make a lot of the same choices. Don't feel guilty." His hands coast their way down my back, massaging slowly along my spine. When he gets to the base of it, he spreads them out, curving around my hips and then down onto my thighs.

"Hard not to."

"For then or now?" The question hangs heavy between us. I should feel guilty. Would absolutely if A.J. and I were a real thing. His hands curl over the insides of my thighs and then make their way up along the inseam. I grab his wrists at the last possible moment and pause the motion.

"Both." I close my eyes and run my teeth over the inside of my cheek before I speak. "I should go home." Even though I don't want to.

He's quiet for a moment but his hands retreat, freeing me to stand, so I do. I grab my phone where it's fallen to the carpet and start to walk away. I can't look at him right now. I'll cave if I do.

"That gnawing ache won't go away on its own," he calls after me.

"Luckily I'm good at taking care of myself."

"My hands or yours, it's still me you're thinking of."

"Good thing you're not the least bit vain."

"Not vain to know what's mine." I stop at the door and turn to look back at him, and he's closed the distance between us.

"I'm not yours." I straighten my shoulders and glare at him now that I can see he's worked his magic.

"Not yet. But the way you come tonight—that's mine."

"You wish." I hurry out the door and into the hallway, making my way to the elevator. Because honestly—I wish. I want. I *need.* And this torture by my sexy, gorgeous, football-playing, smart-mouthed ex is going to kill me. Or wear out my favorite toy. One or the other.

"Goodnight, Madison," he yells down the hall, laughing to himself as he closes the door.

WHEN I GET HOME that night, I practically make a beeline for my vibrator. I need something to take the edge off because the more time I spend around him the more time I can only think about Quentin fucking me. Him lifting me off the ground, pressing me against a wall, and slamming into me until I come, screaming preferably.

Except I absolutely, one hundred percent, cannot let that happen. So I have to settle for a poor imitation. Not that my vibrator doesn't do the job. But he's missing so many of the things I like about Quentin. And Quentin is right. It's him I'm going to be thinking of tonight.

I'm just starting to feel the building swell of my orgasm when my phone rings loudly. I could fucking scream. Can't a girl get off in peace? I look over, and it's him.

I hesitate to answer it. I have no idea what he could want right now, and some discussion about the list or what he needs to get done is going to take me straight out of the mood. Then again hearing his deep husky voice on the line might be the little push I need. I turn the vibrator off, and hit the answer button, putting it on speaker.

"Yes?"

"Not even a hello?"

"What do you need, Quentin?"

"You didn't tell me what I need to wear tomorrow. My tux is at the dry cleaner."

"You don't need a tux. A good suit will do." Fuck. I haven't seen him in a suit yet. At least not outside the photographs I've found online. That's going to kick my crush on him up another notch.

"I've got a few. I'm not sure which one you'd consider good."

"I'll come early, and we can pick one out together, okay?"

"Okay. I have OTAs again tomorrow though."

"I know."

"You sound like you're in a rush."

"I was just trying to get to sleep." It's not a total lie. I need a good rest, and this will help. "And now I'm wide awake again."

"I'm sorry. I didn't realize you were going to bed this early."

"Well... I am."

"Need another massage to help? I can come over..." The word "yes" is on the tip of my tongue. Which means I'm in danger and need to get off this call.

"Funny. Goodnight, Quentin."

His husky laugh in response makes my stomach flip.

"Night, Madness."

I hit the button on the phone and pick my vibrator back up as I shake my head at my situation.

"Fuck. I need to get laid," I mutter before I close my eyes and turn the vibrator on again. Despite the interruption, I'm still close, and I let out a soft moan when it hits me just right again.

"Holy *fuck*. I forgot how good you sound." Quentin's voice breaks my concentration, and I blink for a moment, wondering if my fantasies have just gotten this good. But then I look over and realize the phone is still on and still very much connected.

"Fuck." I reach over and slam the button but miss again.

"Guessing that means it was an accident. Sorry I interrupted—well, not really all that sorry." I can hear his grin through the phone line, and then see it disconnect and go dark again.

uentin

THE NEXT DAY she's at my place before the event, rifling through my closet as she picks out what she wants me to wear. It's some team-sponsored fundraiser that she's going to as well with her brother and sister-in-law. It's the last thing I want to do. She glances back at me when I walk into the room.

"Have you shaved?" Her eyes narrow when she sees my five-o'clock shadow. She's all business today. Not shocking given the oops moment from last night.

"Not yet. I was going to when I shower."

"You need to shower now. You need to be in the car in less than half an hour."

"You want to join me?" I offer up a playful grin and get a raised brow in response. "Or just watch? I feel like I owe you for last night."

"I don't know what you're talking about." She turns her

attention back to my wardrobe and slides another tie to the side before her hands slip over the silk of another one. I'm already imagining it wrapped around her eyes and another around her wrists while I lap her sweet little cunt until she cries for me like she did last night.

"Your 'accidental' lack of hanging up."

"Doesn't ring any bells."

I walk up behind her and run my fingers over her waist, my palm settling over her abdomen, and I can feel her take a deep breath when my lips hover over her throat. I mimic the sound of her throaty breathing and the soft moans she was making.

"Fuck, Quentin. I need your cock so badly," I whisper against her ear. "That sound familiar?"

She turns her head and her eyes flash with disapproval. "I might have said fuck, but I definitely did *not* say that."

It only takes her a moment to realize that she walked into my trap, and I smirk.

"You're awful."

"Come get in the shower with me. I'll make sure you beg for it this time."

"Funny."

"You said you need to get laid."

"My hair and makeup are done," she answers sarcastically because we both know that's not the real reason she won't.

"You look just as beautiful without it."

"Not at a formal event I don't."

"Fine. Have it your way." I pull my shirt over my head with one hand and chuck it on the floor. Her eyes follow the motion and land on it.

"That's rude to the people who have to clean up after you." She bends over and picks it up, dodging me and walking around the bed to the bathroom where she tosses it in the hamper. I follow her, and when she goes to turn around, I grab the top of the frame and lean in against it. Her eyes wander over my chest and then hit the ground.

"You can look. Fuck it, you can touch if you want. Any time you want."

"I have a boyfriend. You know this."

A wry grin spreads on my face, and she raises a brow.

"Can't really find the will to care. You could be married to him. Wouldn't make a difference to me. I'll happily take over where he left off."

Her brow knits and a small frown mars her face. "Don't say things like that."

"Why not? They're true."

"That doesn't make you a very good person, if it's the truth."

"I never claimed I was a good guy."

"Yes, well. That's the problem, isn't it?"

I lean forward, running my fingers under her chin, and bring my mouth within a hairsbreadth of hers. Her lips part, and her eyes drift down to where we almost meet. I can see her doing the mental math of whether it's worth it or not to her to have another taste.

"Not for you. You've always liked my brand of problem," I whisper. I regret it almost immediately because she pushes back.

"Take a shower. Get dressed. We need to be at the event in less than an hour." She walks around me and closes the door behind her.

Some part of her echoes the same feelings I have. I can feel it in the way she talks, see it in the way her eyes fall over me. But how to get her to see that he's the mistake and not me is the part of the puzzle I haven't figured out yet.

17

M adison

It doesn't take me long to find my brother and A.J. I give him an enormous hug that he returns along with a kiss on my cheek for show.

"I see you've already found a partner in crime." I grin at East who's currently drinking a beer and looking at an auction item for a trip to Oia.

"Yeah. We've just been deciding what to bid on and talking off-season plans. Plus I was telling him what a shame it is we're stuck with a second-rate quarterback instead of him." East grins at A.J.

"Be nice," I admonish East. "You might not like him personally, but he's a good quarterback."

"See. You've left her alone too long. Her loyalties are already shifting." East nudges A.J. while flashing a teasing look in my direction.

"I think her loyalties were decided a long time ago." A.J. gives me a small smirk.

"Yes, we'll have to figure out what we do with traitors." East fires a look my way and raises a brow at A.J.

"Oh, both of you... Don't be trying to corrupt A.J. with your feuding nonsense." I glare at East and then take A.J.'s hand in mine. "And you and I need to catch up anyway."

"Guess that means I'll catch up with you later." A.J. nods at my brother and then follows me toward the bar.

"I need a drink," I announce.

"Then a drink you shall have."

I smile at him and squeeze his hand. "I didn't expect you to show up here."

"It sounded like you might need the moral support if you aren't going to collapse under the pressure given the text conversations we've had lately."

I'd been asking A.J. how Operation Get the Wife Back was going and complaining about my own predicament with my would-have-been husband. Mostly I'd been lamenting the fact that I still find him attractive, and explaining how my lack of recent non-fake boyfriends is leaving me incredibly vulnerable to Quentin's particular brand of charm.

"I appreciate it."

"Unless you want to fall back into old habits." A.J. gives me a curious look.

"I mean..." I look up, scanning the room to make sure I don't see him anywhere nearby before we have a repeat of him overhearing things he shouldn't. "I do, but I shouldn't. Not just because of us, but the fraternizing wouldn't look good either. You and then him? At least from the public's perspective, I'm pretty sure I'd get a scarlet letter for that."

"It's none of their business what you do or don't do with your personal life."

"Yes, but the team is likely to have questions about my ability to manage him if I let him... manage me."

We pause in our conversation to put our orders in with the bartender and then slide to the side while we wait for him to make them.

"I maintain it's none of their business."

"Yes, but then there's the reality of it. Not to mention how some of the players might react."

"I worry for my daughters," A.J. mutters, shaking his head.

"Speaking of, how are they?"

"Good. Mia is still working the getting-her-parents-back-together angle pretty hard."

"Well, that might be to your advantage."

"Yes and no. Maya's told her that she needs to accept you as my girlfriend, and we all need to collectively move on."

"Oof. Well... Maya never was the jealous type. I can't blame her really. She's trying to do the right thing. Maybe you should tell her about us?"

"I don't know. I've thought about it. But then I worry that it'll just make me look pathetic. She's out there on real dates, figuring out a new life without me, and I'm just sitting at home wishing I could have my family back."

The bartender slides our drinks to us and A.J. places a tip on the counter before we move to a cocktail table to finish chatting.

"You're doing more than that. You've been working on yourself. You've been working on trying to get a better work-life balance and proving you can be a good dad and pull your weight there. I'm sure she sees all of that. Some of this might be bravado on her part too, you know. That she wants you to think she's fine and moving on even if she's not."

"Maybe..." A.J.'s eyes focus on something behind me, and I tense.

"What?"

"Your guy is incoming, and he doesn't look happy."

"Is he with her?"

"Her?"

"I tried to set him up on a date tonight. Was hoping he'd be with her, and it would keep him occupied."

"No. He's very much alone. He's getting a drink at the bar, but he's already looked this way twice."

I take a step closer to A.J.

"Look at me and talk like we're having some sort of intimate conversation. I really need some distance from him. I made a little mistake yesterday, and he's desperate to make me pay for it."

A.J. slips his hand around my waist and looks down at me adoringly.

"What kind of mistake?" His eyes dance with amusement at my downfall.

"I'll spare you the details, but let's just say he's become very sure he stars in my fantasies," I say, blushing at having to explain this to my friend.

"Does he?" A.J. smirks at my misfortune.

"Does your ex-wife star in yours?" I know it's unfair to snipe at his amusement, but I do anyway.

"Touché," he answers, but it doesn't change the amusement on his face.

"Am I interrupting?" Quentin's voice jolts me back to the present.

"Not at all." A.J. flashes a grin at him but doesn't let his hand slip from my side.

"Did you need something?" I turn to look at Quentin.

"I was just hoping you could introduce us." Quentin nods to A.J. "We've never formally met, and I suppose it might be nice to clear the air about things."

"Clear the air?" I ask.

"Yes. The two of us seem to keep getting pitted against one another, and I just want to be sure there are no hard feelings."

"You'll have to excuse him." I glance back at A.J. "He took a few hits this week at practices."

"I thought OTAs were no contact?" A.J. raises a brow.

I start to reply but Quentin jumps ahead of me. "Some of the guys here are eager to put me in my place. They think rattling me a bit will make me give up. But I don't ever quit when I really want something."

The tone of his voice makes it abundantly clear that he isn't talking about football anymore, and I feel the heat of it in my cheeks. I look to A.J. who's just smiling calmly as he regards Quentin.

"Well, I certainly admire tenacity. It's an important part of the game."

"I'm glad you feel that way." Quentin's mouth turns up in a vicious smile. "Madison here knows all about tenacity. She's been putting me through my paces lately. Fundraisers, working with local businesses, making content for social media. It's almost like she doesn't want to spend any time away from me. Just last night she was at my place and—"

"Quentin!" I interrupt him, and his eyes snap to mine. "I don't think A.J. wants to hear all the details of your PR redemption tour."

"Oh no, I'm fascinated. What happened last night?" A.J. encourages him, and I'd slam my elbow into his ribs if it wouldn't be so obvious.

"See? I think A.J. loves hearing about your life here. He's missing out on so much of it. And you're always so humble. I'm sure he wants the details. Right?"

"Of course. I'm so proud of her."

A.J. is going to pay for this later.

"She was just working so hard trying to get the content right for my collaboration piece that she ended up pulling a muscle in her neck."

"You've got to be more careful." A.J. feigns a concerned look.

"That's what I told her while I was massaging the knot out for her." Quentin smirks, and A.J. raises a brow in return.

"I didn't realize the two of you were that close."

"Oh, Madison and I go way back. Don't we?" Quentin looks at me.

"Shouldn't you be with Fiona right now? I thought she was showing you around."

"I came to get a drink and find you. Wren's looking for you. She has someone she wants you to meet."

"Okay. I'll go look for her. A.J.?" I glance back at him and hold my hand out. He takes it but before he walks away, he turns back to Quentin.

"Nice meeting you."

"You too."

As we walk down the hall I give A.J. a sidelong glance.

"Stirring the pot tonight, are we? I thought you were saving me from him."

"I was until I saw the way you two look at each other. There's no saving you from yourself where he's concerned. If I was your real boyfriend, I'd be counting down the days I had left."

I start to protest, but A.J. just gives me a pointed look, so I shut my mouth instead and hurry to look for Wren.

uentin

WATCHING her walk away with him twists something harder in my chest, stealing a little bit of my oxygen.

"Can I get you something?"

"Whiskey double. Neat."

"Coming right up."

I watch the two of them disappear out the door and I can feel the panic well inside my gut. I hate the idea of her going home with him. Until now I've had to be okay with the idea of them, but it's been a distant sort of philosophical truth that they're together. She didn't go home to him every night. They didn't eat dinner together or watch TV. They didn't spend their afternoons laughing together or share cake for dessert. They didn't spend hours strategizing the next moves for his career or work out the next PR campaign he should participate in. She did all of that with me. She was mine most hours of the day. I only had to be without her when she went home at night. And after last night, I knew some of that time belonged to me too.

But now I'm going to have to watch her laugh with him. Leave with him. I'm not sure I can do it.

"Here you go." The bartender slides my drink to me and I tip him before I guzzle it down in one fell swoop and push the glass back across the counter. I stop myself from ordering another, even though I want one. It's one thing to take the edge off and another to be drunk enough to do something stupid. Like tell her I still love her.

I might need to leave soon if I'm going to stop myself from doing that. Because despite his absence in her daily life, he seems like a good guy. He trusts her. Nothing I said even made him flinch. Which means he knows her well enough and is confident that she loves him enough that he doesn't have to worry.

East walks up to the bar next to me and orders a drink before he turns to look at me, something like pity in his eyes.

"Imagine that's fucking painful."

"What's that?"

"That you stole his spot here and he still has everything you want." East's eyes glitter with the taunt as he takes a sip of his drink.

I hate that he has something on me that lets him twist the knife in, but I won't deny it. Can't deny her. Especially not to her brothers. Because if there's one thing I won't do, it's make the same mistake again.

"Like a rusty spoon being twisted in," I agree and his brows lift in surprise.

"Surprised you admit it."

"Why wouldn't I?"

"Because it'll be embarrassing when you fail. She's not a teenager anymore. She's not going to be easily swayed by whatever charming shit you try to pull. The flowers and ice cream went over like lead."

"I'm not embarrassed for trying again. I'm embarrassed I fucked it up the first time. I don't expect anything to come easy to me. I wasn't born with a dad who had more money than Croesus. I've spent my whole life working for everything I have."

I see East's jaw click, and I know I've hit a nerve. But the two of us are going to have to work through this, and we might as well have some of it out now. He takes another sip of his drink, his throat bobbing on it before he sits the glass down, scanning the room before his eyes meet mine.

"My wife hated guys with money, and I had to work my ass off to win her over. The difference is I didn't walk away when things got hard. I showed up for her day after day. That's the only way a relationship works. The only way a marriage works when you're years in and you're both overworked and stressed and tired." His eyes spark with a warning. "My sister shows up for everyone in this family. Any time we need anything, she comes running to save the day. She deserves a partner who shows up. Someone who moves heaven and fucking earth for her."

"And A.J.'s that guy? Spending his whole summer up in Chicago with his ex-wife and family while she's down here alone? You think he's gonna put her first?"

East's jaw tightens again, and he glances at me.

"You think you're going to grab the ball when he fumbles it then? You think if she couldn't make things work with him that she'll think they could work with you?"

"I think your sister is learning that I've changed a lot over the years. That I might have been a dumb kid back then, but I've worked hard to be who I am today. And I'll show up day after day after day to prove to her I'll be right here for as long as she needs me to be."

East looks me over and shakes his head, but something in his eyes tells me I've gotten through—on some level at least he believes me.

"That's unfortunate. I was hoping you'd fuck off back to Pittsburgh, and I could find a quarterback who knows how to throw a decent fade."

"Yeah. Unfortunately, you're stuck with a quarterback who can run the kind of West Coast offense you excel in. Might even be able to help put your name in the records. But only if you can stop running your mouth long enough to actually play ball."

He tilts his head, his lips flatlining, and I can tell I've got his attention even though he doesn't respond.

"I want to make your sister happy, but I also want to be here. This team has potential. There's no reason it can't be us making a playoff run. You're fucking phenomenal. Just like your brother. Maybe better. He and I put up a lot of points in college. We could too. But we've got to keep all this shit off the field if we're going to do that."

"I can keep shit off the field as long as you don't do anything to hurt my sister. The second that changes is the second any temporary peace between us folds."

"Deal," I say without hesitation.

"Just make sure you hold up your end."

I get a tip of his chin, and he finishes his drink, pushing off the bar and nodding to me before he disappears back into the crowd.

19

M adison

WHEN I GET to West Field later that week after A.J. has gone home, I smile at Wren who's already buzzing around the place, making sure everything is set up and ready to go last minute. In a change of attitude, Quentin agreed to be at the opening for Wren and Easton's new restaurant—conveniently located on the west side of the stadium. I've noticed a shift in the way he and East talk to each other on and off the field, mostly that they do in fact talk now without one of them storming away in the wake of it. I'm too excited at that progress to press either one of them with questions about it, but I'll take the fact that he's here as another win.

He's currently sitting in one of the booths with Fiona, having a beer and chatting with her. I can tell, by the way her face lights and the soft laugh she makes in response to something he's saying, that she likes him. He grins in response to whatever she says, the kind of smile that's genuine and not the forced ones he sometimes puts on for the camera, and I feel the smallest twist inside my heart. I can't be jealous of this—of them. The two of them ending up together—actually liking one another—would be the best possible outcome for all of us.

Quentin and Fiona would make an A-list couple, him as the quarterback and her as a local powerhouse in business and fundraising. It doesn't hurt that they look good together either, like a matching set with their dark hair, blue eyes, and tattoos. I could see them holding hands together, walking red carpets at galas, posing for cute pumpkin-laden fall family photos, and lounging together on a beach in the summer. No family politics in the way. No professional quandaries to worry about. No bitter past to stop them in their tracks.

The thought of it hurts—not just for Quentin in particular, although that's the worst of it, but for the fact that every relationship I've ever had has made me question if they were there for me or my family. Wondering if it was my father or brothers they really wanted access to. Thinking they might be putting up with my career and schedule not because they wanted me but because they wanted what my last name could get them in the football world.

"You're deep in thought." Wren nudges me as she walks by, motioning for me to follow her.

"Just one of those days."

"Anything in particular?" I don't miss the way she glances over at Fiona and Quentin.

"Nope. Bea isn't here yet, is she?"

"No. Not that I've seen. I've been in the back though so it's possible. East has been grumbling about me doing too much and trying to slow me down."

"Well, you do work a lot."

Wren stops mid-stride and blinks at me. "Pot... meet kettle."

"I know. I know."

"Would you want to go remind him it's almost time to get Gramps? If I say something he'll insist I ride over with him to get me out of here for a few minutes, and I don't want to argue about not leaving."

"You do have a manager for this reason, you know."

"Don't you start." Her eyes narrow at me.

"All right. I'll let him know. But at least sit down for a bit at some point? Get your feet up maybe?"

"If they start hurting, I'll get on it," she grumbles.

"It's because we love you, you know." I squeeze her shoulders and run off to find my brother.

LATER THAT NIGHT before I have a chance to even register his presence, Quinten is next to me, following me down a back hall at the restaurant. He's been on his best behavior all night, signing autographs and chatting up the whole restaurant like it's something he does all the time. He's also been incredibly attentive to Fiona because every time I look over, she's at his side laughing or touching his arm, and I'm stuck reminding myself that it's a good thing.

"You've been avoiding me all night."

"You're on a date. I'm trying to let you both have fun and get to know each other."

"A fake date."

"It doesn't have to be fake." Part of me hates saying it, the other part of me—the logical part that tells me getting involved with him would be messy and fraught with difficulties—wishes he would date someone for real. It would keep his attention off me and seal off any ideas about what we could be if circumstances were different.

"It does. I'm only doing this to keep you happy and get things on your list checked off. But another woman could strip naked and crawl in my bed, and I wouldn't notice her." My eyes lift to his when he echoes the comment I'd made about Xander.

"It's not like that between us."

"You're right. I've waited a lot longer."

He takes a step closer to me, and I take a step back until he has me caged up against the wall.

"Where is he anyway?"

"Who?" I ask a stupid question, realizing he means A.J. almost as soon as I do. He smirks at the fact I can't even remember I have a boyfriend right now, fake as he might be.

"Your guy. He already run back to Chicago? He should be able to get back down here in between the Blaze's OTAs. He should be free to be wherever he wants on the weekends especially. And yet he's not down here. Even when your family opens a new restaurant."

"He has kids to worry about and a life in Chicago. He can't just run off whenever he feels like it. I knew that going in. Besides, I'm incredibly busy myself," I say dismissively.

He smirks and leans in closer to me, his eyes studying mine. I make an effort not to let my body respond to it. Desperately trying to think of all the reasons I don't want him.

"Fair enough. But if my girl was down here working so closely with the guy she almost married, lonely for weeks and so needy... I'd be making weekly trips to make sure she was taken care of. Dragging her back to bed any chance I got. On my knees whenever she'd let me."

"Quentin..."

"How long has it been, Madness? A while I'm guessing from the way you sounded the other night. Was it me you were imagining between these thighs?" he whispers against my ear, leaning closer. My eyes start to close, and I can feel the heat of his body against mine.

I hear movement in the restaurant's kitchen, and it startles me. I blink and try to look past where his body is shielding us in the hallway.

"We're in public."

"We can be in private if you want. My place isn't that far."

"We can't do this."

"Because you don't want to?"

"Because of a million reasons, Quentin."

"That's not what I asked. I asked what you want."

I stare into the abyss of the dark hallway. I need to leave. I should leave. I have no business continuing to follow him down this road.

"We can't always have what we want." I finally look up at him again and meet his eyes. "You taught me that."

"But you can have everything you want right now. You tell me, and I'll make it happen."

I start to move. Thinking of going to find Wren or someone who can keep me sane. Back to safety where I don't have temptation at my fingertips. But it doesn't last. A moment later, he pulls me up into his arms and before I know it, I'm pinned against the wall, my legs wrapping around his waist and his lips on mine.

I've missed the way this man kisses. It's rough and claiming. Like he wants to remind me I've always belonged to him and always will. The kind of kiss that makes me want him even more than I already did. The kind that makes ten years disappear in an instant—like I'm nineteen years old and madly in love again.

I could cry from how good it is to feel grounded again. To feel like I'm in the arms of someone who wants me and just me. Not me the Westfield. Not me the fixer. Just me—the girl who sometimes feels lost and lonely.

When we finally come up for air, he presses his forehead to mine and our breathing slows, but he doesn't put me down, leaving me floating in between the two realities. One where I very much need to not fall for Quentin Undergrove again, and another where I want anything this man has to offer. Even if it comes at the risk of everything.

"I taught you a lot of things. Some I'm proud of. Some I wish I could take back. You tell me what it takes to get your forgiveness, and I'll do it, Madison."

"I forgave you a long time ago. It's the forgetting that's the problem." I press back and he lets me drop to my feet again but doesn't move away.

"Then tell me how I can help you forget." He kisses his way down the side of my throat. "Because I've got ideas. Ways I can make you forget everything."

"A.J. is—"

"Fuck A.J. I'll make sure you forget him too."

A throat clears, and we both look up. It's Wren and Fiona, and I swallow hard.

"Fuck..." I mutter under my breath, and Quentin puts distance between us.

"We're looking for Quentin, so he can sign a few things," Fiona announces, shifting on her feet.

"Of course." I smile brightly at her and then Quentin.

His eyes stay glued to me for a second and then he shifts. His demeanor changing back into the spokesperson we've been training him to be as he joins Fiona. They head back out to the crowd, and I smile at Wren, hoping to find a safe harbor when my legs still feel like they're at sea after that kiss.

Wren's demeanor however turns stormy. I'm about to get a sister-in-law lecture, and I know it. She closes the distance between us down the hall and raises her brow at me, crossing her arms over her chest.

"What the hell was that?"

"Nothing. But thank you for interrupting."

"Fiona likes him."

"Good. I'm sure he'll warm up to her. He's just being diffi-cult about the dating thing."

"Because he's in love with you."

"He's not in love with me. He wants to fuck me. Those aren't the same thing."

"What do you want?"

"To keep his career afloat. Keep A.J. safe. Keep East safe."

"What do you want for yourself? Because the way you were just looking at him, it looks a whole lot like he's what you want."

"Don't be silly."

Her eyebrow raises higher.

"Fine. It's been a while for me. With Tobias's drama and work and A.J. and now him... It's been a long dry spell, and Quentin is good in bed. Plus, he looks like... *that.* So I'm fighting the urge to give in to him, okay? I'm only human."

"So stop trying to set him up—with my friends—and fuck him yourself."

"I can't. I'm trying to keep things professional."

"Based on what I just saw, that ship sailed a while ago. Fuck him. Get it out of your system and then figure out where the two of you go next. But if that tension gets any higher between the two of you, it's going to explode."

20

Q uentin

I'M at Cooper's tonight, playing a round of pool. He's kid-free because his daughter's mother gets her every other week, and I'm doing my best to carry on with the list Madison's given me —one of which is to try to make friends with some teammates. Given my offense is the least likely to hate me and the most likely to try to make things work, at least the ones not named Westfield, Cooper and I have formed a loose alliance of shooting the shit on his free nights.

"You ever want a woman you know you shouldn't?" he asks abruptly after he shoots and misses a pocket. The question hits home hard, and I look over at him, but it's obvious his focus is elsewhere, and whatever this question is—it's got nothing to do with me or Madison. My answer, however, absolutely does.

"Yep."

"Did it turn out well?"

"No. It was a fucking disaster." Now we both know who I'm talking about.

"Was Madison worth it?"

"Absolutely."

Cooper grins and takes a sip of his beer. "That's what I'm thinking. Might end in disaster but if the middle part is any good, then it might all turn out, right?"

"Right." I take a swig of mine. "You got someone in mind?"

Cooper leans on his pool cue.

"I shouldn't say. It's fucked, honestly."

"Keeping secrets from your QB now? And here I thought this friendship was headed somewhere."

"Secrets." He makes a derisive clicking sound. "I guess it is one."

"You've been keeping mine. So I figure I owe you."

"I could use some advice."

"Shoot."

"It's Trixie."

"Trixie?" I frown.

"Madison's friend. Xavier's sister?"

Then I put two and two together. "Bea?"

"Yeah. Sorry. I mean Bea. Lizzy calls her Trix, so I started calling her Trixie as a joke and it stuck."

"Oh, right. I heard Madison say something about Bea and Lizzy getting along."

"Yeah. When Tr—Bea used to come to holiday stuff with our parents or visit with Rob. She'd spend time playing with Lizzy and listening to all her stories and stuff. Lizzy just loves her. Thinks she's the coolest. I feel invisible when Trix—Bea... fuck, you know who I mean. Whenever she's around Lizzy's thrilled so... I've been thinking about asking her if she wants to stay with us. I know the hotel is wearing thin on her, and Madison hasn't made up her mind if she's staying in the cottage or getting an apartment. I think she's hoping Madison will get a place with her."

"I wish she would. Anything that would make them more likely to stay..."

"But Bea only has part-time work with the team. She needs something else, and I guess her and Madison's plan isn't exactly going as well as they hoped."

"What plan?"

"I don't know. She hasn't told me a lot. Just that there is one, but it's going very slowly."

"Ah." I'll have to find out more about that.

"So I've thought about inviting her to stay with Lizzy and me to take some of the stress off, and I thought it might be nice for Lizzy to have her around since she likes her so much."

"But...?" I take my turn and then look up at him.

"But... I don't know if I can handle having her in the house."

I let out a low whistle. She and Rob weren't just been a short-term thing. They were together for years. Practically engaged for a while until he met someone else.

"Does she know...?"

"No. Fuck no. She has no idea. I'm Lizzy's dad and Rob's brother to her."

"I mean, I guess Rob moved on from her, so it's not like she broke his heart or anything but still..."

"I know. And she's Xavier's sister. Not exactly someone I want to make an enemy out of."

"I wouldn't recommend it."

He gives me a cheeky grin and takes his turn.

"Speaking of... how's that going?"

"I'm fucked."

"How so?"

"Absolutely fucking leveled over her all over again, and she's got walls up that are fucking unscalable. I've tried every-thing I can think of."

"But behind the walls?"

"She still looks at me the same way she used to years ago. When her guard's down, it's almost like it used to be. But she's with him, and she uses it like a shield."

"So call her out on it. Ask her if she's in love with him or not."

"And if she says yes?"

"It'll hurt like a motherfucker, but you won't keep bashing yourself up against the rocks. You can move on, find a rebound, and get on with your life."

I don't like the idea of moving on from Madison. I haven't been able to in all these years and don't think I can now. But I suppose Cooper isn't wrong either. Something has to give. I can't keep going in circles with her.

uentin

"I THINK everything went really well tonight. The turnout. Everyone getting along." Madison smiles as she fills the containers with the last of the food and places them into the fridge.

We had half the team here, including her brother and his wife, Cooper and his daughter, and my uncle and his family. Madison organized everything on my behalf and it's yet another moment when she feels as much like mine as she can be. The kind of mine that makes me want to have her stay here tonight.

"I think so too. Thanks in large part to you. Getting your brother here and his support."

"You did that on your own when you went to West Field's opening. He knew it took you setting your ego aside to do that, and he's willing to do the same. You both want the same things."

"When it comes to the team at least. He doesn't want me anywhere near you given how many times he brought A.J. up tonight."

She stutters in her steps when she sees the way I'm looking at her but turns to wipe down the table anyway.

"Yes well... he's still a Westfield at the end of the day."

"Half-surprised you didn't make me invite Wren's friend to this."

"We talked, and she didn't want to put on the act anymore." She washes the sponge in the sink and sets it up to dry.

"That annoyed with me?"

Madison turns her head slightly but doesn't look at me. "No. She really likes you. She thinks she could have real feelings for you."

"Ah."

"At least until she saw us in the back hall at West Field."

"Fuck... I'm sorry." I regret Fiona seeing it but not doing it. She was a sweet person. I hope she finds the right guy, but my heart's been tattooed with someone else's name for nearly a decade.

"We can't keep doing those things. It's not fair to A.J."

"Because you're in love with him?" She doesn't answer me, just wipes her hands on the hand towel and walks across the room. "If you tell me you're in love with him, I'll leave you alone. If he's who you want, I'll stay out of the way. But I want you to say it to me—look me in the eye and tell me that you're in love with him, and you don't have any feelings for me."

I see the tense way her shoulders pull together and the way her jaw tightens just that little bit.

"Quentin, it's late, and it's been a good day. I don't think we should discuss this right now."

"I need to discuss it right now." I cross the distance between us, and she turns just as I get close, taking a step back to give herself space from me, and I stop where I stand.

"There's nothing to discuss. I'm with A.J. That's the beginning and the end of the discussion. I like you, I'm glad we're talking again. I'm happy to help you with all of this—that's as surprising to me as it is to you probably. I think maybe we could be friends at the end of all of this. But that's all."

"That's all?" I shake my head. "Which is why you kissed me like you're fucking starved for it and why it's me you think of when you get off instead of him. Right?"

She sighs and shakes her head. "I'm attracted to you, and admittedly I've let that attraction go too far lately. It's unprofessional, and I'm sorry for that. I feel awful about Fiona. I think if you apologized to her, explained that we got confused for a moment—there might be a real chance for things between you two."

I shake my head. "Like there's a real chance for you and A.J.?"

She doesn't answer. Instead, she starts to move like she's preparing to head for the door.

"Because I've been thinking about it. Not just the way you are with me. How you talk about him. How you look when you say his name. I know what you look like when you're in love, and that's not it. I don't know why you're with him. But I don't think it's because you're in love with him. Are you?"

She stops and stares out the windows of my loft before she finally answers. "No."

"So tell him."

"He knows."

"He knows and doesn't care?"

"He's in love with his ex-wife." She sighs before she turns and looks at me.

"What the fuck, Madison? Why would you—" I start but

she cuts me short with a look that tells me I need to listen and not talk.

"I'm trusting you by telling you this. If you say a word..." She shakes her head, but we exchange a meaningful look, and she continues, "I didn't want my father to railroad him after the rumors about him coming here started, and you know my father abhors drama. So we've been pretending to be together. Explained that he was only considering coming here because I was. Plus, my father knows what it would look like if he made firing an exceedingly good athlete a personal vendetta. Something your uncle hasn't learned yet apparently with the way he keeps threatening Easton." Her eyes flash with anger, but all I feel is relief.

"I won't let anything happen to Easton. It's a battle of wills, and my uncle just wants him to fall in line. They're making progress."

"He doesn't deserve to be a pawn between them. He's been through enough."

I nod my understanding. I don't know what all has gone down in that family, but I know when it comes to some things, our families aren't all that different.

"But you and A.J.? There's nothing there? It's all fake?"

"We're good friends from college. I love him, but not like that."

"Why not tell me before now?"

"Because I thought it would make this easier." She looks at me, something in her eyes I can't quite read.

I lean down to kiss her, but her hand darts out to my chest and presses against me, stopping me in my tracks.

"Why?" I ask. "You thought it would keep me away from you? I told you nothing would."

"We can't do this. I should go," she says, her lashes fluttering as she starts to pull away.

"Or you could stay," I counter. "Let me try to do penance in some other ways."

"That would just confuse things between us, and they're already messy. We fuck and then suddenly this dynamic is muddled. I'm not losing everything I've worked hard on just for an orgasm."

"Give me credit. It'd be at least two or three." I try to lighten the mood.

"See. Already mouthing off." She levels me with a look.

"Then keep being the boss."

Curiosity flashes across her face, and the way it lights her up, makes my heart rate pick up. All that blood pools south as I think about having this woman again.

"You don't strike me as the type who could give up control."

I haven't been in the past. But for her, I'll try anything she wants. If the only way she'll take a chance on me is keeping all the control, I'll give it to her.

I kiss the side of her neck. "I'm willing to try. Besides, haven't I been good for you so far? Doing everything you want?"

"Yes," she breathes the word as I kiss my way down her jaw and my hands ghost their way over her curves. "But I'd only be using you for the sex—to be clear. This would just be so we can get this out of our system and move on."

"Understood."

"And whatever happens behind closed doors stays there. Publicly I'm A.J.'s, and you and I are nothing but coworkers."

"Yes, ma'am," I whisper against her lips before I kiss her again.

22

M adison

I KISS QUENTIN TENTATIVELY and his hands are slow and careful as they make their way up my sides. I want him, and now that he knows the truth I've given him everything he needs to know to break down my defenses. He'd already been suspicious. The oops phone call and the kiss had only driven him toward the conclusion he was hoping for—one where I give in. And right now, I'm a weak woman for a multitude of reasons.

I'm lonely and it's been a long time—too long, really. It's been so bittersweet watching everyone around me fall hard in love. Watching time tick past while I keep dating strangers and go home alone because we couldn't even hold a decent conversation. Wishing someone could see past the Westfield name to see me. But it's so much more than that.

I want *him*. I *miss* him. More than anything else in this moment. Want his hands all over me. Want his mouth on mine.

Want to hear him say all the things he used to about how he felt about me. How he loved how beautiful and smart I am, and how I'm the only one who makes him want this badly. Because before everything fell apart, I was convinced this man was the only other person on earth who saw me and saw things the same way I do. Who *wanted* the same things I do. The one person I felt like would love me through anything.

But he didn't. Which means I can only have the shallow end of what this could have been now. I can take the things I want from him and leave the ones I don't. Give him some of what he wants too. But only if I'm careful. Only if I don't lose sight of what this is really about.

He starts to walk me backward, toward his room, and I let him take us that way. His lips are down my neck and over my clavicle, and his hands dip under the back of the shirt I have on. His palms brush over my skin, up my spine, and then down again, slipping over my back and down over the curve of my cheeks before they tighten.

I put distance between us then and grab his belt, undoing it and then unthreading it from the loops. His brow raises as he watches me.

"Lie back on the bed." I nod toward it, and I see the flicker of defiance in his eyes.

Quentin's used to being in charge—on the field and off it. He's definitely used to being in charge of me when we're fucking. He gave me almost all of my firsts. Walked me through each of them slowly, constantly asking questions to see if I was okay and patiently taking me at a pace I was comfortable with. But there was never any doubt that he was in the driver's seat. So the idea that he's going to let me have control now seems a little far-fetched. I'm waiting for him to tell me that he's changed his mind.

But he surprises me when he pulls his shirt off one handed over the back of his head and tosses it to the floor before he climbs on the bed. He lays back and gives me a soft smile and the slight raise of his brow in question.

I use the belt to tie his hands to the back of his bed, tightening it and admiring the way his muscular arms look from this angle—stretched over his head. Every inch of him is sexy as fuck. His tattoos, his chest, the way I can see the anticipation in his eyes. Everything about him has improved with time, and I'm jealous because of it. That I missed all the years in between.

My hands fall to his pants, and I undo the button and zipper.

"Lift your hips?" I ask nicely. I don't know how to do this bossy-in-bed thing either. I'm good at doing it all day at work, but usually, I prefer someone else taking the lead in bed. The idea of Quentin doing that to me, telling me how he wants to fuck me, using me how he wants turns me on so much I can already feel the answering throb in my clit. But first, he has to earn it. I have to know he can do this without abusing our dynamic at work.

He raises his hips for me, and I tug his pants and boxer briefs down his thighs, stopping mid-way so they constrict his movement just a bit, and I see the tattoos don't stop on his stomach anymore. They cover his hips and his lower abdomen, starting again on his upper thighs.

But I can't look long because my eyes fall hard on his cock. He's already semi-hard for me and even bigger than I remember. I always thought I exaggerated his size in my head. Sure that it had been my virgin brain freaking out over its first dick. But now I've had enough to know that my memory was right.

My hands go to my shirt, and I pull it over my head, tossing it to the side while he watches. I go to my shorts next, unbuttoning them and pulling the zipper down slowly. His eyes are glued to my every movement, and I smirk at the way he pulls his lower lip between his teeth as I slide the shorts down and step out of them. I'm thankful I put on the matching lace set I just bought as a midsummer present for myself. Because I want him to eat his fucking heart out for everything he's put me through—then and now.

"Madison..." he mutters and just stares as his eyes drift down my body.

It's one of the most gratifying experiences of my life—like younger me is getting a little revenge. It makes me want more. A chance to torture him for a while before I give him what we both want. I climb onto the bed, carefully straddling him, and then lean forward to test that the belt still has him restrained.

"You sure you're comfortable trying this?" I might want to punish him for hurting me but he'd always been respectful, and I can give him that much back.

"Yes."

"You want to stop, just say so."

"Do I get a safe word?" He grins playfully.

"Pick one."

His eyes drift over my body again before they come back up to mine and then they light with something before he speaks.

"Ice cream."

I realize then why he bought the ice cream for me. Why he was saying it now. I smirk as I look him over, remembering how we got ourselves into this mess in the first place. The night on the deck at my parent's house that summer when he'd tried to stay away and failed miserably. When I'd come out on the deck and started feeding him bites of my ice cream. Ones he'd tasted greedily, just before he'd made a point of tasting all of me.

"Ice cream it is."

 uentin

SHE RUNS her fingers over my shoulders and then down my chest, curling them until it's her nails raking over my skin. She drags them gently over my stomach and stops short when she gets to my cock. I watch her smirk as she studies the tension that's building in my muscles, amused that she has this much control. She runs her hand over me to test me until she hears my ragged breathing. I watch as she wraps her fingers around and starts to stroke her palm over the length of me, feeling the warmth of her soak in. I've waited so many years for her to touch me again. It's all too much, and it makes me shutter my eyes.

"I told myself I couldn't be remembering things right. That you weren't this big, and it was just that it was my first time." Fuck, she's good at this. So good I can barely keep my head straight. I just want to beg her to ride me. But I've got to stay focused. Prove that I can be worth it for her.

When I open my eyes, I nearly break at the sight of her. I can't look away from her golden blonde hair cascading down as her eyes stay locked on the way her hand moves over my cock, watching the way her tongue darts out over her lip like she wants a taste, and the way she studies me and every reaction I have to her. That's before I get to how gorgeous her body is—like a fucking dream, especially in the lingerie she has on. I'm having the same reconciliation with my own memories.

"I knew you were fucking beautiful, Madness. But you're even more gorgeous now." I should have better words than this. Should have practiced what I might say or do if I ever got this chance with her. Instead I'm just half stunned into silence. She doesn't say much herself until she finally grins.

"Hmm." She hums.

"What?"

"You're being good. I'm surprised. I thought you'd last maybe five seconds."

"I last a lot longer than that."

"You think?" She raises a brow at my cockiness.

"I know."

"Guess we'll see."

She lets go of me, and I immediately regret my words—anything that makes her stop touching me is a mistake. But I'm still rewarded a moment later when she shimmies out of the panties she has on and tosses them next to me on the bed. I wait for her to take the bra off, but she doesn't. It breaks my heart a little because I'm dying to have the full effect of her naked, the chance to see how much better she looks ten years later with all the confidence she's built over those years.

She climbs back up on the bed, this time turning like she might fuck me reverse cowgirl. I'm ready to be smug. Make a comment about how she's the one who's too impatient for this plan. Except I have to eat my words before I even say them when she straddles my chest, bending over so that I have a full view of her pretty little cunt hovering just out of my reach. She's glistening already, wet and needy, but I can't touch her. I pull on the belt and groan in frustration when I realize I can't quite get close enough. I can hear the sound of amusement she makes in return.

"This is fucking unfair..." I complain not realizing it's about to get ten times worse. Her tongue runs its way around my cock, and she takes me with her mouth a moment later. She's perfect in the way she teases me with soft touches and swirls and then follows with the stroke of her hand and the comfort of her mouth. It's once, twice, and I'm already feeling my balls go fucking tight as she starts to pick up her pace. She's loving it, getting wetter by the second.

"Look at how soaked you're getting teasing me. You need my tongue?" I try to tease her, but she's concentrating hard on my torture.

I shouldn't be surprised she's this good. I taught her years ago after she asked for my help, and she knows every fucking touch and rhythm I like as a result. But something about the fact she remembers so much of it—or at least seems to—makes it that much better.

"Madness... fuck. Please." I beg—I'm not above it. "Please let me have a taste of you."

She releases my cock from her mouth and leans back for the briefest of moments, her cunt grazing over my tongue, giving me the slightest taste before she's back on my cock again, working me over like she's been dying to have me like this for years. It's so good I'm ready to concede defeat.

"Fuck, okay. I don't think I can take anymore..." I groan and I uselessly pull against the belt again, desperate to be let loose and touch her, put my mouth on her, and bury my tongue inside her before I suck her clit until she screams for me. But I get none of those things because, the second I warn her, she releases me and pulls away. I'm left hanging on the precipice, so close to coming I can barely stand it. She moves away from me, delicately pulling her leg back over and sitting on the edge of the bed.

"Fuckkkk," I growl, and she turns to smile at me.

"Admit you can't handle it, and I'll let you loose and finish you off." A taunting smirk paints her gorgeous face, her lipstick slightly smeared at the corner from how diligently she's been working me over, and I can't give up on her now.

"No. I can handle it."

She grins and grabs my pants, pulling them the rest of the way off along with my underwear and socks and tossing them all in a pile on the ground. Her bra comes off a moment later and tops off the little mountain of discarded clothing she's created. I can't help but stare at her. How every single curve of hers is so perfect, the way her nipples bead up under my watch, the swell of her hips and thighs. She's everything I've ever dreamed about.

"You sure you can take more?"

I nod and she grins, climbing on the bed and over the top of me. She spreads her legs wide and leans back, using her left hand to brace herself on my thigh. She's hovering just over my cock, and it gives me the perfect view when she starts to play with herself—the pads of her fingers brushing over her clit in small circles before she dips her fingers inside.

"This is what you liked to do, right? Watch me touch myself, so you knew how I liked it?"

I might die right here, tonight.

"Holy fuck, Madness. You're fucking evil." She's so close I can feel the heat of her against my cock and the backs of her knuckles brush the underside.

"Am I?" She grins and looks at me from under lowered lashes. "Why's that?"

"You had me so close and now you're making me watch...
It's too fucking much."

"You want me to take the edge off for you?" She grins.

"Please. Anything. Just please."

She spreads her legs wider and slides over my cock, teasing
both of us with the way she uses me.

"Oh fuck. Yes. Use my cock how you need me." I groan the
words more than speak them.

She's not the shy girl she once was. She's confident and sexy,
everything I loved about her and more. It's all bringing me to
the fucking edge, all more than I can take after this many years
without her. I grit my teeth.

"I'm begging you. Ride me. My cock or my face, I don't care
—just put me out of my misery."

She kisses her way up my chest and gives me a devious
smile, her head turning to my nightstand. "Condom?"

"In my bag." I nod to it across the room.

She gets up and pulls one out, tearing the wrapper on her
way back and then slowly puts it on, rolling it down my cock
like we both have all the time in the world. When she's done,
she climbs back on top of me, but instead of taking me, she
leans up and reaches for the tie on the belt.

"I'm going to let you go, okay?"

24

M adison

THE LOOK in his eyes is almost feral, and I can feel his heart pounding under mine as I reach up his body to where the belt's still holding him in place. My fingers fumble over it, and I feel his sharp inhale like he doesn't want to say the next thing but feels compelled to anyway. I look down at him again and his eyes are a brilliant piercing blue, a warning in them.

"You should fuck me first. You let me go like this, and I'm going to bury myself in that cunt so deep you'll forget you ever had anyone but me."

I smirk in response and his brow furrows.

"That's what I'm hoping for. Be a good boy and make me come hard, yeah?" I grin, watching his face as it turns to surprise and then determination.

I undo the belt as quickly as I can, and when it finally drops, he grabs me. His broad hands wrap around my back and my thighs and he pins me to the mattress beneath him. I spread my legs wider, and he takes the invitation and slides inside me, his cock so fucking big that I gasp a little when I feel him all the way in. I don't know how my virgin self handled this because my experienced self needs a moment to adjust. I guess it all just hurt, and I didn't realize it might have hurt a little less if I'd been with someone more average in size. Not that I'd trade having him first for anyone else in the world.

"Fuck..." He groans as his eyes shutter. He stills inside me, and I get a moment to adjust to the way he fills me. My hands ghost down his sides, taking in all his skin and muscle. A moment later he comes back to me, his eyes opening—a new sort of determination in them, and he starts to fuck me deep and slow.

One of his hands wraps around my hair and pulls my head back, exposing my neck, and his tongue slides its way up my throat. A desperate whimper escapes me as he starts to fuck me harder, his fingers tightening their grip in my hair, and his lips and tongue working their way over my flesh. I forgot how good this can feel when you have a man who knows what he's doing. A man who fucks like this. One who actually cares if you come.

"Fuck..." I mutter. "You're so good, Quentin. So—fucking—good."

"That's my girl. Taking me so fucking well. The kind of cock you actually need, isn't it?"

"Yes." I wrap my leg around his and raise my hips up to counter his strokes. "You get so deep. I hate you for making me think it would always be this good."

"It is always this good." He nips at my neck. "When you fuck *me.*"

"So vain," I mutter, smiling despite myself.

"Just truth." He kisses down my throat and starts to take me faster. "I know it because I've been just as desperate for you."

I can't think straight as he pushes me closer to the edge, my breathing and his are the only things I can hear as he hits me perfectly with each stroke—a sort of white noise that bathes me in near bliss. The building wave of my orgasm has me matching him, and I'm crying out his name over and over as I beg for him. Too desperate to come to think about anything else.

"Fuck me, you feel so good. So fucking pretty the way you flush like this for me. Let me hear you come."

"Quentin, please. Harder," I plead one last time before I feel the crash of it through my whole body. Waves of it drag me under and make me almost see stars from how good it feels.

"That's right. Come for me, Madness. Let me feel this cunt tighten around my cock. I've been waiting years for it." He groans as he starts to come inside me, the feel of it pulling the last few waves of pleasure from my body, and I hate the loss of him when I finally feel the last stroke of his cock inside me.

He collapses next to me a moment later, his breathing as heavy as mine, and we both just lay there taking a moment. I'm senseless right now because all I can think is how I want him again. How I want him like this every single day. How much I've missed having him.

But that's all too heavy right now, so I run my fingertips down his forearm, grinning up at him with the most playful smile I can muster. This is just sex. I can handle it—even with him.

"That was fun." I break the quiet when his breathing slows.

"Fuck me, Madness. I might be what you remember, but you aren't anything like you used to be."

"I grew up."

"I noticed." He looks at me with something I can't quite read before flashing me a bright grin that melts my heart.

A heart I can't afford to be melting. I sit up on the edge of the bed, reaching for my clothes before I stand to go to the bathroom. I need to get cleaned up and get out of here. I can't do the post-fuck cuddling I want with him because the only way this works is if there's a deep line drawn between the two versions of us. The one we can only have like this, and the one we have to be everywhere else. There's no middle ground where I chase after him like a schoolgirl again. I have to be the grown-up. I need it to be clear for us because otherwise, we'll both be in danger of losing everything. I refuse to let him, A.J., or anyone else I care about down like that.

"Leaving already?" he says it lightly, but I can tell there's disappointment behind his tone.

"Work in a few hours. Demanding client. Need a couple of hours of sleep." I shrug with a small smile as I close the door to the bathroom, thankful that he doesn't argue with me about spending them here.

I lean against the sink as soon as I'm inside and stare at my reflection. I'm playing with fire by sleeping with him because there's no way I won't fall for him again. Not when he's trying so hard to make me believe he can be the right guy. But he did this all once before, only to leave me stranded—broken in a way I never totally recovered from. My heart couldn't take it again.

WHEN I GET BACK to the cottage, the sun's already up, and I am nowhere near ready for the day. I need a shower, a nap, and then desperately some water and caffeine. I slip my sunglasses on and toss my bag over my shoulder for the short walk inside, only to come up short when I see my brother sitting on the small porch with two mugs of coffee.

"Morning, Mads." His pale blue eyes slide to meet mine.

"Morning."

"Imagine my surprise when I came over with some coffee to see if you wanted to walk the property with me, only to find out you were already up this morning. Early morning errand?"

"Yes. I had to... get something."

"What was it you had to get? Clothes? Are you down to the last set? Because I swear that's what you were wearing at Quentin's last night. And yet there's no bag. Or is that in your car?" He peers around me dramatically.

"Okay, Easton. Cut the shit. Point taken."

"I hope it was worth it."

"It was."

"Worth losing A.J. over?"

"A.J. and I aren't actually together. It's a ruse for Dad's sake."

He shakes his head, his mouth flatlining like it's all making sense and pissing him off at the same time.

"Which is why Wren told me I should talk to you when I told her I was concerned about the way you were with Quentin last night. How long has she known?"

"A minute. She's my sister you know. I have to have someone I can confide in."

"You have Bea. Don't make my wife keep secrets."

"She's only known since I got here. I had to tell someone."

"You could have told me."

"And then you would have been lying to Dad and complaining about being in the middle. Not that you should be taking his side."

"I'm not taking his side. I just think one of us has to have a détente with him. Know what the fuck he's up to. I don't want any surprises from him or Mom. And I don't want Mom to feel like we've given up on her. I still love her."

"I don't care what he's up to. It's never anything good these days. He's leaning all the way into his narcissism. I don't want any part of it."

"You still talk with Mom."

"Trying to talk her out of her Stockholm syndrome. Telling her to get a divorce and find a younger guy. She's been due one for what... nearly thirty years now?"

Easton gives me a look. His parentage isn't a secret between any of us, but the outside world doesn't know that he has a different mother. Our parents did a good job of keeping the Vegas showgirl a secret, and East was raised as if he was my mother's child. I'm thankful to my mom for bringing East in like her own. I love him to death and have no idea what I'd do without him, but I never could understand her forgiving our father.

At the very least I'd hoped when we were all eighteen and grown that she'd find herself again, start over somewhere new with someone who could treat her right. Instead, she stubbornly continued to stand by my father, telling me I had no idea what it was like to be married. That much, at least, is true. And if that was what marriage looked like, I didn't want it. At least not anymore.

"I agree she's due a better life than the one he's given her. But after all these years, I have to assume she has her reasons."

I sigh and collapse in the chair next to him on the deck. "Is this for me?"

"Yes. Or at least it was until you decided to turn traitor."

"Traitor?"

"Crossing lines with the enemy. You remember how that turns out historically, right? Romeo and Juliet? Hatfields and McCoys?"

"Romeo and Juliet is fiction."

"Probably based on facts."

I roll my eyes at my baby brother and shake my head. "I'm not a traitor."

"So you didn't sleep with him?"

"You really want details of my sex life?"

"No, but I need to know if you're fucking my quarterback. The one who's been trying to get me kicked off the team. Remember?"

"He's not trying to get you kicked off the team. His uncle might be. But he's not."

"His uncle... the one who brought him onto the team. The one who orchestrated this whole nightmare. The one who helped raise him—that uncle?"

"The quarterback who's been nothing but patient with you? The guy who came to the opening of your restaurant like he was a circus act to help draw a crowd for you? Don't get yourself all in a twist. Especially not this early in the morning when I haven't had enough caffeine."

"I'm not in a fucking twist. I just think you're playing with fire. And West Field would have done just fine without him. Wren is a fucking master at that shit."

"I'm sure it would have been fine. But he definitely helped. You know it. You just don't like it." I can't believe I'm defending Quentin this hard but then I don't like the way East talks about him either. Neither of them has a fair opinion of the other, and I'm desperately trying to get them to see each other as team-mates if not friends.

"I liked it better when I could taunt him about you being with A.J. Now that's ruined," East grumps.

"You did not!" I punch him in the arm.

"Might have, a little. He had it coming."

"You're such an ass, East. Your wife needs to put you on a shorter chain."

"She does. Just usually it's on Saturday nights."

"Again—not enough caffeine."

"You started it. Speaking of, does he know you're not with A.J.? Or was he just on board with the cheating?"

"He knows. I told him we have to keep things secret. That means you too." I give East a pointed look as he sips his coffee.

"You're not going to carry on like this, are you? You remember you fucking work together?" East's brow furrows.

"I'm going to do whatever I damn well please. I'm not hurting anyone."

"You'll hurt yourself if you get attached to him again. He's not the kind who sticks around, Mads."

"You don't know what kind he is. Besides, you weren't the kind either and look at you now, living in domestic bliss. Just like our brother. Xander. It can happen... If you all can, he can."

"I didn't leave Wren when she needed me most."

"You had an easier life than he did. You know his uncle raised him because both of his parents bailed. Our father might have been a miserable excuse for a loving parent, but we had him and Mom."

"And that's an excuse?"

"No. But it's something I can give him some slack for. Anyway... I'm not expecting him to stick around. I'm just expecting to get some good dick while I can, okay?"

"Jesus Christ, Madison. There isn't enough caffeine in the world for you to say shit like that to me. Especially this early in the morning."

"Then next time send your wife to sit and ambush me. She'd at least give me a high five."

East side-eyes me and finishes the last of his coffee. "You want to walk with me or not?"

"I do, but I'd better get a quick nap and a shower. I've got meetings later today. Rain check?"

"Works for me." East starts to walk off, but he turns back. "You know it's because I love you, right? I don't want to see you hurt again."

"I know. I love you too."

East nods and takes off down the steps, heading for the trail that snakes through the woods sitting on his property. I hurry back inside, desperate to get a hot shower and more caffeine. At least we're all in on this secret now, for better or worse.

25

M adison

"THE AGENT FOUND a piece of property for us. It's honestly perfect and everything we hoped for." Bea pushes the listing across the table to me, and I stare at a gorgeous perfectly trimmed and maintained lawn with a massive old house that has a ridiculous amount of character and charm. It's everything we ever wanted and hoped for in Colorado for half the price we could have gotten there.

"Wow," I whisper as I page through the pictures.

"Ten rooms. Seven bathrooms. A huge caterer's kitchen. A sunroom that would make a perfect yoga studio. A wraparound balcony where we could have art classes in the summer. A horse barn and two small cottages so we could have some of the staff live on-site." Bea starts rattling off our dream list.

"It's... perfect."

"Then why do you look like you've seen a ghost?" Bea eyes me carefully.

Because I think I'm falling for Quentin all over again. Or maybe I never stopped being in love with him. I'm not sure yet, but I definitely feel the heavy weight of guilt fall over me as I stare at page after page of perfection. The feeling of wanting to say no to all of this is my gut reaction, knowing that it's not even remotely logical. Bea and I have been planning this for over a year. We've poured blood, sweat, and tears into this dream, and I can't abandon her now when we have the perfect property sitting right in front of us just because I slept with him. But the idea of leaving him hurts.

"I just can't believe it."

"The price tag is reasonable though, right?"

"Right. Two million isn't hateful. How much are they estimating in renovations?" I look up at her and something about her demeanor isn't quite right either. But it's probably because she can sense that something's off with me—the way best friends always can.

"Another quarter to a half million. It depends on what we want to do."

"Again, not terrible considering what we were facing in Colorado."

"Exactly. And this one has access to city water and its own well. No water concerns. No nearby forest fires in recent history. All the things we want. I honestly can't believe it's real."

"Me either."

"But it's so soon. We thought we would have more time to come up with the financing."

"Yeah, I definitely don't have a million plus sitting around right now."

"Me either. And some of our investors have fallen through now."

"Right. I haven't spoken with A.J. recently, but... I can't imagine he'll want to invest anymore either. The way that'll look to his ex-wife if he puts that kind of money in for me."

"And we know Xander and Tobias are out since they've been putting all that money into the museum in Seattle."

"Right."

"We're still agreed that we're not asking the parents?" Bea flashes a look of uncertainty.

"Not in this life or the next one."

"So... thoughts on new investors?"

"I'll have to think about it. East and Wren are a no considering they just put all that money into West Field. I might be able to ask a couple of other people. If things work out with Quentin, I may get a nice bonus but not enough to put a dent in this. You have any leads?"

"Not many."

"How fast do they think it'll sell?"

"The agent said that properties of this size and price usually need the right buyer to come along. They usually tell the sellers to expect sixty to ninety days on the market, but it could go at any time. Obviously, she said the faster the better."

"Well... crud." I stare down at what could be the perfect PR retreat. The kind of place I would love to go if I were trying to escape the media and the limelight to reset. "It really is perfect."

"I know a quarterback who just came into a very nice signing bonus and is very fond of one of the potential owners," Bea muses out loud.

I give her a surly look. "No way am I asking him for money. Especially not after everything."

"Everything?" Her eyes go bright with interest.

"I might have... given in to that particular problem we discussed before."

"You slept with him?" She grins.

"I don't know why you're this happy about it."

"Well... watching you put everything about your love life on hold while you hurry around fixing Tobias's problems, A.J.'s problems, and working on this deal... I hate that you never take time for yourself."

"Hi, pot. It's me, kettle." I raise a brow at her.

"I know, but I also don't have a guy who's been in love with me for years following me around like a lost puppy, wide-eyed and eager to do anything I want."

"You sure about that?" I raise my brow higher because I've seen the way Cooper was around her at the party.

"Cooper's just being nice, and it's nowhere near the same. You and Quentin were engaged. You had this, like, epic Romeo & Juliet love affair thing going."

"That was so many years ago."

"And yet..."

"And yet, I can't ask him for money."

"Fine." She sighs but then she lights up again as she studies me. "But how was the sex?"

"Good."

"Good?"

"Really good. Better than I remember. Better than anyone else. It's depressing, honestly. I was hoping it would be disappointing. That my younger self had just built it all up in my head, but I hadn't."

"Oh, Mads!" She grins so brightly and pats my arm excitedly. "I'm so happy for you."

"Happy about what? I still have a boyfriend. Quentin's still a client. Not just a client. A job—the whole job. Money I desperately need, and if the front office finds out about it, I'll lose my job in seconds and have a hard time finding another if the rumor spreads."

"It's not like that."

"I know that. You know that. But other people won't know that."

"Well, I obviously won't be telling anyone. You don't think Quentin would?"

"No. I might have lost my mind, but I trust him. He's been... thoughtful and kind about everything. Not to mention he's invested in the outcome of all of this too. It's his career after all."

"So then nothing to worry about, right?"

"Hopefully not. But it can't happen again. It was just a one-time thing to get it out of our systems. So we can refocus."

She laughs, softly at first and then it crescendos until she's half doubled over. "Oh, I think you really believe yourself when you say that. Don't you?"

"I mean..."

"Mads. I love you, but you know that's not going to work."

"It has to work."

"Does it? As long as you're discreet, I don't see why you can't have your cake and eat it too. Or why he can't, anyway." She smirks at her clever wordplay, and I shake my head at her.

"You're a menace."

"I am not! I'm just being supportive. Making sure my partner in crime gets some much-needed time off."

"Uh-huh. Speaking of... back to business. How are we making this happen?"

"I don't know. I guess we just try to brainstorm this week and come up with some ideas. Then we'll reconvene and formulate a game plan. Hope that the place doesn't sell in the meantime."

"But what if it does?"

"Then I guess we find another place."

"But this one is so perfect..." I stare down at the pictures again spread out over the table.

"It really is. So... Where there's a will there's a way. You work your connections, and I'll work mine. We'll figure it out." Bea gives me a determined smile, and I return it.

We can do this. Somehow, someway, this is all going to work out for us. Even if it means some sacrifices along the way. After all... what thing worth having in life doesn't require at least one or two? Eventually, there's always a fork in the road.

uentin

"SHE WON'T ASK YOU, so I am." Bea looks at me, brushing her curly brown hair back over her shoulder.

"Okay. What's the big ask?" I smile, thinking it must be some sort of sponsorship Madison thinks I'll hate and is sending her softer-hearted emissary in her place.

"It's for the place in the mountains. The one we're trying to buy. Has she shown you the pictures of it yet?"

"No. Didn't know she was looking to buy at all." I get a sinking sensation in my stomach.

"Oh. I thought she might have mentioned it by now, but maybe she doesn't want to talk about it." Bea frowns.

"Well, you can't leave me hanging."

"I mean, it's not really a secret. Everyone knows we've been working on it for a while. Our first set of plans fell through in Colorado. Then we lost our investors. That's how she ended up on the team here instead. How I ended up kind of jobless myself."

"I'm sorry. I know it hasn't been easy for either of you."

"Well... growing pains when you're trying to figure this business stuff out, you know?"

"I can imagine."

"We've been planning to put together a sort of PR retreat. It'd be a place people could go when they're having trouble— going through a divorce, long-term recovery from an accident, rebranding, whatever the case may be that they've suddenly been thrust into unwanted limelight. Not a rehab facility or anything serious like that. We're not qualified if they need medical interventions, but after—if they want help with the next steps when they've finished with the medical profession-als, they'd come to us. Somewhere to get away from the flashing lights for a bit and rethink things. We'd be available to strate-gize and then they'd have resort facilities where they could relax and recenter."

"Huh. Not a bad idea."

"Yeah. Madison came up with it last year when her brother was going through it. The bad press was making him spiral while he was trying to recover from the accident, and he really just needed a place to escape. She wanted to make sure people didn't have to go through that in the future."

"Makes sense."

"We'd specialize in athletes too since Madison and I both have experience in that realm. Would have been perfect for someone like you during your transition from Pittsburgh to Cincinnati. You know?"

"Right. I can see that. I could have used a resort." I laugh. "So would you oversee it from here or?"

"No. We'd move to head the place up. We might be able to hand it off eventually. Start a second one out west, but we'd need to be onsite initially. We'd be the main draw, obviously, with our experience as far as brand and PR strategy."

"And where is this place?"

"Mountains of Virginia. It's a gorgeous place. Former B&B." My heart sinks hard.

"And you're buying this place? Or you've already bought it?"

"That's where the ask comes in. We're looking for investors. We don't want to ask family, and our brothers have all been investing in their own charities and projects. So we're looking elsewhere for someone or someones who can see the benefit of this kind of place. We've got numbers all drawn up if you'd like to see the portfolio our business manager put together."

"But you want me to invest, so you can buy the place?"

"Yes. Not all of it. Just a portion. You'd get returns commensurate with the investment." Bea's all business as she explains, blissfully unaware that the idea of watching Madison disappear to some far-off place again is actively shattering all the plans I have for the future.

"I see. And how much investment are you looking for?" I can only hope this place is so absurdly expensive they'll need a while to get the investors for it. Give me time to show Madison that I'm worth sticking around for. That once she and A.J. are done faking it, she could have something real if she wants it.

"Five hundred thousand."

"That's it?"

"Well, I mean... I'd love to have more if you're interested and willing. The total funding we need is two point five million."

That's nothing. I mean, it isn't nothing. Not really, but in the world these two women lived in where they're surrounded by athletes and celebrities, they could probably get the money in just a short while.

"I'll do it."

"You're in?" Bea grins.

"Yes. I'm in for all of it. Just one catch."

"All of it?" She's wide-eyed. "But there's always a catch..." Bea scrunches her nose. "Hit me with it."

"Let me be the one to tell Madison? I'll need a couple of weeks to get the money together and have my accountant draw stuff up. You can send over whatever yours has in the meantime. But I want to tell her if that's okay?"

"Okay. Just don't wait too long. I'm terrible at secrets, and I'll let something slip without meaning to."

"Fair enough." I nod.

"Thank you so much, Quentin. You don't know how much this will mean for us."

"Of course. Anything I can do to help." Bea wraps her arms around me to hug me, and I hug her back.

"Just let me know when you've told her. Or she'll probably run to tell me. She'll be so excited." Bea grins so brightly that I feel ridiculous for not being able to return it wholeheartedly.

But I love Madison and want whatever she wants for herself. If that means a new world, a new business, away from here then I'd be happy to help her make it happen. I just wish I had known earlier how limited this time we'd have would be. I'll have to make the most of it while I have her. Which is going to start with explaining to her why I left her in the first place.

27

M adison

"I NEED to tell you something I should have told you before now," Quentin says as he sits down at the table across from me.

"You're secretly married?" I joke.

"Worse than that." His voice is flat, and I feel my heart seize in my chest. I look at him and there's guilt in his eyes. My stomach twists, and I feel goosebumps rise on the back of my neck like my body already knows it needs to prepare for the worst.

"Okay... tell me," I say softly.

"When I left Colorado that summer, I got a transfer to another team—another school. It meant getting off the bench and getting a second chance. A second chance to fix all the things I'd fucked up and get drafted."

"I know..." I nod. "I saw you that season. The end of it anyway."

"You watched?"

"I mean, I was hoping you'd still do well. That you were okay wherever you were." I shrug. "At least until she kissed you."

"She?" He frowns.

"Whoever you were seeing at the time. After the championship game. Hurt a little to see you happy. I was still bitter at the time. Broken heart and all."

"I wasn't seeing anyone. I don't remember anyone kissing me, but I didn't see anyone for a long time after you. Definitely long after that. I couldn't get you out of my head."

"But you didn't answer my messages." I state the obvious, trying not to get emotional. I'm not angry anymore, not in the way I was, but I still feel sorry for my younger self. The way I pined so hard for this man for so long. The way no one else compared. It was part of the reason I went back to fixating on my crush on Xander.

"That was part of the agreement." He takes a breath.

"Agreement?" I echo. A sick feeling hits me hard. The dread that comes with having an inkling of where this is headed.

"I only got a second chance if I stayed away from you." I can hear the heaviness in his voice, feel it like a pall that falls over the room.

There's only one person who would have given him that kind of deal. One person who would have kept him away from me on the pain of ending his career. Even his own uncle wouldn't have been that cruel—but someone else would. My father.

"That's what he promised you to make you go away so fast? I wondered what he could have said. How he scared you off so completely."

"He used his connections to get me on the new team. Talked the coach into giving me a second shot at life, at football, at something besides working a minimum wage job when it was all over."

"And you got drafted and got a championship out of it. Pretty good deal." I feel my blood run cold. The anger I thought I'd buried blooming again.

"No. It's always felt tainted. Part of the reason I've felt so careless about all of this. But I didn't do it for the career. At least not the way you think."

"No? Then for what?" I'm trying to find my professional side right now. The side that says Quentin is just a client of mine, and I need to take all this in objectively, but my heart feels like it's being crushed in a vice. All the old pain I felt over him is resurfacing.

"Your father pointed out that if we got married, with the way things were—the only life I could have offered you would have been difficult at best and soul-crushing at worst. He told me he'd disinherit you, cut you off from your family, and quit paying for your school. That he'd do whatever he could to crush any chance I had of getting off the bench, and I'd be left with whatever job I could get with a high school diploma. One that wouldn't pay the bills and would force you to work long hours with me. That you'd never get to travel, never get to finish college, never get any of the things you deserved." He stops for a moment to catch himself as tears start to form in his eyes. "I couldn't do that to you."

"Why didn't you tell me? Give me a chance to have a say in it. I would have told him to go to hell."

"Because I believed it. All the shit he said... I could see it all playing out that way. Having to watch you wither away because I'd stolen the chance of something better away from you. You were so good to me, Madison. So trusting and loving in ways I never deserved, and I knew you'd be loyal to a fault."

"It should have been my choice to make." I feel the fury rise

—that my father had fucked up more things in my life that I didn't know about, and Quentin had allowed him to do it.

"It should have been. I should have told you. If I had it to do all over again, I would."

"I deserved to know he was manipulating you that way—manipulating us."

"You did, but you have to understand, Madison... I came from nothing. I was embarrassed. I'd fucked up everything at that point, and only saw myself fucking up more things in the future. I couldn't believe you even wanted me." I hear his voice break with his pain and it guts me.

As mad as I am, I feel sorry for him—or at least the younger version of him. He'd been through so much. Abandoned and hurt by so many people when he was a kid. His father. His mother. His grandparents all thought he was too much. I'm sure it was hard for him to trust or believe in anything that wouldn't lead to more heartache.

"I wanted you. I would have done anything for you. It broke my heart when you disappeared."

"I know." His voice is raw. "I know I fucked it up. I know I hurt you. I'm so sorry for it. I wish I could take it back."

I sit for a moment, catching my breath and collecting myself before I reach out and take his hand.

"It was a long time ago. He took advantage of you too—your situation. He didn't like that he couldn't control you the way he controls everyone else, so he found a way."

"I should have known better, done better. At the time, I just kept thinking about how my mom was after my dad went to jail. How she was left to pick up all the pieces because he couldn't hold it together. I didn't want to be him. Didn't want to see any of that happen to you because of me."

"You weren't going to jail though."

"No, but... my senior year, my dad got out of jail. He didn't have anyone left, and he'd seen me playing on TV. So he came up to live near the college in a halfway house. Said he wanted to spend time and get to know me finally, since he'd missed so much of my childhood. And you know... At the time I was vulnerable to his story. Vulnerable to what I thought he could offer me. My mom and I, we had a strained relationship. We still talked some, but she had her new family out in California. A much better life than we'd had, and she was trying to focus on it. My younger brothers took up a lot of her time, and she didn't care much about football. So I thought with my dad, maybe he could be that somebody for me, you know? And maybe I could be his reason to stay on track with his post-release program. That we'd support each other and be each other's family."

"I understand." I run my fingers over the backs of his. I can see young Quentin standing in front of me again. Can still see the lost look on his face that summer.

"But then he was having so much trouble readjusting. We got into a couple of arguments that last season. He said he needed me. I'd have practice or an away game, and he'd tell me I was a shitty son for leaving him alone like that. That he needed me, and I was too busy. I'd feel guilty and skip a practice or a class here or there to try to make it up to him. It never seemed to be enough to make him happy though. Then one day he texted me a few times. He'd been kicked out of the halfway house for repeatedly breaking the rules and drinking, needed money for a place, and I didn't answer because I had a game. So he tried to steal some liquor and cash from a local stop and go. When I got back, someone from the halfway house had contacted me to let me know what had happened. When I went to see him, I couldn't afford the bail. He was a repeat offender, and you know... I was twenty-one. No money. No one wanted to give me shit as far as a loan. He was furious. Told me I was worthless to him, and to fuck off. It spun me out so bad. I was drinking and fucking around to try to drown it out. Going to practices still drunk. Passing out in the locker room. Skipping classes I needed to keep my grades within range. Just fucking up left and right."

"Did Tobias and Xander know? Why didn't they help you?"

"No. I was too embarrassed to tell them. My uncle knew, but then he never liked my dad. Felt like he fucked up everything he touched. Me. My mom's life. He told me to stay away from my dad when he got out, and when I didn't, he told me those were the consequences of my actions. I was a man and had to deal with them."

"Fuck your dad and your uncle."

"My uncle—he warned me, and I didn't listen. He's not a bad guy. He's just not a very forgiving man either. He says what he means, and if you can't respect it..." Quentin takes a deep breath. "He wasn't wrong about my dad. I just was looking for a relationship I was never going to be able to have. I saw the other guys on the team have it, and I wanted it. I didn't think logically about whether my dad could really be that for me."

"I don't blame you. You were just hoping to have a family. But you know Tobias's relationship with our dad wasn't all that great. Practically nonexistent now. Xander and his father's either really."

"Which is why we got along. We could all relate to that. Your father at least had a lot of faith in Tobias's career. Easton's too for that matter."

"Only because he wanted a legacy. Not because it was out of love."

"I think... well, it's not for me to say."

"No, say it."

"I think your dad loves all three of you somewhere deep down. I just think he loves himself and his vision for you more. I think he meant well when he drove me off. He was probably right about the kind of poverty we were headed for. He didn't want to see you go through that."

"He didn't want it to reflect on him. But it wasn't his decision to make. And you're right. That man always puts himself first, and I'm tired of it."

"I didn't tell you this to dredge things up and have you fighting with your dad. I've just been dreading you finding out from him rather than me, and I wanted to be the one to tell you."

"Well... thank you. For telling me. It still hurts to hear... But I know we were kids back then. You weren't much older than me, and you went through a lot worse than I ever could have imagined. We made the kind of decisions kids make because they don't know better. I know you were just doing what you thought was right."

"I did it because I loved you." He turns his hand over and takes mine in his, squeezing it. "I still love you. Pretty sure I always will."

I stare down at our hands, and I feel my heart swell and twist in my chest.

"I don't need you to say it back. I'm not telling you all this to try to get you to say it back to me. I just don't want this to be in the way if you ever decide this could be more between us. That you could love me again. Because I love you. I never stopped loving you. I meant it then. I mean it now. I'll wait however long you need. But I'll walk away too if that's what you need from me."

"I love you, Quentin. I've always loved you. I tried hard to stop. Tried hard to hate you, honestly. But even when I had to watch your games, telling myself I was going to root for you to be sacked as many times as humanly possible, I'd still find myself cheering for you."

"But..." He looks up at me.

"But I've made a promise to help A.J. You and I—we work together here and if people find out about us, we could both lose our jobs. I might lose my whole career if they think I fuck every player I work with. I'd hate to hear what the gossips would say if they think I'm dating one and fucking another. It's dangerous for me. And all this history between us. It's a ton of baggage. The kind that casts a shadow over everything."

"I know. And the last thing I want is for you to wind up hurt because of me again."

"So this is all we can be for now. Whatever this is... I know that's probably not what you want to hear. Not enough but I... I need time to work through everything. Get my head straight, and I can't even start thinking about that when I'm spending all my time on yours and A.J.'s careers."

"Anything you give me—especially now that you know the whole truth—is enough. Even if it's just forgiveness."

"I need time. Time to process this all. Like I said, I know you were just a kid. I just... the decisions you made changed my whole life. It could have been so different, and I never even had a say."

"Take all the time you need. I just wanted to be honest with you."

"I appreciate the honesty. More than you know."

We sit for a few minutes in silence before I realize I probably need to make my own confession if we're going to clear the air like this.

"I have something I should tell you too. I haven't brought it up yet because there hasn't been a good time, but I don't want you to think I've been keeping it from you."

"You and A.J. secretly got married?"

"Ha. Very funny." I roll my eyes at him. "No, it's me and Bea. We've got plans. It's why I haven't looked for an apartment, and she's been staying with Cooper for the time being. There's a property we're going to buy and renovate. Turn it into a resort for athletes to get away when they need a break—the yips, a divorce, a scandal they have to work through."

"Like your brother?"

"Like my brother. Yes."

"Bea mentioned it to me when she was looking for investors. I asked if I could talk to you about it on our own time. I wanted to give you a chance to bring it up or for me to find a good time."

"She did?"

"Yes. Remember I know Bea from back in Pittsburgh when she dated Rob. I would have been someone she would have asked anyway. She knew you wouldn't want to because of our history."

"She shouldn't have asked because of our history."

"It would have hurt my feelings if neither of you asked."

"I don't want you to feel pressured."

"I'm not pressured. If it's what you want. If that's your dream, then I want to support you. You're helping me do this. I can help you do something for yourself."

Him saying that makes it so much harder to say the next part.

"I'll be moving away at the end of the season."

"But I've got you for a whole season first." He offers up a small smile.

"That's true."

"So then we do what we can with the time we've got."

28

Quentin

WHEN WE GET TO SEATTLE, we drop our stuff off at the hotel and quickly hop back into our rental car to head to Joss's, a friend of Madison's. She's the photographer who's taking the photos for my tech company sponsorship, some sort of deal Madison's set up for us, so we have some editorial control of the content. The tech company was more than happy to agree to it because Joss Marks-St. George is apparently famous and has worked with athletes and celebrities the world over. I haven't heard of her, but I've also never had this kind of sponsorship before. This is all Madison and her magic.

I'm nervous coming here, not because of the photos but because we're about to jump straight into Tobias and Xander's world. Joss's husband, Colt, is their quarterback and from what Madison has told me, a very good friend of theirs. They're also all friends with Madison and I have no idea how much they know about our past. She's only warned me that they don't know anything about our present and she wants to keep it that way rather than involve more people in the web of secrets we're all currently entangled in.

So I'm preparing myself for a potentially icy reception and a very long awkward day. One that will turn into an awkward weekend when Madison meets up with Bea and goes to Xander's engagement party tomorrow while I stay at that hotel before we fly back. She offered to book me earlier but I wanted to be here with her as long as I could. Especially if it meant we got some time away from prying eyes on the team and in her family. But also because I want another chance for us to talk.

I surreptitiously glance over at Madison as we wait at the door. Ever since I confessed to her she's been quieter, more closed off. I can tell her wheels are turning, and she's still processing everything. I'm trying to give her the space she needs and not suffocate her while she works through it, but she has me worried. So once we get through the job obligations today, I'm hoping to take her to dinner and talk more tonight.

WHEN THE DOOR opens a woman with long black hair and brilliant green eyes answers, grinning brightly and then jumping forward and wrapping her arms around Madison.

"Mads! I've missed you so much! How are you? Flight okay?"

"It was fine. Took a while to get off the tarmac because of the weather between but we made it."

"Well, I'm so glad you survived. I hate flying but it's a necessary evil, I guess." She lets Madison go and then turns to me. She extends her hand and I take it. "And you must be the infamous Quentin Undergrove."

"I don't know about infamous, but yes."

"You will be by the time I'm done with you. Turn around for

a second." She motions as she lets my hand go, and I reluctantly circle around. "Yeah, I see why they wanted him. They gave me a list of the shots they want. You willing to strip down a little?"

"I suppose. I let the boss here decide most of those things, and I just do what she says."

"Oh, that's cute." Joss flashes a look I can't quite read to Madison, and Madison tilts her head and narrows her eyes as a result. "Well, come on in. I made some margaritas. The boys are inside."

"The boys?" Madison asks as we walk into the cottage-style house. It's smaller than I would expect knowing how much money Colt makes. He's one of the best quarterbacks in the league—if not the best—and he's off his rookie contract and making real money now. A fuckton of it. So I'm surprised that they don't live in a sprawling mansion somewhere outside the city or on Mercer Island. But the walls and space are covered in artwork and photos, every square inch littered with the kind of personality that makes my loft back home feel like a blank slate in comparison.

"Colt and Nick. They're playing video games in the game room downstairs next to the studio. I thought Tobias would be over, but I guess he and Scarlett had somewhere to be today. Sorry."

"Oh, no that's probably for the best." Madison flashes a look at me. "Tobias doesn't know I'm here on business too. Just thinks I'm going to be here for the engagement party so..."

"Really? Why not tell him?" Joss asks.

"Well... Quentin, Xander, and Tobias don't have the best history. It's a long story."

"A long story, huh? Is Colt in on this? He didn't mention it when I told him you guys were coming today."

"I doubt it would have come up in conversation on its own."

"Hmmm." Joss hums as we follow her down the stairs.

"Oh fuck. She made margaritas from scratch. I wonder if the tequila is down here. Dollface!" I hear a man talking and then yell out the nickname just as we round the corner.

"Speak of the devil and she appears." Joss leans in and kisses him. I recognize him immediately—Colt St. George.

"Sorry. Didn't realize you were right there." He looks up and then behind her. "Or that you had company."

"Yes. I have the photo shoot today remember?"

"Oh shit. Yes, I'm sorry." I see the recognition in his eyes. "Undergrove. Nice seeing you off the field. And good to see you again, Madison."

So no, Xander and Tobias had not informed him of the past. I might have a little bit of a reprieve today after all.

"Madison?" I hear another male voice ask from around the corner and then a guy with dirty blond curly hair rounds the corner. He's an inch or so shorter than me, and I don't recognize him. But when his eyes land on Madison, they light up like a kid on Christmas morning, and he hurries over to hug her. Grabbing her up off the ground and spinning her around. "Fuck, I didn't know you were coming, Maddy girl. I've missed you."

"Nick!" She hugs him back and grins brightly as he spins her and then sets her down on her feet. They obviously know each other, *well*. And I have to control my reaction, biting the side of my tongue as I watch it play out. I feel the swell of irritation at how familiar he is with her. It's obvious as fuck it's more than just friendship on his part, and while he'd have zero clue that she's secretly with me, he should at least be respecting the fact that she's very publicly dating A.J. Does it make me a hypocrite given my own approach to her? Maybe. But I'm starting to think this afternoon is going to be even more painful than I thought.

They're busy talking as Joss introduces me to Colt more formally and takes me to see the studio she has set up in her

house. She explains she has another one we can go to if need-
be but that this one is her favorite, so she thought we'd start
here. She shows me a room I can change in, and I set down the
bag of clothes I brought with me, pulling some of them out as
she shuts the door behind me. I was hoping Madison would
help me pick something, but she's too involved in talking to the
others and Joss fixing her a drink to notice, and I don't want to
interrupt. I immediately feel like an outsider here, even more
than I did with the Chaos, which is saying something.

I CAN SAFELY SAY that I officially hate Nick who I've discovered is
a former all-pro Ivy Leaguer and now the long snapper for the
Phantom. He's a team favorite, a fan favorite, and a darling of
this friend group. And apparently, a huge fucking fan of
Madison judging by the way he's been glued to her side all
afternoon. She can't move without his eyes on her, can't talk
without his rapt attention, and every chance he gets he presses
closer to her to whisper something in her ear or make a joke
that sends her into a fit of laughter.

When Madison follows me to the downstairs bedroom after
Joss whispers something about the next change of clothes, she
shuts the door behind her and smiles at me. She's gorgeous
today, maybe more than usual for all the laughing and smiling
she's been doing, but I'm too riled to enjoy it. The envy is eating
me from the inside out, and I'm trying to quell it.

"What?" she asks as her fingers brush away a small piece of
fuzz caught in the five o'clock shadow I have. "I know it's a long
day."

"Just feel a little out of place here."

"Really? I thought they were being nice."

"Oh yeah. Nick's being *very* nice. To you." I look up at her
and her brow furrows.

"What are you talking about?"

"Did you guys have a thing before? It's very obvious he's doing his level fucking best to keep your attention. Can't stop flirting with you."

"He is not flirting with me. He's just a friend."

"Just a friend," I snort. "If that's a friend…"

"Excuse you?" I hear her temper flaring in her tone.

"All that whispering between the two of you. That's friendly?"

"We're trying not to interrupt the shoot. Yes, it's friendly."

"You might think of him as a friend, but he definitely sees you as more than that. Which would be fine if you were single, but he knows you're with A.J."

"He's just joking and chatting," she reiterates.

"So he's never given you any indication he's interested in you?" I ask as I pull off my shirt.

"I didn't say that."

I fucking knew it. I toss my shirt and stare at her silently before I speak. Trying to choose my words carefully but they come out jealous and bitter anyway.

"So he just doesn't care that you have a boyfriend. Thinks he can work his way in anyway."

"Oh, I know you're not judging someone else for that," she admonishes.

"That's different."

She shakes her head, and I can tell I'm about to get business Madison instead of my Madness—another thing that's grating on my nerves today.

"You need to take a breath."

"I'll take a breath when he stops touching you. I'm tempted to say something."

"You are absolutely not saying anything. It'll make it awkward. He hasn't done or said anything inappropriate."

"A guy can fucking tell when another guy is trying to go

after his girl, Madison. It's obvious as fuck, and I don't like this where I just have to sit here and watch it happen."

"Because you're so worried for A.J.?" She makes a sarcastic comment and it pricks.

"You *know* why."

"And you know you have no business telling me what to do. These might be friends of mine, but this is work. We're at work right now. Joss is doing this as a professional courtesy. Her name will help your brand. Part of the reason you got this sponsorship deal was because I told them who would do the photographs. You make things all awkward and uncomfortable out there for what's going to look like no good reason? You're going to embarrass both of us."

"I don't need pity handouts from your friends."

"Actually, you do. You need any and every kind of help you can get right now to help you win over the fans and have them see you as a household name. This brand deal helps you in more ways than one. It's good for your image—makes you look like you fit in with Colt and the rest of the golden boys who play ball in this league."

I feel the sting of that. I didn't go to an Ivy League or come from money. I don't have a championship ring. My reputation in the league has left me as a gruff, wrong-side-of-the-tracks unrefined underdog—lucky number thirteen as they always like to say. A reminder that I don't fit in with the rest of them. That I don't fit with her.

"Makes me look like something I'm not, you mean. Pretending and faking to try to sell them something that isn't real. The same way you are with A.J."

Her head tilts back, and she studies me for a moment.

"What has gotten into you today?"

"I told you. I don't like seeing him all over you."

"He hasn't touched me."

"He had his hands all over you the second we walked in.

Grabbing you and spinning you around like you're in some sort of trailer for a Hallmark movie."

"Are you hearing yourself? He's my friend. He was excited to see me."

"He shouldn't be touching you."

"You don't decide who touches me or doesn't touch me. I don't belong to you."

"You've made that very clear."

"I knew this would happen." Her lips flatten and she shakes her head.

I start to say something but there's a throat-clearing noise and the rap of knuckles on the door.

"Come in," Madison says, taking a step back and putting distance between us again.

Joss opens the door and steps inside a moment later, her eyes shifting between us and narrowing as she looks us both over.

"You almost ready? Everything okay?"

"Yep. Just trying to figure out what to wear. Madison was just making sure I'm staying in line." I put on a fake smile, but I can feel Madison's eyes on me.

"Sorry, it's taking so long. I was distracting him," Madison apologizes and when she flashes a look back at me, I realize the comment is meant for both of us. She follows Joss back out the door, and I'm left feeling like I'm fucking things up once again.

29

M adison

BY THE TIME I get back to the room after the day at Joss's house, I'm a frazzled and weary ball of frustration. Worried that I made a mistake by sleeping with him so soon or that I slept with him at all. That everything in my life revolves around him professionally, and I'm losing perspective on him and our relationship in my personal life too. The delicate balance I was hoping for is already unraveling, and I'm as furious with myself as I am with him.

I stare at the door, tempted to knock on it. I don't even know what I'll do if I see him right now. I barely made it through the car ride and up the elevator. Half of me wants to lecture my client on his behavior this afternoon, how important all of these things are to his career and mine, and the other half of me wants him to make me forget everything again. But I'm still working through how I feel about his confession. What it means for us now all these years later. If it's enough to mend all the shattered edges of my heart.

He's also made it clear that he doesn't care about professional boundaries or what anyone thinks. He was barely able to keep his temper in check this afternoon when he thought Nick was overstepping. I spent most of the day terrified he was going to say something that would make our secret public. So I'm the only bulwark between us and disaster and that means I've got to keep it all together.

I have to get him out of my head, but being with anyone else holds no interest for me. Which means the only way I'm taking the edge off this, is by myself. I can at least think about someone else while I do it. Imagine it's Nick on top of me holding me down and fucking me senseless. He could probably fuck me without holding back the way Quentin does. Look at me like I'm not some precious thing that he might break again. No baggage would get in the way of us fucking and enjoying it.

I grab my toy out of my bag, the one I brought for just such an emergency, and toss it on the bed. I'd already stripped halfway out of my clothes in anticipation of taking a shower, so I crawl into bed. I close my eyes and try to picture Nick's face. His curly blond hair and his bright smile. I hear the sound of his laugh and imagine it's him here next to me telling me how much he wants me. How he can't stop thinking about me.

I slip my hand between my legs, gently running my fingers and then my palm over my clit. Spreading my legs wider while I try to imagine him telling me how much he wants to taste me. But his hair turns dark and tattoos appear all over his skin. His genuine smile turns into a wicked grin. Suddenly it's not his hands slipping down over my stomach to touch me but tattooed knuckles. I let out a silent scream and open my eyes again, staring at the ceiling of the hotel room.

I can do this. I just need to concentrate. And use something that will do a better job of distracting me. I slip my vibrator out of its bag and flick it on. I run it over my body first, dipping it under the cups of my bra to tease my nipples and then down over my stomach. I tease it over my abdomen and my upper thighs, trying to build up Nick in my head again.

I slide the vibrator between my legs, over the cotton of my panties, and then I close my eyes again. The vibration starts to tease life back into my clit once more, and I can feel the desire starting to bloom. Nick's blue eyes are on me, kissing his way down my body until he grabs the edge of my panties, pulling them back to place a playful kiss underneath. He starts telling me how gorgeous I am and how much he wants to fuck me, and I click the vibrator up a notch—moaning when I feel the first little aches of want spread through me. Nick's eyes shift down between my thighs as he bites his lip, and he tells me what a good girl I am for him.

"I can hear you."

The fantasy bubble bursts, and Quentin's standing there instead of Nick. Glaring at me like I'm a traitor. This time the scream is less silent. There's a loud knock at the door between our rooms, and I turn the vibrator off, shoving it back in its case.

"Open the door, Madison." Quentin's tone is demanding, and the audacity of his insistence paired with my desperate need for a fucking orgasm riles me to the absolute edge.

I jump out of bed, grabbing the robe I'd left draped over the desk chair, and wrap it around me, angrily tying it closed before I grab the door and wrench it open. Stormy dark blue eyes meet mine, and they narrow as they drift down my body.

"What do you want?"

"I can *hear* you."

"And? I don't care. Turn the TV on. Go down to the bar."

I can't help but take in his shirtless state though. He's wearing nothing but his jeans, and my eyes are drawn to every hard curve of his chest before I can tear them away. This is going to fucking ruin any attempt I make to get back to Nick. Nick is handsome, lush lips and cheekbones to die for. But he can't compete with Quentin. I'm going to have to do double time now to try to erase him from the fantasy. I start to shut the door, but his palm hits the frame and braces it open. His mouth draws up in a self-assured smile.

"If you need me, you don't have to settle for a toy."

A shocked laugh pops out of me. The absolute gall.

"You're so incredibly vain, Undergrove. Like I told you when you thought you could *hear* me on the phone, it has nothing to do with you."

"We bicker all day. You're frustrated and grumpy the whole way back here. The first thing you do when you get back is take out your vibrator, and I'm supposed to think that has nothing to do with me?"

I flash him a bright saccharine smile.

"I spent all day hanging around Nick after not seeing him for months. He flirted with me the whole day, and I can't stop imagining what his mouth would feel like on me. But I can't have him because I need to be loyal to A.J. So I'm frustrated and grumpy, and the first thing I do when I get back here is imagine him fucking me senseless while I use my vibrator to get me off."

I watch Quentin's face darken with this information, his jaw goes tight, and his eyes study mine before they drift over me again.

"Then let me watch."

"Excuse me?"

"I want to watch you come while you think about another man, Madison. Let me see it. It can cure me of this sick fucking obsession I have over you for good. Remind me why I can't ever have you because you want fucking Ivy League cock instead of me. You won't forgive me. *Fine.* Punish me then, and let's get this fucking over with."

He makes his way into my room and shuts the door behind

him with a loud click. Every step back I take, he takes one forward until my legs hit the bed, and I'm staring up at him. He's furious. His eyes are dark and every muscle in his body is rigid.

His hands go to the tie on my robe, undoing it and letting it fall open before he slips them underneath and slides it back off my shoulders. It falls to the bed, and his eyes drop to my chest. I'm breathing heavily, and he can tell—he watches the rise and fall as he unhooks my bra. The clasps open, and he tugs it down. There's a soft sound of approval when he finds my nipples hard underneath. His fingers sneak under the band of my panties next, the gentle version of him that asks permission long gone, and he wrenches them down my thighs.

His fingers slip between my legs, and he brushes them over me, letting the pads dance over my clit before he dips them inside. His eyes shutter and a soft groan comes when he feels me.

"Oh, fuck. Look how wet he's got you. You'd soak his fucking cock, wouldn't you?"

A small sound escapes my throat, and his eyes snap to mine.

"Get on the bed, Madison."

"You don't tell me what to do."

"Don't I? That's how you always used to like it."

I lean back until my ass bumps the mattress, then I crawl backward until my shoulders hit the pile of pillows at the top. Half-confident that he's going to follow and climb on top of me. Hoping he will.

But he doesn't. Instead, he grabs the chair from the corner of the room and drags it in front of the bed. He sits back in it, his legs wide, and he kicks one foot up on the footboard.

He nods at my thighs. "Spread those wide for me, Madison. I want to see how good he makes you feel. Want to watch you soak yourself and that bed while you think about him."

I roll my lip nervously between my teeth. This isn't the Quentin I know. I've only ever experienced the gentle side of him. The one who treats me like I'm glass that needs to be handled with gloves and soft careful touches. This man is the one I haven't met yet.

"You want the vibrator? Or you think he's so good you could come with just your hands?" He glances at the bag on the bed before his eyes fall back on me.

"I don't need it," I say absently, my eyes dropping to where his hands are undoing the button and zipper on his jeans. "What are you doing?" The last words I speak are barely above a whisper.

"You need him. But I need you. It's always you when I close my eyes. So I figure I might as well have it one last time. Will that distract you? I don't want to ruin the fantasy for you." He pulls his cock out and wraps his hand around himself, his eyes lift to meet mine in question.

Mine drift between his and his cock. I swallow hard, and he starts to stroke himself.

"Is it okay like this? You can pretend like I'm not here. Just imagine your golden boy between your thighs."

"I..."

"Go on. It's awkward if it's just me imagining the two of you."

I slip my hand between my legs, tentatively letting my fingers trail over my skin. I'm in too much shock to know what else to do but follow his orders.

"Touch your clit for me. Run your fingers through, gorgeous. I want to hear how wet he has you."

I lightly touch myself, letting my fingers brush over my clit as I stare at him. The muscles of his arm and chest work as he runs his hand over his cock.

"Quentin..." I whisper.

"Nah, gorgeous. Nick. That was his name, right? Say his name for me."

"Quentin, please." I falter.

"No, baby girl. You're getting confused. His name is Nick." His jaw tightens, and he lets out a breath as he starts to stroke himself harder, faster than before. "Touch yourself. Don't let me do this alone."

I'm so fucking desperate to have his cock in me, I slip my fingers inside, easing them in and out while I grind my palm over my clit. I'm torturing myself because none of it is as good as him.

"There you go. That's how you like it. I remember when you showed me the first time. Did you show him yet? How you like to be touched. Did he memorize it like I did? Spend all his time trying to figure out how to make it better for you?"

"Please... I just... Please," I whisper, risking a glance at him again.

"Please what, Madison? Say his name and tell him what you want. Tell him how badly you need his cock inside you right now. Beg him for it."

"Qu—"

"*Don't.* You say my name again, and it'll be my cock in you. We know you don't want that." His tone is lethal as he mocks me. I close my eyes, trying to swallow. My mouth is like cotton, and I try to lick my lips, but I barely wet them.

"I can't see him. Every time I try... You're there."

"You just have to try harder, baby girl."

"Don't call me that."

"No? What would he call you? Something sweet I bet."

"You're an asshole."

"Yeah. I know. Yell at me some more. Fuck I love when you do that. Gets me so fucking close."

I sit up and open my eyes, staring at him while he fucks his hand. There's a devilish grin on his face, and I have a sudden urge to slap it off him. I've never been violent in my entire life but fuck if this man doesn't inspire every new feeling I've ever had. I get off the bed and cross the room until I'm standing over him, and he looks up at me nonplussed. The curl of his lips sharpens as his eyes fall over my body.

"Oh, fuckkkk..." he groans, his eyes drift closed for a moment, and I look down at his cock, a drop of precum already there. His eyes follow mine when he opens them again. His thumb slides over it and drags it down his length. "You think it'll be big enough for her?"

"For who?"

"The new girl." There's a wicked smile—one the devil himself couldn't pull it off. "Fuck, I hope she can suck cock as well as you do. That she gets as wet as you do for... what was his name again?"

"Quentin!" I growl, and like it's a magic fucking word, he jumps out of the chair, rising to his full six-foot-four frame that towers over me when I'm barefoot like this.

"I warned you." His hand wraps around the side of my throat, his thumb on the side of my jaw. He smears the precum over my cheek and presses his thumb into my mouth as his eyes bore into mine. My fingers wrap around his jeans and boxer briefs, and I start to pull them down.

"So do it." It's my turn to taunt him.

"Take them off me," he orders, nodding down to the clothing I still have wrapped in my fists. I pull them down, and he steps out of them. Then he walks me backward until I hit the wall, and he tilts my head up, forcing my eyes to meet his. "Say it again."

"Fuck me," I say sharply. "Quentin."

He grabs me and pins me up against the wall, his cock slamming inside me a second later. He fucks me rough, and I have one hand wrapped around his neck while he braces my other wrist against the wall as I slide up and down his cock. I'm begging for him. Whimpering his name over and over again while he curses about how fucked up over me he is. I hate him for how good he is.

It doesn't take long before he's coming hard inside me, and I follow him within seconds, the feel of him filling me up is the thing I never knew I needed this badly. He fucks me through the last waves of my release and then carries me to the bed, setting me down gently. His brow is furrowed and his jaw is still tight. I'm surprised by how wound-up he is. My heart goes soft after the way I came apart; I assumed he would too.

His hand slips between my legs, gliding over the tops of my thighs where his come and mine have started to make my skin slick. He gathers it with his fingers and then pushes them back inside me. His lips are at my ear, and I brace for what he's about to tell me.

"That was just the first time, Madness. I'm gonna fuck you all night. Fill this cunt up until you can't even say another man's name without thinking of me. And you're gonna be a good girl for me, aren't you?"

I can't breathe for a moment. The words have broken any ability I have to think, and I just stare at him until he kisses me, nipping at my lower lip as his fingers dig into the flesh of my hip, urging me to answer him.

"Yes," I whisper.

There's no other answer. Never has been. I'm his whether I want to be or not, and the sudden desire to please him the same way he works so hard for me wraps around my heart. "Whatever you want."

"Perfect," he breathes against my cheek before he kisses his way down my jaw, and his thumb circles over my clit, teasing me. I gasp at the contact, and he releases me. "Do you want me to draw you a bath or would you rather take a shower?"

30

 uentin

I HEAR the shower running and occasionally the sound of her moving inside. I set up the water, towels, and washcloth for her, making sure she had everything she needed before I left her alone to process—fuck, give *myself* a chance to process—what I've just done.

I've managed to put myself halfway back together, and I'm sitting in the chair, staring out over the Sound through the window. I drag a hand over my face. I fucking snapped. The idea of losing her, the idea of her and some other guy together while I'm right here, broke the last bit of my self-control. I've always been good about being careful with her. Never pushing her. Never asking for too much. Making sure everything I did was well within her bounds, coloring so far inside the lines with her that I didn't even have to worry. She had the reins. She had all the control. I even liked having her tie me up because it meant I couldn't fuck up.

But now I have. I'm sure I've fucked it all up. If she couldn't forgive me before, she won't be able to now. The amount of time she's spending in the shower should tell me all I need to know. I grab my jeans and start to get dressed again, looking for my belt and finding it just as I hear her getting out of the shower. I should make myself scarce so she doesn't have to see me again tonight. She can tell me to go fuck myself in the morning. I'd get a plane back early, and she could go to the engagement dinner without me. It'd give me time to figure things out back at home with my uncle and the Chaos. Explain how I couldn't handle losing her, so I treated her like she was mine to do what I wanted with.

Just as I reach for the handle, I hear her say my name. I turn around, and she's standing there hair wet, her brow furrowed.

"Where are you going?"

"Back to my room. I'll get a flight out in the morning. That was... I'm sorry. I crossed lines I shouldn't have." I move to leave again.

"You promised all night," she snaps at me, and I turn back to look at her. She gives me an expectant look, as she stands there in nothing but her robe, her eyes running over the place where I'm touching the door in disappointment.

"I... what?" I blink. "I'm sorry. I should go. We can discuss it when you're ready."

"Let's discuss it now. I forgive you. For the first time. For my dad. For all of it. You were young too. You were struggling. You did the best you could. You did what you thought was right, and you were afraid that we'd choose the wrong thing. That I'd choose the wrong thing and that we'd both hate you for it. I forgive you for all of that, Quentin."

"But..." I say in return, sure there's about to be one.

"But if you walk out on me now because you think I chose wrong again, it'll be the last time you do it."

I let go of the handle.

"I love you. I thought it would make this easier. That having grown up and loving you hard enough would show me how to fix it all. But I'm still fucking up. I shouldn't have done..." I look back at the chair. "That."

"I have bossed and berated you since the moment you came back into my life. Running you through your paces and making you check every damn box on my list. You've done it all with minimal complaint. Then you apologized for events that were as much out of your control as they were mine and bared your whole soul to me. So I panicked and told you I was leaving town."

"You have to chase what makes you happy, Madness. I know that."

"You make me happy. I'm just scared I'll lose you again. That if for a second I lose control of this, if I can't make it all perfect, I'll lose you all over again. I'm ragged with the stress of it. That..." Her eyes shift to the chair and then the wall. "That was the most grounded I've felt in a long time."

"I see." I stare at the chair and wall again, replaying it in my head.

"Is there a way I can get that without you being furious with me?"

"You want that side of me?"

"Not always, but on nights like tonight? Yes."

I run a hand over my face and lean back against the door as I study her.

"You're not going to lose me. Whatever happens, I'm here for you always. The last thing on earth I want is you stressed out over me. Fuck, if I could take all your stress away, I would. This is messy as fuck with everything going on. Our families.

You and A.J. Working together. It's more than messy—it's a clusterfuck of epic proportions, but I'm not going anywhere."

"Even after a day like today?" She looks at the door again, reminding me I tried to leave.

"I thought after you came down from it, you'd be pissed as hell and wouldn't want to see me. I didn't even ask if you were on the birth control. Fuck..." I feel the worry flash through me as I look at her.

"I was thinking through everything and working through my feelings. Then I realized I probably owe you an apology for pushing you away instead of talking to you. Being so heinous today." She closes the gap between us and her palms land on my stomach. "And I'm on birth control. I would have said something otherwise."

"You weren't heinous. Like you said. You're stressed and frustrated. Even if you were, you're allowed to have bad days, Madness. I was out of bounds with some of the way I acted at Joss's. You don't owe me an apology."

"You could have been better at Joss's. Especially after I told you how important it was. What it could mean for your career to have that opportunity and more like it. You have to trust me right now to lead you through this the way I trusted you all those years ago."

"I trust you. I just didn't trust him."

"If you trust me, you don't have to worry about him. When you're the man you can be, Quentin, no other man on earth comes close to you. I see it and other people will too once they see you through my eyes. That's what I'm giving them. It's not fake or pretend."

"Even if they're the same eyes that watched me walk away?"

"I didn't even get to watch you, did I?"

I let out a rough breath at that truth. "I'm sorry for that."

"I know and I forgive you. And you're going to spend a lot of time helping me forget, right?" Her eyes glitter with the question.

"Yes."

"Good."

Her fingers inch under my waistband, and she tugs me forward. I follow her until she stands me in front of the chair. She takes her time, undoing my belt and jeans. Tugging them down my hips, then pushing me back in the chair before she slips her robe off and tosses it on the bed.

Her body looks gorgeous with the light pouring in from the window shimmering over her still damp skin, the curve of her hip, the soft indent of her belly button, her full gorgeous breasts that I can't fucking stop staring at.

"What are you doing?"

"You said all night. So I figure I should start by rewarding you for being good. Maybe try to earn some forgiveness of my own."

She hits her knees, and her hands are on me a moment later, freeing my cock and stroking me slowly. Her tongue laps along the underside before she takes me in her mouth. I feel like I'm about to come out of my body with the determined way she sucks me and takes me deep. I will do any and everything this woman wants when she has me like this.

"The way you suck me... Nothing feels this good. You remember the lessons I gave you so well."

Her hand works over the base of my cock while her tongue teases the tip again, and she has me cursing by the time she brings me close—my cock swelling as she takes it again, so sloppy and sweet. Her lips are bright pink from how she's working me over. The wave of the orgasm hits me like a fucking tsunami.

"Oh fuck... Fucking hell. I forgive you. You take my cock like this, and I'll forgive you for anything you want." I groan as she collects the last of me on her tongue. Some of it lingers on her full lower lip, glistening in the dull light. I swipe it with my thumb, pressing it back into her mouth. She swirls her tongue over it, and I watch her throat bob on the swallow. Her eyes glitter with satisfaction that she's put me in this state, and I can't help the smile that forms.

"Smug, are we?" She grins in return.

"Sated more like..." I lean forward to kiss her. "Loving the way I taste on your mouth."

"I love the way you taste too. The way you look at me when you come... You always make me feel like I'm the only woman you've ever wanted." She kisses me one more time before her hands brace on my knees, and she stands a moment later, reaching for her robe and slipping it back on. "Do you want some water or anything?"

"Sure." I pull myself back together and put my pants back into some semblance of order.

She walks to the small kitchenette and grabs a water out of the fridge, opening it and taking a sip before she hands it to me. I take a long draw off it before I hand it back to her.

"I want you to get your toy and come sit in my lap."

"I can wait until you're... recharged." She raises a brow at me.

"Nah you started all this with that toy. I want to finish you with it. At least before we take a nap and *recharge* together." I smirk at her.

A playful smile flits over her face, and I almost think she's going to protest but instead, she does as I ask, handing me the small vibrator before she sits in my lap.

"Lean back and spread your legs for me."

She lays back against my chest, hitching one leg over the arm of the chair, and I use my knee to brace the inside of hers on the other side. She wriggles a bit and then settles comfortably against me. I flick the vibrator on and slip it down over her chest and stomach, watching as goosebumps rise in its wake until she lifts her hips expectantly.

"Fuck. You were going to go to sleep like this?" I whisper as I rest the vibrator lower, gently teasing it back and forth over her clit.

"With the promise of more dick later, yeah." It's her turn to smirk.

"You'll still get some later, but we have to take the edge off if you're this greedy for it."

"I'm not normally. I just... forgot I guess, how good it can be, with the right person."

"Is this good?" I ask quietly.

"A little more." She grabs my wrist and adjusts for me. A ragged breath comes from her as she bites down on her lip. "Right th-there."

"Fuck, you're so sexy like this. Pull your robe back a touch for me." She pulls it back and exposes herself. The way her chest rises and falls, her breasts moving gently with it, the subtle rock of her hips as she chases more friction. It's captivating. Her eyes close, and she looks like an angel.

"It won't take long," she murmurs.

"Hold it for me?" I ask her, and she takes the vibrator from me, adjusting it. I slip two fingers inside her and start to fuck her slowly with them.

"Oh, fuck."

"That's how you like it best, right?"

"Yes. Just like that. Oh god," she whimpers and kicks the vibrator up a notch, her hips rocking down to counter my fingers. Her breathing stutters, and she cries out softly as she falls over the edge of it, using me and the vibrator to take her through the last surges. As she finishes, I take it from her, setting it aside, and then pull her close to me. I kiss her forehead and down her jaw.

"I'm right here. Always, Madness. To take care of you

however you need. Whenever you need. I'm not going anywhere."

Her eyes flutter open, and she wraps her hands around my neck, kissing me like it's the first time.

"Take me to bed then and get naked. I want sleep and cuddles until you need me again."

"Yes, boss." I smile, kissing her, and then lift her into my arms.

31

Madison

I'M STILL LAUGHING to myself about something funny Quentin said this morning when someone knocks on the door. I check the time, and it seems way too fast for room service to be bringing our breakfast but then again, a lot of what we ordered could be put together quickly, so I suppose it's possible. I might tip them extra for the speed because I'm starving after being up with Quentin all night. I stumble out of the bed, tossing my hair up.

"Just a minute!" I call out because Quentin's still in the shower, and I'll have to answer it. I glance down at my naked state and cringe, grabbing the robe off the mattress, wrapping it around myself, and tying it tight. It's still rather obvious I'm naked underneath but at least the essential bits are covered. Plus I'm sure room service has seen worse. I hurry across the room to the door a moment later, opening it and expecting to see a cart with a tray of food. But instead, it's just a man. A familiar one. I look up to see my older brother staring at me.

"Tobias!" I blink.

"Mads!"

He grabs me and hugs me tight. We haven't seen each other in a few months. I've missed him but his timing is atrocious. I hug him back, glancing behind him, thankful that there's no Scarlett right now. I try to make a furtive glimpse behind me before he scruffs my hair. "I came here to get you and tell you to come stay at the house. It's ridiculous that you're in a hotel when you could be with us. I think you're hurting Scarlett's feelings, honestly."

"Well, I just assumed with you being freshly engaged that you'd want your alone time." I give him a pointed look.

"We're at the condo half the time anyway, and the house is huge, Mads. Don't be crazy. We were fucking the whole time you were there for Christmas, and you weren't bothered." My brothers are nothing if not blunt.

"I had earplugs, and I'm fine staying in a hotel. I was planning to call you in a bit so we could make plans."

"I'm here now—what plans do you want to make? Scarlett wants to have you over for an early dinner. She wants some alone time with her future sister before the party tonight. Think you can make it?" Tobias's grin drops as I shift on my feet. "You're in bed kind of late."

"It was a late night last night. Just catching up on some beauty rest."

"Is that room service?" I hear Quentin call out and dread sweeps through me.

Tobias goes stiff and his eyes travel in the direction of the voice. I hear the sound of footsteps and then they abruptly stop.

"Late night, huh? Well, I guess that explains why you didn't want to stay at the house. Not our fucking you were worried about." Tobias's voice is flat, and I can see the tick of his jaw as the muscle tightens.

I turn around and a shirtless, wet-haired Quentin is standing next to the bed, just this side of the bathroom, staring back at my brother, looking like he's just been shot.

The last time the three of us were in a room together was ten years ago and one of the worst days of my life, so I'm bracing myself for impact. Quentin's smile disappears, and he straightens as his eyes meet my brother's.

"It's not what it looks like," I say softly, trying to break the building tension.

"No? Cause it looks like..." Tobias doesn't finish the sentence, tucking his tongue against his cheek and shaking his head instead.

"I'm here with Quentin. I just haven't had the chance to tell you that yet. He has a brand deal with one of the tech companies. He had a photo shoot yesterday for it with Joss. It was fun, but it was a long day."

"And what? The shower wasn't working in his room? Had to come over here?" Tobias's eyes fall on me, an accusation in them.

"It's none of your business, Tobias." Quentin's voice has an edge to it that I've never heard before, not entirely unlike the one he had last night but different all the same. One that sends a nervous flutter through my chest. I can't have these two fighting.

"Oh, it's my business, Undergrove. She's still my sister. Not that you ever seem to remember that."

"Your grown sister."

"I don't care how old she is when it involves you. You obviously didn't."

"Would you have had the same problem if it was Xander or were you just afraid I was beneath her?"

"I never treated you any differently until you fucked my baby sister in *my* fucking house." Tobias takes a step forward.

"Your father's house," Quentin taunts.

The mention of my father has Tobias's fists balling up, and I press my hands to my brother's chest.

"Please. *Please*. Both of you just calm down." I shoot a look over my shoulder at Quentin.

"I'll calm down when this asshole stays away from my family. Trying to get East kicked off the team and now he's trying to ruin your life too."

"He's not trying to ruin my life. There's a lot you don't know, Tobias, so I suggest you talk less until I have a chance to explain. Remember when you lectured me on the way I talked to Scarlett the first time we met?" I flash my brother a warning look and his shoulders relax the slightest bit.

"This isn't the first time we're meeting."

"It's the first time in a long time."

"Start talking then," Tobias grits out.

"There's a lot about the past that isn't mine to tell. But I've forgiven Quentin. There are no hard feelings, and we're both moving on. I think you would too if you knew. And you should also know, A.J. and I aren't really together. That's between us. I'm doing it to protect him from Dad while he figures out what he's going to do. He's hoping for a spot elsewhere, and you know what Dad would do if he found out. He was furious enough when he heard about Cincinnati wanting him. But he's got his ex-wife and kids to think about in Chicago. He knows about Quentin. No one's cheating," I explain as quickly as humanly possible.

"What about the part where he's your client, and you essentially work for him?"

"Are you implying he pays me for sex?" I glare at my brother.

"I'm implying that the optics are bad. You of all people should know that."

"I'm well aware of the optics, but I don't work for him."

"Trust me. If anyone works for anyone around here, I work for her," Quentin muses and Tobias shoots him a look, but I see the slightest twitch of his lip like he's entertained by the idea. I frown at both of them and continue.

"We're coworkers. Neither of us reports to the other. The Chaos pays the bill, not Quentin."

"So you've reported it to management?" Tobias looks at me skeptically.

"Obviously not. Since when are you such a stickler for the rules?"

"Since this last year."

"This is nothing like that."

"And it's just a coincidence that you ended up at the same organization at the same time?" Tobias levels Quentin with a suspicious look.

"Stranger things have happened," I counter.

"Not exactly. She was part of the bait my uncle used to get me there," Quentin answers, and I whip around to stare at him.

"What?" I ask before Tobias can say anything else.

Quentin has the decency to look slightly sheepish. "When my uncle saw you on the new hire list after they brought him on... He might have mentioned it to me."

"So you knew when you were in negotiations—when they were edging A.J. out?"

"Might have..." He lifts a shoulder.

"See, I told you..." Tobias mutters.

"Oh stop." I look back at my brother. "It's exactly the kind of shit you would have pulled if it was Scarlett."

My brother tilts his head in a half-admission.

"We're going to talk about that later." I narrow my eyes at

Quentin. "But in the meantime... Yes, I would love to come to dinner *if* I can bring Quentin as my date."

"I can stay here at the hotel. Got room service coming," Quentin offers.

"Don't be fucking stupid," Tobias grumbles. "You can both come to dinner. I'm just not speaking to him, so I hope you and Scarlett can keep the conversation going."

I think about arguing but then think better of it. Scarlett and I can manage the two of them, and I know Scarlett will be on my side in this once I explain things to her. I'd planned to let Quentin stay at the hotel tonight for the engagement party, but maybe if I can get him and Tobias talking we could smooth over a decade of bad blood. Maybe.

"Fine." I nod and give them both a look that tells them they'd better behave.

"Good," Tobias agrees. Quentin stays silent.

"What time do you need us there? Can I bring something?"

"We'll eat in a couple hours. You can come over whenever you're ready. Don't need to bring anything."

"All right. Just let me get fixed up, and I'll bring some dessert."

Tobias sighs and pulls me in for another hug. "Love you. See you in a bit."

He gives a slight chin tip to Quentin and then heads out the door, and I lean back against it after it closes.

"That went better than I imagined." Quentin looks at me hopefully.

"Don't get too excited. You remember Tobias doesn't do rage. He does anger in the Westfield way. A slight simmer underneath the surface and then straight for the jugular when the time comes. You might still end up dead before the night's over. Especially since you didn't tell me you knew about A.J. and me being here when you took the job." I raise my eyebrow.

 uentin

DINNER IS LESS awkward than I expect it to be with Scarlett and Madison leading the conversation and Tobias and I just following it wherever it leads. After we clear the table and help get the dishwasher loaded, the girls hurry off to the library, so Scarlett can show Madison some of great-grandmother Westfield's letters. Which leaves Tobias and I awkwardly alone.

"I have some whiskey in the den if you want a glass. The good stuff's upstairs in the library, but I'd rather let the girls have their moment."

"Any whiskey is good whiskey." I nod for him to lead the way and follow when he takes me back to another corner of the house. "House is nice by the way."

"Thanks." Tobias pulls the top from the decanter and pours two glasses, pushing one my way and motioning for me to sit on one of the leather chairs.

"If I thought you'd have answered the phone, I would have reached out before now."

"Yeah, well... you didn't answer the phone either, did you?" Tobias looks up at me over the glass before he takes a sip.

"No. I didn't. I fucked up."

"How long did it take you to figure out that one?"

"Minutes. But it didn't matter once it was made."

"I had to hug her and hold her hand through all of that. Knowing it was my friend who broke her. Someone I thought was my friend anyway. Fuck... it's ancient history, but when I think about it again, Quen, I still can't believe it. I trusted you..." He shakes his head.

"I loved her. Still love her."

"Hard to believe."

"If I'd have stayed, she would have clung to me no matter how shitty things got. Your sister—she'll fight for anyone, stick by their side through anything if she believes in them. And at the time, I was headed down a road to nothing. I didn't know if I could even go back, and if I could whether I'd get off the bench. She was ready to fire sale everything she owned to try to raise a little bit of money for us, and I had nothing to give her in return. I would have made her miserable."

"And you just suddenly came to that conclusion after you took advantage of her?"

"No. Your father helped me reach that conclusion. It might have been different if I was Xander or someone else, but he didn't want me or my family name anywhere near her."

"Might be one of the few things we've ever agreed on. You were fucking up left and right—and for what? I've never understood why you pissed it all away like that."

I sigh, rolling the last sip of whiskey around the glass and downing it before I explain everything about my father that I've already gone through with Madison. And answering a few more details about games I missed that he remembered.

"I wish you would have told me. Xander and I might have been able to help you."

"Like I told Madison, I was embarrassed. My uncle told me to stay away, even my mother who was tuned out half the time told me to stay away. And I knew I should have... but I wanted that. What you had—or at least what I thought you had with your dad.

And then there was your dad... He was determined to put me at odds with you and Madison. He told me if I tried to contact either of you, he'd disown her. Make her miserable if she chose me. That I'd be responsible for ruining her life and destroying all the opportunities she'd have in her future without me. I couldn't do it. Couldn't live with the idea of me taking anything away from her that she deserved."

Tobias purses his lips and lets out a sigh. "Yeah, everything you thought you saw there was an illusion about him being a good father. The man only wants extensions of himself, ways to make his reach extend beyond its bounds. We're nothing without him in his mind. I hate that he tried to destroy your relationship with Madison. The man is selfish as hell. Thinks he knows better than everyone."

"Funny that Xander turns out to have the best parents of the three of us, given what a dick Senator Xavier always was about him playing."

"Turns out, best is relative."

I nod and slide my glass back on the desk.

"Do you love her?" He gives me a pointed look.

"Always have. Always will."

"You won't deserve her, you know. Ever—no matter what you do. Guys like us never do."

"I know. But I'd rather spend the rest of my life trying and failing than not have her in my life."

Tobias pours another finger of whiskey and holds it out for me to take, clinking his glass against mine when he does.

"To trying and failing until we get it right. Or death. Whichever comes first."

We both down it and set our glasses back down.

"Don't fucking hurt her again." His eyes lift to meet mine, and I see the threat there.

"I won't."

"Good. Glad that's settled. You want a tour of the house then? I got the old college jersey properly preserved and framed."

I smirk at my old friend. "Yeah. I'm going to have to see that for myself."

A FEW HOURS later we've migrated from Tobias's house to his condo that he shares in the same building as Xander. Xander's hosting his engagement party downstairs, and after stopping at the hotel to change, we've come to Tobias's place to hang out and have a few drinks until the party is in full swing. We're chatting over a bottle of rosé when there's a knock at the door. Tobias answers it, and I hear a voice I haven't heard in years. It's one I miss hearing tell me jokes and slap me on the back, but a man I know hates me almost as much as Tobias did for what happened between me and Madison under their watch so many years ago.

My eyes drift to Madison, and I see her smile go bright when she sees Xander, and I have to tamp down hard on the jealousy that threatens to claw its way up my throat. She's done everything in the last twenty-four hours to tell me I'm the only one she cares about, and she's told me again and again that she doesn't want him. But the way she jumps up to hug him still makes my heart skip.

"Maddie girl! What are you doing here? I didn't think you would make it. Harper's gonna die."

"Harper might know. I saw Joss yesterday. We had a photo shoot."

"We?" Xander frowns and then looks up to see who's with her. His eyes land on me, and the transformation in his body is immediate. "What the fuck?" His eyes go to Tobias.

"Madison works with Quentin these days. She's his PR person at the Chaos. Trying to get people to like him as much as they do East. Work that magic she has." Tobias tries to smooth things over.

"Fine. Why the fuck is he at your house? He's not coming to mine."

"Xander." Scarlett's voice is harsh, and his eyes snap to hers. She shakes her head subtly, but his eyes return to Tobias.

"I'm sorry. Did we all just forget the shit he pulled?" His eyes are back on me, searching me and finding me wanting. "Because if it had been Bea, you wouldn't be walking this earth. Fuck, if Tobias and Madison hadn't talked me out of it, you wouldn't be able to play football at all."

"Don't talk about him like that." Madison's voice is sharp, and the look on her face could kill.

Xander's face softens as he looks at her and shakes his head. "Listen, I know you've always had a soft spot for him but he's —"

"He's the best man I've ever known. He made some mistakes when we were kids. So did I. But I've forgiven him, and we've moved past it. We're friends now, as well as coworkers. I'm not going to listen to anyone say a bad word about him. So, if that's how you feel, I'd like to go wish Harper a happy engagement now before the party starts, so we can leave without making a scene."

"Madison, don't. You can stay, and I'll go back to the hotel." I stand, feeling awkward that I'm at the center of this altercation.

"We talked. I think if you two talk, you'll see a lot has changed." Tobias stands up for me and my heart swells with relief. The two of them are like brothers, and even back in the day, I felt like an outsider to it. With years of animosity, I feel like Tobias saying anything on my behalf to Xander is a huge fucking leap of support.

Xander's eyes flash between Madison and Tobias and then return to me.

"If she vouches for you. Fine." Then like I've been dismissed from his attention, he turns to Tobias. "Do you have any extra bottles of champagne? Harper's worried the caterers didn't bring enough."

"Yeah, I have some if we need them. Do you want them now or just if they're needed?"

"Just if they're needed. Just trying to figure out if I have to run to the store right now, or we could call it good."

"No problem," Tobias agrees.

"Perfect. Look forward to seeing you later, Madison. You too, Scarlett." Xander nods at them and then leaves. When the door shuts, Tobias turns to me.

"Sorry. He'll take some work. You know how he is. When he makes his mind up about something..."

"Yeah. We're not too different there. Hopefully, I get a chance to talk with him. If not... It is what it is. At least you're talking to me again." I offer half a smile, and it seems to smooth the room over. Madison returns to my side, and I kiss her forehead when she sits down, forgetting myself for a minute.

Scarlett's brows lift in question and Tobias cringes. Thankfully, Madison is there to save the day.

"So, I hoped I wouldn't have to drag you in on the secret." Madison gives me an accusatory side-eye. "But A.J. and I aren't really dating. It's a bulwark against Dad and a bunch of politics going on behind the scenes. And stuff between me and Quentin just sort of happened."

"I mean... I was going to tell her later, and then just tell her to keep it quiet so..." Tobias shrugs.

"Your secret's safe with me. I understand." Scarlett gives Madison a reassuring smile and pats the back of her hand.

"I appreciate it." Madison smiles and then looks up at Tobias. "Gossip!"

Tobias starts to protest but Scarlett shakes her head. "He is. He got me in trouble. Be careful, or he'll be telling everyone."

"He better not," Madison warns, glaring at him.

"I mean... if you don't think Xander just read in on your protective girlfriend act there." Tobias shrugs. "Plus, Joss will have you dead to rights in two seconds flat."

"Well, that's true," Scarlett muses.

"Not true. I spent the whole day flirting with Nick yesterday. He was there hanging out with Colt."

"Oh, then she definitely knows." Tobias and Scarlett laugh.

"Like I said, if it makes you uncomfortable or Xander... I can hang at the hotel. Get some room service. Read a book or watch something," I offer.

"No. We'll just have to act more like we normally do when we're working. Since we're amongst spies and traitors." Madison looks at Tobias skeptically.

33

Quentin

WHEN I ROUND the corner with drinks, I see Nick leaning into Madison and whispering to her as she laughs. She looks fucking stunning tonight, and just getting to look at her across the room like this again makes everything worth it. When he touches her arm again though, I'm ready to break up their little tete-a-tete.

"Pomegranate fizz as requested." I hold out the drink for Madison and she takes it, smiling at me. Nick takes a step back and eyes me furtively. I'm sure he's trying to decide how exactly I factor into her life that she'd bring me here.

"Thank you. Nick, you remember Quentin. Quentin, you remember Nick." I can tell by the tone of her voice she's reminding me to keep my cool despite last night.

"Friend now, am I?" Nick muses and they exchange a knowing look. It stokes the jealousy I've done my best to put out. But the memory of her saying she was thinking of him yesterday is still fresh. Which means I could do with less of Mr. Ivy League's charm around my girl.

"I think so." They exchange a look.

"Fair enough. Except the only girl who interests me is taken. Where is A.J. anyway?"

I take a sip of my drink to keep from saying something.

"Busy. Family vacation with his kids."

"That doesn't bother you?"

"No. I trust him."

"Well... if he ever disappoints." Nick grins at her, and I clear my throat.

"He's just kidding." Madison excuses Nick's behavior.

Nick looks at me again, and he must see the annoyance on my face because he excuses himself a moment later and takes off.

"I don't think he's kidding," I mutter once he's out of earshot.

"Not entirely."

My eyes snap to hers. "Did you have a thing? Is that why he was the center of your fantasy yesterday?"

"Eh. Just a little flirtation. When Tobias and Scarlett were figuring out they had feelings for each other, their friends set Scarlett and Nick up. He was in on it, but I think he was still feeling a little odd man out by the end of it."

"And you fixed it?"

"Not like you're thinking. Like I said, it was just flirting. He's too young and sweet for me anyway."

"Because you prefer them old and bitter?"

"I prefer them older and with a little more grit, yeah. As you're well aware." She leans in closer. "And you can remind me again later when we're back at the hotel." The devious grin she gives me has me wanting to take her here and now, but I bite my tongue to keep from saying or doing anything that would get us unwanted attention.

"Have you talked to your other lover yet?" I scan the room for Xander.

She flashes me an amused look. "No, I haven't seen him or Harper here yet."

And like I just summoned them, they walk up to us. Or what I assume is Harper given that I've never met her, but she's walking hand in hand with Xander.

"Madison!" Xander's fiancée greets her, and they exchange a hug while Xander and I nod at each other. Tobias must have laid groundwork because Xander's already less icy to me than earlier.

"Let me see the ring!" Madison takes her hand, and they exchange excitement over the massive rock and the wedding that's coming.

"Looks like a nice turnout. I'm jealous of you and Tobias. Being with the same team all these years. Must be nice to have a lot of the same friends and a place that feels like home," I say to my old friend.

"Yeah. It is. I count myself lucky that I might be able to retire with the same team I started with. I know that's rare. Listen... Tobias caught me up a little." Xander talks softly, letting the girls' voices overtake us. "I wish we'd known more sooner. Still might have decked you for touching her in the first place, but Tobias and I would have taken your side. We could have helped."

"I was too proud for all that." I shake my head dismissively. "Especially from you."

"Fair enough." Xander sighs and motions for me to follow him to get a drink. I don't need another, but I can tell this is about more than that. When we get to the bar he speaks again, low enough for only me to hear. "I shouldn't get involved. But given my own experience... Don't waste your time. I don't know the whole story. If she's really seeing A.J. or not, Tobias said he couldn't explain details of what's going on now, just that you two are back on good terms again. If you want her though, don't wait any longer."

"I don't plan to. If she gives me a chance, I'll take it."

"She missed you for a long time after. She'd ask me sometimes and tell me not to tell Tobias. Want to know if I'd talked with you or if you'd reached out. Broke my heart to tell her that we hadn't spoken and to see the way she looked."

I take a deep breath and nod. "I fucked up. I know. It'll take a lifetime to fix."

"As long as you're committed to fixing it. For what it's worth, I'm rooting for you two. I think you guys balance each other out."

"Thank you. It means a lot to hear that from you. I've fucking missed you and Tobias."

"We missed you too. Fucking hard thinking back on college without thinking about all three of us. I can't promise I won't still sack your ass when we play, but I'll try to hit you a little less hard." He laughs.

I laugh along with him, and I feel like my life might finally be on the right track again.

"Fair enough. *Fair enough...*" I grin.

34

M adison

THE PARTY'S still going strong a few hours later, and I finally get a chance to catch up with Bea who is playing hostess and keeping trays stocked as guests make their way through her brother's house.

"I know Harper's super grateful you're giving her the night off." I smile at my friend as I follow her into the pantry to grab some of the food the caterer left behind when they closed up for the evening.

"Well, the caterers did most of the work. I just have to be back up for some of the extras. Also, I definitely don't think they planned for everyone to be here this late." Bea makes a face at the pantry door. We were hoping the party would be smaller by the end of the night, and we could all spend some time catching up with our Seattle friends, but so far very few people have left.

"They throw a good party though." I smirk, lifting my champagne glass and swallowing the last of it before I set it on the shelf to help her with the cookies.

"At least my parents left early." Bea flashes me a look. She doesn't have nearly the strain on her relationship with them as I do with mine, but Senator and Mrs. Xavier were still demanding in their own right.

"How's that going?"

"My mom wants me to come stay at the house for a couple of days, and I am not remotely interested. I'm trying to use Cooper as an excuse, but she's not having it."

"Speaking of Cooper..." I raise my brow in question because Cooper came with Bea to Seattle.

"He's just here as a deterrent. She badly wants to play matchmaker with one of her friend's sons who's in town, and I am *so* not interested. We went to the same prep school, and he was an asshole then and I can't imagine anything's changed."

"And Cooper just volunteered for that job?" I grin in amusement.

"He's a good friend, Mads. You remember that I was all but engaged to his brother?"

"Oh, I remember." Bea's ex had started out promising and turned into a jerk of epic proportions by the time they called things off.

"Besides, don't you have enough on your plate with the boyfriends you have?" It's her turn to taunt me and I frown.

"Fine. Fine. Point taken..." I mutter as we make our way out to the table and start plating the cookies. No sooner than Bea is out of the pantry though, someone is summoning her across the room. "Go. I got it." I shoo her off and she mouths "Thank you" before disappearing into the crowded room again.

As I watch her go, I see a group of people talking. I start to look away until one of them steps to the side. I see a woman pressed up closely to Quentin, her hand on his forearm as she laughs at whatever story he's telling her. She's clearly enamored with him and I feel a little spark of jealousy light under my skin.

"Oh, I think you might be in danger of losing your man to Nora. Or one of these other women. They've all been chattering about him tonight. I know I always needed a pick-me-up, fuck-me-down situation after going to engagement parties like these. Thank God, I have one built in now." Joss's voice startles me out of the people-watching I was doing. Person-watching really.

"Nora?" I ask now that I have the name of the woman who can't stop flirting with Quentin.

"She's Violet's sister-in-law. Violet, Ben's wife? You've met her."

"Oh yes. I remember Violet. Just not Nora." Violet is best friends with Joss and Harper and is married to Ben, one of the wide receivers for the Seattle Phantom and a close friend of both my brothers.

"Nora is new around here. Well not really. She's Violet's other best friend. That's how she and Ben ended up together in the first place. But she's newly divorced now, so she's been spending more time out here with them."

"I see. Also, Quentin's not my man. I just have a vested interest in who he goes home with. Don't need any scandals." I try to sound disinterested but when I look back at Joss, the bemused look on her face tells me I'm a terrible liar.

"The way you two were bickering at my place? If you're not fucking, you should be."

"I'm with A.J." I shake my head.

"Well, you should be under Quentin. Do yourself a favor before Nora beats you out for it. The way he looks at you, you'd be silly not to take advantage of it. Just a tip. I'll leave you to your brooding though." Joss grabs a cookie off the table behind me and disappears back into the crowd.

Nora's fingers play over Quentin's bicep again, and I can feel the jealousy creep up my spine, my fingers dig into my glass a little tighter as I watch. I could do this. He did this plenty for me. Plus it's good for him to be seen like this. Keeps the suspicion off us. Except... right now I want to walk over there and kiss him just to prove a point.

He chooses this moment to look over, and the irritation must show on my face because he smiles and excuses himself. He closes the distance between us, pretending to just be taking something off the table but then turns and stops at my side.

He leans over to whisper in my ear, a devious look playing over his face.

"Are you jealous?" Quentin asks, his eyes going wider with surprise. "Oh, fuck. You are, aren't you?"

"I'm not jealous. I just think they could keep their hands to themselves when they're asking for autographs."

"Because you don't like when other women touch what belongs to you?" He smirks. It's so self-assured and so wicked that I melt a little under the weight of it.

"I didn't say that. You're putting words in my mouth. I'm just saying, she was a little handsy."

"You've worked in this industry long enough to know that's not exactly unusual."

"Yeah well... it should be. What if you were in a relationship? Do you think she'd care then?"

"No. But I would. Is that what we are? A relationship?"

"We're... I don't know. I'm just saying..." I say, flustered with the discussion.

"Which is why you're so jealous right now? Because this is so casual?"

"I'm not jealous right now."

"So I could go home with Nora and it wouldn't bother you?"

"What you do is your business," I lie because he knows I am, and I'm not about to cede ground on this. Admit that I'm having the same jealousy issues he had over Nick.

He looks left and then right like he's checking to see who's watching and then he grabs my wrist, taking me across the room and dragging me out onto the terrace. No one else is out here and it's dark. The sounds of the city at night buzz in the background, and the only light out here comes from a few strings of lights. The door slips shut after us, and he spins us around, backing me up against the brick wall behind me.

"What I do is *your* business," he repeats the statement.

"During the day what you do is my business. If you want to have a bunch of women feel you up at parties at night, I guess do what you need to for your ego. Just don't expect to come back to my bed after."

"Oh, fuck. You *are* jealous. Look how fucking riled up you are." He cages me up against the wall, and I can feel his breath against my neck.

"Please. I am not."

"You are. But jealousy is fucking hot on you, Madness. Such a rare thing and fuck is it getting me hard to see you all pissed off." One of his hands slips under my skirt and up the inside of my thigh as his lips drift down my neck.

"I just don't like the way she touched you. I'm not pissed off. You're just being such an ass about this. I still hate you sometimes." His fingers slip under my panties, and he groans against my throat.

"Yeah. I can tell by how wet you are how much you hate me."

"I do hate you."

"Awfully jealous over someone you hate so much."

"Fuck off," I mumble, biting my lip as his fingers push inside me, and he uses his thumb to stroke my clit as he moves them in and out.

"Yeah? You want me to fuck off? Or you want me to get you off?" he mutters against the shell of my ear. "Because I think you should spread these pretty legs and let me have a taste."

I gasp when he grabs my skirt and wrenches it up my hips. He fists my panties and drags them down, making me step out of them, and tucks them in his back pocket before he pins me up against the brick. He lifts one of my legs over his shoulder, and I have to brace my hand against the brick to get purchase.

"Quentin, anyone could come out here..." My protest is a weak one because having this man on his knees for me is everything I didn't realize I wanted tonight.

"Good. Hopefully, it's Xander or Nick. They can watch you come all over my face and mark me as yours."

He doesn't spare another word then, his mouth closing over my clit as he starts to suck and his fingers sliding gently inside me. The two sensations have me melting back against the wall, and a small whimper comes out of me before I can stop it. I sound desperate and hoarse—like I can't think of anything else but him getting me off. Which is fair because it's true. I can't even bring myself to care that several other buildings around here look over this terrace. That anyone could look out and see the Chaos's brand-new quarterback on his knees, his face buried between my thighs.

He takes on a punishing pace with his tongue and his mouth, alternating them as he keeps up the rhythm of his fingers inside me. It's like being back on that deck the summer I was nineteen, and I got to have his mouth on me for the first time. But this time he isn't tentative or careful. This time he takes me like he knows me well—like he owns me. Because I've given him all the ammunition he needs to know I'm stupidly fucked up over him all over again.

I gasp when he sucks harder, and my fingers skim over his head, my nails grazing through his short dark hair. I've started rocking my hips without even realizing it, and I stop myself, embarrassed at how carried away I'm getting. He pulls away from my clit and looks up at me with a smirk.

"Don't stop, Madness. Fuck my tongue. You taste better

when you're desperate for it." His fingers press deeper into me, curling inside as he works to hit every spot he can and drags his tongue through my wetness again before he swirls it over my clit. The teasing sensation of it is just too much, and I coast my fingers over the back of his head, once again starting to rock my hips forward, chasing the pressure I need from him. Fucking him like he belongs to me.

"Fuck. You're such a good boy, Quentin. I need more. *Please*," I say the words I know he wants to hear, and he delivers in kind, sucking my clit again and using his fingers to bring me to the edge.

I come hard a few moments later, whimpering and gasping as it finally hits me. The brilliant bloom of pleasure spreading through my limbs makes me weak. I have to lean against the wall to stay upright, and he slips my leg back off his shoulder so I can regain my balance.

He stands to his full height again, his fingers slipping under my chin, and his mouth crashes on mine. I can taste myself on his lips, and he kisses me roughly, one hand caging me against the wall again and the other gripping my ass. I can feel how hard he still is, and I'm desperate to give him the same relief he gave me. My fingers go to the button on his jeans, in a hurry to try to undo it and have him inside me.

"You can fuck me here if we're quick," I whisper, grinning up at him. But he lets go of me and puts his hand over mine.

"No. It's my turn to be jealous now. I want you naked and spread out on a bed for me like you're my girl, and I have all the time in the world. I want to watch how wet you get and how much you beg for me when I tease you. Take my time with you knowing Nick, Xander, and all the rest never get to touch you again."

"Okay," I reply, my heart thumping hard in my chest. Because the idea of him forever is the only thing I want right now.

uentin

WHEN WE GET BACK to the hotel, I follow her into her room. She gives me a sidelong glance but doesn't move to stop me.

"There a reason you're coming in here?" she asks coyly as she steps out of her shoes and sets her purse to the side.

"I told you what we're doing tonight."

"Oh yeah? And you expect me to just do whatever you want."

"I know you will. I've got questions first though."

"About what?"

"Xander among other things. We settled things. We're good. If that wasn't obvious."

"No, the weird back-patting and grunting thing you guys did at the end of the night wasn't obvious; I assumed that was the two of you sealing some sort of new friendship pact."

"Well, now you've made it sound weird. But yes. I think we're friends again. He seems to be coming around."

"Well, I'm sure if Tobias can forgive you, Xander will. It wasn't his sister."

"Ah, but it was his fangirl I stole."

"At least temporarily."

"You *were* kidding about that, right?"

"About what?"

"Being with Xander after."

"And if I wasn't?" She gives me a devious grin that lets me know she's just playing along.

"I'm going to have to punch him before we leave tomorrow. Going to make the apology and new friendship pact a little harder when he has a black eye, but he'll understand I'm sure —if I'd done the same with Harper. He did say I wouldn't be walking if it was up to him."

She rolls her eyes. "No one is punching anyone."

"Because he didn't touch you?"

"He let me cry on his shoulder a bit about things before Tobias took me home the next day. It's not like I told him all the details. But Xander and all his chivalry? He would have never touched his friend's girl. Even if she was ill-gotten gains." She smirks at me, and I ghost my hands up her sides.

"Listen... I just did what I had to win you."

"Like seduce me in my bedroom with my brother sleeping in the next room?"

"I maintain you seduced me. I tried to stay away. Literally laid there at night counting sheep and thinking unsexy thoughts, but then you were asking me questions about how to get guys off and walking around in that thin white T-shirt with no bra. What was I supposed to do?"

"Exercise self-control?"

"I tried."

"Like you tried when you edged A.J. out of his spot here?"

"Fuck..." I groan. "You're going to make us go over that again?"

"This is the first time I'm hearing about it. That it wasn't a coincidence."

"It was in a way. My uncle ending up as coach was just a fluke. Or fate. He was available and had a good season last year, you know this."

"But you ending up on the team?"

"A.J. can't run the kind of offense he wants to run with the Chaos. He plays your dad's sort of ball. Meanwhile, he raised me. Spent all those nights and weekends in my teen years coaching me how to play. I can run a lot of his plays with my eyes closed. So yeah... he wanted me there. Call it nepotism if you want. I guess it is in a way. I'm sure I'll be hearing that in the locker room for a while."

"But you didn't want to play for him?"

"I did and I didn't. It's complicated. I love him, but he's harder on me than he would be on any other player because he taught me. Because he expects more out of me. It means I don't get to have down days or off days. His sons don't play. So I'm his legacy in the same way your brothers are your dad's."

"I see."

"This isn't getting us in the shower with all that perfect water pressure." I press my lips to the side of her neck, but I feel her brace her hand against my chest even as she melts into me.

"Don't distract me, Undergrove. You said I was bait."

I grumble, kissing her one last time under her ear before I pull away.

"Like I said, he saw you on the staff and used it to his advantage."

"How did that happen?"

"He called me up and said, 'How'd you like your PR person to be a Westfield?' I asked him what the fuck he was talking about. He said they'd just hired you on contract, and he thought he could make it work to my advantage."

"So he thought I'd just fall in line?"

"No. He said he thought if anyone could make me fit in at Cincinnati, it'd be you. That I'd have to win you over but you'd be the key to your brother and to the city. That I'd probably get my ass kicked repeatedly first." I laugh at how true that turned out to be. She put me through the fucking wringer.

"I thought he was trying to get rid of Easton."

"He would if he thought it would help. He'd get rid of me if he thought it would help. He's ruthless with those kinds of decisions. No emotion. No special treatment. Just business for business's sake. But I don't think he wants Easton gone. He just wants to remind him that he's the coach, and East has to play ball his way."

"So you had to win me over to make your job work?"

"I had to win you over because I'd been living in a world without you in it. One that wasn't worth living in most days honestly. Having you there again, even yelling at me and telling me how awful I was... made me feel alive again. Made me want to try."

"Here I am teasing you, and you're being all sweet." She kisses me softly.

"I can be *not* sweet if you need me to be. I was trying before this little shakedown here."

"Hmm. I think I like that. You can be the stalker who moves across the country to be yelled at."

"Stalker? I think that's a little harsh."

"Really? I think I like that. Might be into it..." She laughs softly against my lips before she kisses me again.

36

M adison

"I'M into anything that gets you into the shower with me right now." Quentin's voice has taken on a demanding tone that makes me want to do everything he asks for.

"Well, after earlier... you get what you want." I grin at him.

We make quick work of our clothes, losing them in a trail on the way to the shower. I turn on the water to warm it up, and he grabs me and lifts me onto the counter. He kisses me roughly, and I wrap my leg around the back of his, pulling him closer.

His hands run over my skin, up my thighs and sides, and then down my arms again until they come to my breasts. He cups one and leans down to brush a kiss over the tip of my nipple before he takes it into his mouth. I gasp at how good it feels, and he uses his tongue to tease the peak.

His free hand drifts between my legs, slipping through the

wetness he finds there to torment me more, and I slide to the edge of the counter. I wrap my hand around his dick, stroking him as slowly and torturously as he is me. His mouth drifts upward, kissing a trail to my neck and I lean back, spreading my legs.

"Fuck me. Please."

"No," he whispers against my skin. "I told you. I'm taking my time. I want to hear you beg. Tease you until you're whimpering my name so much you'll give me anything I want."

"That's a big ask."

"I'm very fucking determined." He nips at my neck and then looks back at the shower, seeing the mist finally roll out from the hot water, he picks me up and carries me in. He sets me down on my feet under the spray, and we stand there for a minute, taking turns and letting the warmth soak into our bodies while his hands drift over my skin.

My fingers make their way down his chest as the water falls over both of us, and I pause at a set of tally marks that sit directly over his heart. I'd been curious when I'd first seen them and more so now. A set of five followed by another set of four. My finger traces over them, and his eyes follow the movement.

"What are these?"

"A reminder."

"Of?"

"You."

My heart skips in my chest, and I look up at him. His eyes meet mine and they go soft as he studies my face.

"One for each year we were apart. All because I fucked up. I was giving myself until ten to do something about it. The last one would have been added when the season started this fall."

"The last one?"

"I figured if I had ten years to fix my shit, find you, and

make up for it and couldn't do it, that I deserved to live without you."

"You were cutting it close..." I say quietly. "If you hit ten, then what?"

"Then I was going to say goodbye and try to figure out how I would live life without you. Figured I'd crack open one of those expensive whiskies I've been holding on to and end my dry spell."

"Your dry spell? You stopped drinking?" My brows knit together because I'd seen him drink plenty around me.

His lips tug to one side, and his hands slide down my arms until they reach my wrists.

"Nah, Madness. I stopped f—being with anyone."

I take a step back, blinking as I try to make sense of what he's just said.

"Being with anyone? You don't mean..."

"Yes..." The silence after that yes stretches on for a minute before he explains, and I stare at him in shock. "That's what I mean. I felt guilty at first. Felt like it was the least I could do after I took your virginity and left you like that. After you trusted me with all of it, and I broke your heart. I didn't want anyone else anyway. I tried a couple of times, and I just couldn't do it. I always saw your face and heard your voice. It felt like I was cheating on you, and I wasn't being fair to them. Made me feel fucking awful. Plus I didn't want to risk someone getting attached to me, knowing I'd leave them in a second if you ever came back."

I stare at him, wide-eyed because, of all the things he's told me, this one is the hardest to process. I saw him photographed and out with what seemed like dozens of women. Before me, I knew there had been plenty. Not as much as Tobias and Xander. He didn't do girlfriends, but he did usually have a regular friend with benefits. One he exchanged at regular intervals.

"That turn you off?" he asks when the silence stretches on.

"I just have a hard time believing it. All those women you were photographed with. The way you were before me..."

His smile twists and fades as he looks down at the floor. "I told you. I had—have—a sick fucking obsession with you, Madness. I'm not saying I wasn't tempted. That I didn't want to bury my cock in someone else to try to forget, but I couldn't do it. I went out on dates sometimes. One of my friends would be seeing someone and would set me up with her friend. Someone I met while I was out. I didn't lock myself away. I just didn't take them home."

"I see," I say softly. "But I didn't wait for you."

"Oh fuck. I don't care about that. I knew you were living your life. I didn't wish anything different for you. I hoped you were out there, traveling Europe and doing all the things you wanted. The only thing I hoped was that it wasn't Xander. I knew if he ever caved, he'd wake the fuck up like I did and see what he'd been missing all along. That jealousy would have eaten me alive."

"That's why you were so mad when I joked about it."

"Not mad. Just jealous. I could never be mad at you. Especially not for chasing the person you wanted. That would make me a fucking hypocrite when I spent a fucking decade chasing you."

"I didn't want Xander. I mean originally, yes. But all these years. He was just a stand-in for you. When people would ask why I wasn't dating or why I didn't stay in a relationship, I'd joke and say it was because I was in love with him and waiting for him to notice me. But it's because I was in love with you, and no one lived up to you in my head."

"Now it's my turn to be skeptical, Madness, because I've heard you were pretty fucking down about Xander getting married. Your brother made sure to rub that in my face in the locker room at the beginning."

"Because I figured if he was married, you definitely would be. I couldn't bring myself to look you up. I avoided your games and mentions of you as much as I could because I didn't want to know. The thought of you married, with kids... not that I wanted you to be unhappy. I wanted you to be happy, I just didn't want to think about it personally. You know?" I look up at him, and he's smirking. "What?"

"I know. I tried to stay away, but I'd look you up sometimes. Brace myself for when I had to see the boyfriend or the engagement announcement. Held my fucking breath that it wouldn't be anyone I knew. That it wouldn't be Xander..."

I stand on my tiptoes and wrap my arms around his neck, my fingers running down the sides of it as he looks at me.

"It was never going to be Xander. It was always going to be you."

I kiss him and he answers it, deliberate and consuming passes of his lips and tongue over mine. He wraps his arms around me and presses me backward, pinning me up against the wall. The cool tile shocks my skin and brings me back as he pulls away, studying me.

"Or A.J? Or Nick?" His eyes lift with a hint of jealousy in them.

"You know they weren't real."

"The thought of it though..." His hands brush softly over my sides until they come to rest on my hips.

"Like you going home with Nora?"

The wariness fades as a grin spreads on his face.

"Fuck, that was hot. The way you got so fucking heated over that. Then so flustered trying to cover it up."

"I think I was more flustered over what happened on the terrace. Thought you weren't the fuck-in-public type, Undergrove?" I lift a brow.

One of his hands slips over my abdomen and then slides up my middle, over my breastbone and clavicle until he reaches my neck. His fingers wrap around my throat, and his amused smile turns shameless.

"Turns out I'm a fuck-you-wherever-I-need-to-so-I-can-remind-you-you're-mine type." His hand tightens just a bit. He leans in, his cock gliding over my wet skin and pressing into my belly. "Anytime you need me to put you in the right mindset on that, you just let me know. My cock, my tongue, whatever you need. Because they're the first you ever had and they're going to be the last."

"You sure about that?" I taunt him, and the challenge flickers in his eyes.

"Oh, I'll prove it to you, Madness." His grip on my throat tightens, and he pulls me forward, kissing me roughly before he turns me around.

He presses me up against the glass of the shower roughly and moves behind me. The cool slick surface presses against my cheek as his cock nudges against my ass. His mouth is at the side of my throat, kissing and nipping his way down as one hand wraps around me and dips between my legs. His fingers start to massage my clit, and I start to writhe underneath him, so desperate for more I could cry.

He doesn't give it to me though. His free hand drops off my shoulder and down my arm. He stretches it over the glass and threads his fingers through mine, wrapping them both around the edge of the glass wall. His cock slips between my cheeks, and he groans as he grinds against me.

"Look at you, Madness. How pretty you are when you're dying for my cock." His lips brush over the back of my ear. I open my eyes and see us reflected in the mirror across the room through the foggy glass. "That desperate look you get in your eyes for me. Saw it every time I closed mine and thought of you. Came so many times alone with that image. So much better in person though. So sweet and demure when I've got you like this, like you know who owns you." He pushes his middle finger inside of me, roughly pumping it in and out, and I rock against him. "Fuck, yes. Just like that."

I'm slipping down the glass, bent over and practically begging for his cock when he pulls his hand away. I whimper at the loss of him but he grabs a fistful of my hair and stands me back up again. He wedges me against the glass, and his cock nudges me, but he's controlled, just teasing me with the tip. His breathing is ragged, short puffs of his breath playing over the back of my neck and shoulder when he speaks again.

 uentin

"I NEED to know I'm the one. I need to hear you say it. Because as long as I breathe, I belong to you. My heart will go out beating for you," I confess, my heart hammering in my chest.

"You're the one. You were always the one."

A ragged breath rips from my chest at that admission because now I'm about to ask her for a thing I don't know if she'll be willing to give me.

"Then I want you to end things with A.J. I don't want to do this in secret anymore. When you leave to go build your empire with Bea, I want everyone to be very clear on the fact that no matter where you are—you're mine."

She lets out a shaky breath, and her eyes close. Everything seizes up in my chest and time feels like it hits a standstill. I'm afraid she'll say no—that she's gearing up for an explanation of why she can't.

"Okay. Can I... can I do it after the first game? To give him a chance?"

The way she asks so softly makes my heart melt. She hasn't spoken to me like this in years. Not since the last time she trusted me to help her make decisions. It's how I know in my bones that she means it when she says she forgives me, that she wants us.

"Of course. Whatever time you need, we'll make it work. I know he's your friend. But I..." I don't want to sound selfish.

"You want me to put us first. I want that too." She gives me a small smile, and I kiss her shoulder.

"I love you," I say the words so softly, I'm not sure if she can hear them over the water. But my heart feels fuller than it ever has.

"I love you too," she answers easily. "But Quentin?"

"Yeah, Madness?"

"Right now..." Her eyes lift to meet mine, and the fire in them makes everything inside me spark like a tinder to a flame.

"I have a lot of time to make up for."

She smiles and my hands fall back to her hips. I line myself up with her and wrap my hand around my cock, stroking it and teasing her with the tip. She rocks back against me. Begging me with the way she moves, her hands trailing down the glass, leaving evidence of her desperation.

"Please," she mutters when I slip over her again.

"Scary how much I need you. How you're the only one who gets me like this." I tease her one last time before I take her hard, and she moans out her approval.

"Fuck. Your cock is so good..." she curses, using the glass to balance herself as she counters me. I start to fuck her harder and faster, and she unravels in front of me. Watching her fall apart is one of the most gratifying experiences I've had in my life. Rivals everything I've ever felt out on a field. Because I know it's for me. That I'm made for her.

"Glad you approve because it's the last one you'll ever get." I dig my fingers into her hips and take us closer. But I need more from her. I want to watch her fall apart for me. So I retreat, and a muted growl of frustration comes out of her as she looks back at me.

"Quentin..." Her brow furrows, but I turn her around and pull her backward with me to the marble ledge in the shower. I sit down and her eyebrow lifts for a moment before she realizes what I want. She climbs into my lap eagerly, straddling me, and she kisses her way down the side of my neck. I wrap my hand around my cock and another around her ass, helping to guide her way down until she's fully seated.

"I want to watch you ride me. Watch you fall apart on my cock. So take me like you need me."

She starts to move almost immediately, bracing her hands on my shoulders and writhing over my cock with shorter more determined passes. She sits back where I can get a better look at her, and her teeth bite into her lower lip. My hands wander. One over her hip and ass and the other between her legs where I use the pad of my thumb to work her clit.

As she fucks me harder, she starts to curse and moan, breathing so heavily that I think she might pass out from the exertion until she cries out, telling me how good I am and how much she loves my cock. The way she grips me when her orgasm hits sends me tumbling over the cliff with her. I lean back against the tile, closing my eyes as I feel myself filling her.

"That's my girl, taking all of my come in that pretty little cunt of yours. Fuck, Madness. You feel so good."

She slows her pace and collapses in my arms. I run my fingers up her spine and kiss her cheek and jaw. She buries her face in the crook of my neck, and I pull her tight to my chest as I feel her breathing start to slow.

"I need you," she whispers.

"I need *you*."

Whatever happens while we try to figure out our future, I've got my girl back. The one who always should have been mine. The one I'm going to spend every waking minute of my life trying to keep happy from now on.

38

M adison

THE DAY of the home opener I wake up in Quentin's bed. The sun isn't even up yet, but I can hear him in the shower already, so I make my way out to the kitchen to get the coffee going and the food started. I shouldn't have stayed, if it was a road game I couldn't have, but he'd been very persuasive with his mouth in more ways than one, telling me I was his lucky charm.

When I get to the kitchen, there's an envelope lying on the counter with "Madness" scrawled across the front in his handwriting. I open it, and inside is a note and a check.

However things go today, I want you to be able to chase your own dreams. You've given me all of mine.

My heart swells with the note, and I feel tears sting my eyes. I'm not the kind of person who cries over sentimental things. It's not in my nature—not how I was raised in my tough-as-nails guide to life upbringing. But Quentin brings out every soft part of me that I never knew existed. When I flip the check over, I nearly choke on it though. It's not the five hundred thousand that Bea told me they discussed. It's the full two and a half million that we need.

"Oh, fuck. That coffee smells good right now," Quentin mutters as he walks into the room. I whip around and hold up the check.

"What is this?"

He gives me a sheepish look in return, his steps faltering.

"The money for the resort."

"All of it?"

"You said investors had special perks. If that's the case, I want to be the only one getting them." His lips pull up to the side in a cheeky little grin.

"That's an expensive monopoly."

"Worth it though." He kisses my cheek.

"Except you don't have one. One of the investors already gave money."

A stormy look overtakes his face and his brows grow heavy. "Who?"

"Cooper. He gave five hundred thousand."

The cloud lifts immediately. "Yeah, I'm not worried about Cooper. His special interests don't involve you."

"What do you mean?" I perk up.

"Not my place to say."

"Well, you've already said too much. You might as well tell me what you know. Is there something going on between him and Bea?"

"I don't know details but if there was, I wouldn't be surprised."

"I mean... they are living together but... he's Rob's brother. And Bea is so sweet. I feel like Cooper would be... a lot for her."

"Maybe she wants a lot." Quentin raises his brows and pours himself a coffee.

"One cup." I glance down at the mug.

"Yes, boss."

I'm still processing the idea of Bea and Cooper together. If it's possible. Bea is a by-the-book sort of person. She's a lot like her mother. Quiet, reserved, put-together. I can't imagine her with someone as rough and brooding as Cooper in a regular scenario, but in the scenario where she had been Rob's live-in girlfriend, it seems utterly impossible. Something she would think was too uncouth to consider. I was going to have to get caught up on whatever was going on. If Quentin was right and my quiet bestie decided she needed "different" for a rebound. Although rebounds don't usually sign half-a-million-dollar checks.

"What's going on in that head of yours?"

"Thinking about Bea with Cooper. How that would work, if it was in fact, *working*."

"Probably the same way we work."

"We're different. We're both from sports families. We know this world. We make sense."

Quentin's eyes go wide.

"Madness, I promise you. The only way we've gotten away with this for as long as we have is that no one thinks the West-field Princess is letting me put my filthy hands on her."

"I like your filthy hands. And your filthy mouth. And just really everything." I stand on my tippy toes to kiss him, and he wraps his hand around the back of my neck, threading his fingers through my hair. He kisses me until I feel like I might be tempted to drag him back to bed. In fact, I suspect that's exactly what he wants to do. But we don't have time. It's the home opener. Which means it's our big day today. He relents slowly when I start to pull away, kissing me one last time for good measure.

"We're going to finish that later." His eyes drift over me before he resumes drinking his coffee.

"Your uncle doesn't suspect?"

"My uncle doesn't want to know."

"Fair enough."

"At some point though, if we keep up like this..."

"I know. With the season starting, I'm sure A.J. and I can conveniently go our separate ways soon. I was just hoping he'd have a few wins under him first. Something that reinvigorates his support before my dad can try to go in for the kill again."

"Even if he does... your dad is your dad. Vindictive as fuck. Willing to hold on to something to make sure it delivers a KO. I assumed he told you a long time ago about me. Shocked he didn't."

"Yes, well... he was probably saving that for the day we ended up back together. He'll be sorely disappointed you took that away from him."

"Good." He kisses the top of my head. "Gonna start getting ready. You making breakfast or did you want to order something?"

"I'm making my guy breakfast for his big day, obviously." I flash him a playful smile.

"You're the best, Madness."

WHEN I GET to the box it's already nearly time for the team to come out. I'm nervous as hell. Quentin's social media numbers have been up, and he's had tons of positive press. Plenty of articles that have welcomed him as a new era, and all the talking heads on sports media this morning have been saying this is one of the most anticipated games of the day. The stadium is absolutely packed and given the less than stellar season last year, that's a good sign. The potential that Quentin and I have convinced fans he can be the kind of person they want to see out on this field long term.

I glance out into the sea of jerseys and Chaos gear beneath me, and I even spot a not-insignificant number of Undergrove jerseys. Brand new ones with the "13" practically gleaming across their backs in gold.

Bea steps up next to me, handing me a drink.

"Think I'm going to need it?"

"Yes. To toast to your success."

"I'm terrified they'll boo him."

"Oh, someone will. They always do. But I think you're going to be surprised at how excited they are for him."

"I hope so. I've been wondering if I'm losing my edge since..." I don't fill in the blank because there are other people in the box today, friends and Undergrove family who I don't think need to know our business just yet. They can find out with the rest of the public.

"Speaking of, does... know?" Bea's eyes drift to the sidelines indicating Coach Undergrove.

"I don't know, actually. I'd guess he suspects. Probably a plausible deniability situation if I had to guess."

"How do you think he'll react?"

"Better than other coaches I know."

Her mouth flattens, and she raises her brows in recognition of that truth. We don't have time to discuss that problem though because a moment later the lights are coming on, and the player tunnel is set up. I reach out and grab her hand, and she squeezes mine in return.

They start introducing the offensive players, one after

another they come out of the tunnel, and I scream loudly when they introduce Easton. It garners a few looks from other people I don't know in the box, not that I care. Let them talk shit in their group chat if they want.

When they get to Quentin though, the butterflies kick up in my stomach, and I'm bouncing on my tiptoes waiting for him to come out, hoping that they don't boo him so loudly it drowns out the announcer. I squeeze Bea's hand tight and close my eyes.

"And now... for our brand-new quarterback. Lucky number thirteen—Quentin Undergrove!"

The crowd erupts into cheers so loud that if there are any boos, I can't hear them. I open my eyes to watch him run out onto the field, the clapping hits a crescendo, and they show a couple of the "Welcome to the Chaos #13" signs that people are waving around to greet him. I can see the smile on his face as the camera pans to him, and the rest of the team gathers around him before they head to the sidelines.

"See. I told you. It's fine." Bea grins at me.

"Thankfully."

"So... Question." I sit down next to Bea in the box during halftime. She's off in a corner alone sipping her drink and answering messages on her phone, which gives us a little bit of privacy for this conversation. Because as excited as I was this morning to have the money for the property, thinking about leaving this man now feels wrong. Throws a pall over the whole celebration really. I'm wondering though if I'm as alone in that sentiment as I thought I was.

"Answer, maybe." She smiles at me and tucks her phone away.

"How are we feeling about the property?"

"Like we still don't have the money."

"But if we did. If we had all of it and could make a cash offer this week. How do you feel about it?"

"Do we have all the money?" She studies me.

"We do. As of this morning. And then some because of the money Cooper gave you."

"So we have Quentin to thank."

"Yes."

"And you don't want to leave because you're in love with him." Bea doesn't say it with any emotion. It's just a statement of fact. Her wanting to know if it's true or not.

"I'm having my doubts, if I'm honest. I don't want to change course for a man. And trust me when I say I see the irony in changing course for a man who I thought wouldn't change course for me once upon a time. But more importantly, I don't want to let my best friend down." I look over at her, and she gives me a small smile, her eyes going soft.

"Mads, you could never let me down. You've been there through everything. All the crap with Rob. Made sure you found work for me when Colorado fell through. I don't want you to do something just for me. I want you to do it because your heart is in it, and you think it's a smart business decision."

I squeeze her arm and lay my head on her shoulder. "I love you, you know."

"I love you."

We sit in silence for a moment. Overtaken by the sounds of the halftime show and chatter in the booth. I'm trying to think of how to ask her the next thing without prying too much. If she hasn't shared, there could be a reason, and I don't want to make her uncomfortable.

"Did Cooper give you the money for the same reason?"

I see her wince a little, but then she straightens her shoulders and sits back.

"No. He's not in love with me."

"But something's going on there?"

"Maybe." She shifts in her seat.

"If there is... and it makes you happy, I'm glad. Rob was awful to you. Especially at the end."

"He's still his brother."

"The only opinions that matter are yours and Cooper's."

"And yours." She looks at me, a question in her eyes, searching to see if I'm judging her or not.

"I told you my opinion, and it'll always be the same. If it's right for you, if you're happy—I'm right here to support you."

"Thank you. I appreciate that."

"I'm also here for juicy details whenever you're up to share them. We can get some wine and some of those good chocolates from Graeter's."

"Quentin converted you with all those ice cream pints, huh?" She laughs.

"Yes. I think I might be a Graeter's girl now. Which might be part of the reason I'm not ready to leave this city."

"I think the bigger reason is out on the field though. It's okay to admit that. That you're in love, you know. As long as I've known you, you've been so focused on your career. Taking care of other people's lives and making sure they're happy. It'd be nice to see you happy for a change."

"I mean... that one Scottish guy I dated made me happy for a while."

"The way Quentin does?"

"No." I grin brightly and laugh.

"So no resort then," she says with conviction.

"Well, wait. I don't think we have to say no resort. Maybe just no resort in Virginia. I know there are a couple places in Eastern Ohio that are gorgeous. In the foothills. Or maybe we get a big farm with therapy animals. We just have to rethink it, you know?"

"Or we could just start a PR firm of our own. We'd have a few clients already. The city has a football team, a hockey team, a soccer team, and a baseball team... that's not counting the colleges or people who compete nationally."

"Yes, Quentin has a cousin who fences."

"And there's how many big cities within a couple hours of here? Not to mention, nothing says we have to be geographically limited. Once we're established, we could travel and represent clients all over."

"I like the way you think."

"Me too."

"But it's what you want? I want this to be something we're both agreed on. I don't want you to just do it for me. You're always so kind, Bea. You always put everyone else before yourself, and I don't want you to do that here."

"I'm not ready to admit it to anyone but you, but I don't think I was ready to leave this city either." She stares out at the field as the players start to come back into the stadium, and I see her eyes trail after Rawlings.

"Gotta say though. If your brother hated Rob, I hate to hear what he has to say about Cooper."

"I honestly think Cooper might be the nicer brother."

"Well, he was kind to Quentin when he got here. I think he was the only one who was willing to reach out to him at first. So I can see that."

"So this week. We come up with a name and a plan?"

"As soon as we put in our notice."

"Good point. I didn't see any noncompete in the contract, did you?"

"No. I specifically asked when they brought me on since I was still working with some of the other Blaze players in addition to A.J."

"Good. To us." She holds up her plastic glass, and I hold up mine.

"To us." We clink plastic together and take a long drink. And while it might not be the fanciest cup or the best drink I've ever had, it tastes like it might be the sweetest.

39

Q uentin

"WHERE'S MADISON?" I frown when I don't see her after we get out of the presser.

"She's still up in the box. After the news came out, she had a billion more calls, and she already had a lot of sponsors after the first half of that game you played."

"Second half wasn't bad either." Easton grins.

"Yes well, I'm sure she's positively buried now." Wren looks at me. "You could go up and rescue her."

"Okay. But what news?"

"You don't know?"

"No. The game and then the presser..." I wave a hand in the general direction of the conference room.

Wren looks around almost conspiratorially, noting who's in the room with us and then looks back at me.

"It's A.J. He's back with his ex-wife. Someone got photos of them together and the media circus has ensued. Madison's been trying to help put out some of the fires and deal with her dad. Bea's helping but..."

I don't need to hear another word. I take off like I didn't just play the hell out of a game, jogging toward her in the box. Because I can only imagine that she's going to be overwhelmed with everything right now, and I want to be there for her.

When I get to the box, Bea is just leaving. I motion to the door silently asking the question about whether Madison's still inside.

"She's on a call, but she's still in there."

"She okay?"

"Yeah. I think things will be fine. She told Kenneth that they broke up a while ago, she just didn't want it to cause friction during the first part of their season. He calmed down after that. You have a lot of new fans. You should be proud."

"I am, but I'm worried about my girl."

"Your girl, eh?" Bea smiles at me.

"If I get any say in it."

"I think you do." Bea gives me a knowing smile, and I look at her with a question. "She'll tell you."

When I open the door, Madison's winding up the call she's on. Nodding and smiling along as she answers the last of the questions and stares out the glass to the stadium that's nearly empty now. Mostly just workers cleaning up what's left of the mess behind and people on the field cleaning up the gear and equipment.

"Okay. Thank you. Yes. I'm sure he'll be excited to hear that offer." She turns around and when she sees me she lights up. "Talk soon. Thank you. Good night."

She puts the phone back in her purse and grins at me. "You are the man of the hour. You should be out celebrating. Not up here."

"Oh, I'm celebrating. Wren told me you and A.J. are done."

"Yes. Good god, people online are nasty. I'm a home wrecker who's been thrown in the trash for good. Did you know that?"

"Hadn't heard that one yet. But fuck them." I grin as I pick her up to kiss her.

She wraps her legs around me and kisses me like I've just won the whole damn thing. "I'm so proud of you."

"Me? You did all this. All your magic made them think I was worth giving a shot."

"I helped. But you did the work. And the way you played today. Quentin..." She shakes her head in disbelief. "You do that every week and—"

I cut her off with another kiss. "Let's not get ahead of ourselves. It was a good game. It was a good day. My girl is free of her fake relationship. I'm fucking happy as hell."

"Me too. But there's something else I need to tell you."

"What's that?"

"I'm quitting this week."

"What?"

"I'll give them a few weeks' notice to bring someone else on, but Bea and I are starting our own thing sooner than planned."

My heart bottoms out. "Not to be a prick, but I think I regret giving you that check this morning a little bit."

"No. You giving me that check made me realize I don't want to buy that property. But I had to talk to Bea first. And it turns out she doesn't really want to leave either. So we're not doing it." She pulls the check out of her purse and rips it in half.

I'm stunned speechless. "You're not leaving?"

"No. We're going to start our own PR company here in town. She's got Cooper on board already, and Easton will come over of course. I'm thinking if I can get a certain quarterback to sign up... it might be enough to get things started. Bea and I can figure it out from there, but there are enough teams here in the city and within a couple of hours that I think we'll do well."

"Holy fuck, Madness. You gotta lead with that next time." I set her down on her feet and kiss her again.

"Does that mean you'll be my client?"

"I don't know."

"You don't know?" Her face falters.

"I mean if you're going to have the same rules about no fraternization, I'm out. Now that you're free and quitting the Chaos, I plan on convincing you to actually date me in public."

"Oh." She laughs. "I mean, we can figure that part out."

"I'm happy to pay extra. Sign an NDA. Whatever you need, boss." I grin at her, and she slaps my arm playfully.

"Stop! It's not like that."

"It's absolutely like that."

She rolls her eyes and goes to grab her purse. "You're terrible. Also, we'd better go. You're going to be wanted at the team party after the game. You'll be the main attraction."

"Which means hours of chatting and being out, when all I want to do is get my newly single girl home so I can devour her."

"We don't have to stay long. Just an hour or two."

"Yeah. I don't think I can wait. I think the public version of us starts now."

"I have to give my notice first. We're still going to have to be careful. A.J. and I need to make things officially over with a statement. There are loose ends to tie up."

I glance behind me at the door before I turn the small knob. "Good thing this door locks."

Her eyes shift up to meet mine, a question in them.

"Quentin..."

"Madison..."

"If we get caught..."

"We won't get caught. Not if we're quick. And the risk is minimal now. You're a single woman starting her own business."

She bites her lower lip and glances around before her eyes meet mine again, fresh desire in them, and I can tell from the color rising on her cheeks she loves the idea. I kiss her then, wrapping my hands around her sides and backing her up to the counter that runs the length of the suite, looking out over the field.

"Slip out of those jeans for me and turn around."

She starts to turn, but her fingers hesitate as she reaches for the zipper on her jeans.

"Here?" Her eyes widen as she looks back at me. I'm already undoing my pants, so fucking hard and desperate to be inside her.

"Here."

"Are you sure? You've got to be tired, if you sit down over there I could—"

I slip my hand over her mouth and turn her around, her back to my front. I kiss my way up the side of her throat, and she melts into me.

"No. I want this view. The place you run behind the scenes, and I run out on that field. Watch you come apart with this background knowing we own it. That seventy thousand people are out there cheering my name this season because Madison Westfield convinced them to take a chance. That you could have any guy you want and you still choose me. Your brothers might be very good at this game, Madness, but they're not the ones who inherited the real family legacy. The ability to make kings out of nobodies. You do that." I slip my hand down the front of her panties, gliding the pads of my fingers over her clit. "And knowing you have that kind of power and I'm the guy you use it for? Fuck. I'm lucky as hell. Add that to the fact I can get you this wet? I promise I'm never too tired to give you anything you need."

"I want you inside me. Where you belong."

Fuck, do I love this woman when she's bossy.

"Anything you want."

She steps out of her pants and bends over the counter, the jersey she's wearing with my name on it long enough that it still covers half of her sweet little ass.

"Spread for me, gorgeous."

She shifts her feet and bends further as I line myself up, teasing her with the tip a few times before I take her. She clenches down on my cock, and I grip her hips, too fucking high on the win and the way she feels to go slow. I feel like a god with her in my hands and this stadium under my feet. Like everything I ever sacrificed or suffered through was worth it for this moment. If I never get a ring or a trophy, it won't matter. Because I have her. I have this—and it's all I ever wanted.

She moans softly, her hips countering me as I fuck her faster and harder. The sound of our fucking echoes against the walls, and I just hope no one chooses this moment to wander the hall outside the suite. They'll get a fucking earful if they do. The sound of her moans and whimpers too fucking good for anyone but me to hear.

"Fuck, Madness. When you whimper like that... I can barely take it. You're so good for me. Take me so well..." I can hardly think to talk, and I'm just muttering every little word that comes into my mind. So gone for her I can't do anything but tell her how perfect she is.

A few moments later, I can feel her coming hard around my cock, hear it in the sound of her voice as she cries out my name and collapses forward onto the counter. It pulls me down with her, taking both of us under until my vision goes black, and I feel like I can barely get enough oxygen in my lungs. She might have been right that I needed more recovery time after the game, but I don't give a fuck when I open my eyes and see the image in front of me.

Her bent over, breathing heavily, desperately trying to catch her breath. A sated smile on her face as she glances back at me.

Set across the backdrop of the place I plan to spend the season turning into my own home, finally, after so many seasons playing for teams that didn't matter to me. Wasting days and hours just getting by. It feels like everything finally matters. Everything in my life finally counts for something now that I have her and this chance. Neither of which I plan to waste a single second of.

40

M adison

"Did you want me to make the salad?" I call to Wren from the pantry as we prep dinner in the kitchen.

"Yes, if you don't mind. Hopefully, East is back soon. Some of the herbs he's supposed to be getting are what I need for the salad dressing," Wren calls back.

East and Quentin have gone on a walk out around the lake, so East can show Quentin the garden he created and the greenhouse he has set up, and allegedly to get the herbs we need to finish dinner. The ones that have yet to show up. I peek out the back window to see the two of them in the distance staring out at the lake, East gesticulating wildly at the water, and I'm sure Quentin's currently getting the story of how East sunk a bunch of their old Christmas trees in there to create a habitat for the fish. He claimed he was going to have it be a fishing pond for him and his future kids, but instead, he mostly seems to be keeping the fish as pets.

The doorbell rings just as I'm bringing out the croutons and bread from the pantry and Wren's brow furrows.

"Expecting anyone?"

"No. Not that I know of. Maybe a package or something? I never know what East orders. The weirdest things show up when he's in one of his new-hobby modes."

"I'll go answer it."

"Thank you!" Wren calls after me as I make my way down the hallway to the front entrance.

I wipe my hands on the apron I'm wearing and open the door to look for the package. I'm startled to find two people standing there. More startled when I realize they're my parents.

"Mom. Dad."

"Oh good! We were hoping we'd get to see you too." My mom grabs my hand and squeezes it as she walks past me, following my father who just barges right in without waiting to be invited. It doesn't surprise me that I got no warning of their visit. I'm not really speaking to my father and barely speaking to my mother because of the way he handled Tobias's PR problems and then the loss to his team at the championship.

"Um. We're in the middle of dinner. It's not the greatest timing."

"Why not? We haven't eaten. Sounds like perfect timing." My dad flashes one of his characteristic smiles.

"I don't think there's going to be enough food."

"Oh, honey. Wren works at a bar, you know. She always knows how to scrounge something up. I'm sure it'll be fine." My mother dismisses me as they make their way down the hall. She still can't seem to grasp the concept that Wren owns the bars she supposedly works at.

"Wren! Your mother and father-in-law are here!" I call down the hall, hoping that the two seconds of warning might mean something. Especially if East and Quentin have started to make their way back in.

I hurry behind them, rounding the corner just as they do and making a face of panic at Wren when she blankly stares at our visitors.

"Oh. Hi, Donna. Hi, Kenneth. I wasn't expecting you to visit."

"Well, we were going to be in town anyway, you know." My mother laughs.

"If I can't come a day early to see my children, then what am I doing? I run that fucking team. Least they can do is let me come a day early. Plenty of other coaches to take the plane tomorrow morning, and I'll be there waiting to kick their asses when they arrive." My dad chuckles to himself before he looks at me.

"Oh, well that's nice. Are you staying downtown?" Wren asks because the bigger skill that owning a bar has given Wren is the ability to have casual conversations with almost anyone. Even the biggest assholes.

"Yes. Got the penthouse suite. Has a nice view. Though the Ohio River isn't exactly Lake Michigan, you know." My mother flashes another perfectly white smile, and I cringe.

"Well, that's true. It has its charms though."

"Definitely not that chili. We tried it for lunch. I can't understand why people fucking like it around here," my dad grouches.

"Well, don't worry. I think we have enough for everyone. We're just having salads and burgers though. I hope that's all right for you."

"Oh, yes. I love all that bar-food stuff you make," my mother answers.

"Bar-food stuff? You know they have burgers in some of the fanciest restaurants now. Some are hundreds of dollars depending on the grade of meat and the toppings."

"Oh, are we getting hundred-dollar burgers?" My dad laughs.

"No, but you also weren't invited to dinner," I snap.

My dad's face darkens, and I hear Wren clap her hands together. "We finished the den we were working on the last time you guys were here. Did you want to see it? East had the contractor put in a gorgeous built-in table and bookshelves."

"Oh, yes. I'd love to see it!" My mom flashes me a look from behind my father's shoulder, telling me I should shut my mouth before I make things uncomfortable for them.

"Yes. I'd love to see what you've been working on. East has put so much work into this house, always nice to see the progress." My father's distracted from my mouthing off and disappears down the hall behind them.

I check on the sauce for the mac and cheese Wren has going on the stove and then turn my eyes to the guys. They've disappeared and even when I lean on the windowsill I can't see them anywhere in the backyard. I turn up the hallway, dodging past the side hall my parents went down and try to see if they've gone out by the cottage or somewhere else. I need to warn them. Need to get Quentin out of here because none of this will end well if my father sees how cozy we've all become. Even if he doesn't know quite how cozy.

I've nearly reached the side door when it opens and the guys come busting in, laughing, and chatting loudly about whatever they were doing outside. It warms my heart for half a second to see my brother and Quentin so close. Right up until I feel the swell of panic. I start to open my mouth to speak, but Quentin spots me and grins brightly at my appearance.

"Oh fuck. You look so domestic in that apron, Madness." He closes the distance between us and wraps his arms around me, kissing me. I kiss him back for half a second and then try to tug him into the guest bathroom. But it's too late. Wren's tour has apparently ended and my father is standing at the other side of the hall.

"Was pretty clear I didn't ever want to see your hands on my daughter again."

"Fuckkkkk..." East grumbles and rubs a hand over his mouth. He steps out in front of Quentin, making himself a human barricade.

I feel Quentin's entire body tense up, and his eyes open, staring at me.

"Surprise," I whisper.

Quentin starts to pull away from me like he wants to protect me from the ensuing fight, but I grab his hand, threading my fingers through his. If we're doing this, we're doing it together. He squeezes my hand in recognition, knowing exactly why I'm doing it.

"Your daughter is a grown woman."

"Who had a boyfriend. A respectable one who she's been seeing for months."

"You know that's over."

"I told you it was coming if you kept staying down here working with him. Which is why I told you to come up to Chicago. Told you I'd make sure you had the same job and more pay up there."

East and Quentin's eyes flash to me, and I feel the heat rise up my neck. It was an offer I'd never even been willing to consider, so it hadn't been worth mentioning.

"Well. I like my job here."

"You mean you liked wading back into the trash here."

"Dad," East warns my father with a look that's almost as frightening as the one my father makes back.

"Son, I know he's your quarterback, but let's be honest, shall we? I don't think Quentin will begrudge us honesty. Will you, son?"

"Not your son," Quentin replies tightly.

"And like I told you once before. You never will be." My father grins like he's just remembered that tidbit of information. His eyes shift to me. "Because you see, Madison, this desperate fucking felon's child was only too happy to be bought off to stay away from you. I just had to flash some money and few connections in front of him and suddenly you were the least shiny thing he was interested in. But then we all know that's why you wanted her. Thought her money and connections would solve your problems for your lazy ass."

"I'm well aware you tried to manipulate him. And you should be aware that if you speak about him like that again, what little speaking we do currently will end," I warn.

"Be smart, Madison. I don't know what his interest is in you right now. I'd guess the fact that your last name and your brother are currently saving his career from the death spiral it's been on the last two years. Thanks to his uncle. But I promise you he'll be balls deep in some trailer-park princess the second the chance presents itself."

"I—" I start but Quentin squeezes my hand.

"Madison is the love of my life. Making her happy—that's my only interest in her. The only one I've ever had and ever will have."

My dad laughs, loudly. So loud it echoes off the wall. "You couldn't make her happy if you tried. The only man who ever could, she couldn't catch because she already fucked his best friend."

The tears choke my throat, and I cover my mouth. Wren gasps and she moves back between East and me, her eyes turning on them as she grabs my free hand and squeezes it.

"That's it. Get the fuck out of my house!" Easton bellows.

"Don't speak to your father like that," my mother scolds.

"You're going to let my father speak to *your* daughter like that?" East never, ever contradicts our mother, and her eyes go wide at the realization.

"It was crass but he's upset." My mother defends him, and I shake my head, the tears falling hard. Quentin wraps an arm around my waist and tugs me close, clinging tightly to me.

"You heard East the first time. Get out," Wren repeats, holding ground beside me. My mother's brows lift, and my father's face darkens. They've never been particularly fond of Wren. They wanted my brother to marry a trust-fund princess or the daughter of another sports dynasty like ours. But my brother never saw anyone but her, and since he's long been the favorite, she's been accepted despite what they felt were her perceived shortcomings. My mother in particular has grown fond of her and the look of shock on her face tells me that Wren has been far too nice to her for far too long.

"We're going to discuss this later. When you've calmed down and can think rationally." My father acts like he has any say at all, and then storms back into the living room and out through the front door. My mother hurries behind him like she's been forgotten to the wolves. He'll probably lecture her on the ride back to the hotel about how her calling him "crass" undermines his authority over us. It was the kind of thing he always did to her. The kind of thing I always hoped she could escape, and my heart hurts to watch her follow him.

When they're gone, the house turns into a flurry of activity. My brother and sister-in-law reassure us both that my father and mother are awful people who we shouldn't listen to, reminders that they treat everyone this way and we can't expect anything different. There are lots of promises to one another over dinner that we won't let them ruin anything else in our lives going forward. But something in my gut tells me that it's not the last we've heard of my father on this front.

41

Madison

MY SUSPICIONS about my father are well founded. The next day at the game it only takes minutes, barely halfway into the first quarter before I start to see his plan unfold. One that involves a singular goal—sacking the quarterback as hard and as often as possible. His defense is leaving men wide open and making rookie mistakes. Ones that have us climbing the board with an early lead but leaving Quentin on his ass on the ground more than he has any time this season.

It starts that way at least. Legal hits that just have them focusing so hard on the pass rush that our offense is trying and failing to adjust. But by the second quarter, the hits have come harder. Guys are leading with the crown as Quentin goes to shield the ball and take the sack, slamming into him helmet-to-helmet in a way that threatens to snap his neck. His body hits the turf again and again, even on the plays he manages to get the ball off to his receivers, he's being hit late and not a single ref is making a call.

I'm on my feet more than once, screaming through the glass in the box. First cursing their names and then begging them to do anything to protect him. Anything that even remotely resembles throwing a flag has my attention, but again and again, they let him fall. A direct hit to his knees, gloved hands that reach inside his facemask and drag him down to the ground, and a brutal late hit that sends the back of his helmet bouncing on the turf are all ignored.

Bea's up on her feet screaming along with me, and the home crowd boos again as the refs ignore what should be easy penalty calls.

"This is insane. It's like they're doing it on purpose. I can't believe the refs aren't calling it. It's blatant."

My heart sinks in my chest, and I stare down at the small figure of a man on the sidelines. A man so small that he would do something this fucking cruel. Another play has Quentin launching the ball down the field and one of our receivers catching it to run it in for a touchdown. But it's impossible for me to celebrate as I watch a defender headhunting Quentin after the play.

"It's because he is."

"What?"

"He's doing it on purpose. His fucking vendetta against Quentin. He doesn't care if they win or lose this game as long as he destroys Quentin's career in the process." I stare down at him.

"What? He wouldn't... He wouldn't be that unhinged, would he?" Bea frowns down at the field.

"I would never underestimate the depths of that man's cruelty. But I'm not letting him get away with it." I grab my purse and hurry out of the box, on a mission to make the person who was supposed to be my father see reason.

. . .

I'M WAITING for him at the edge of the tunnel, mindful of the cameras I know are aimed this way and the security guards who are eyeing my badge like they don't quite trust it. But when he rounds the corner, he sees me.

"We need to talk." My voice is just above a whisper.

"I have a team to coach, Madison." He uses the same tone he used when I was an errant teenager.

"This will only take a moment."

"Speak." He pauses in his steps and looks at me. I beam a bright smile in his direction, hoping that any cameras that might catch this think I'm just some nice representative of the facility or if they do recognize me as his relation, think we're just having a heartfelt father-daughter moment.

"Call your guys off. What you're doing is beneath you. It's beneath your players."

"I have no idea what you're talking about."

"You *know*. If you don't stop, I'll spend every waking moment making you pay for it from now on."

I grin brighter, and my father's blue eyes meet mine. He's looking at me the same way I've seen him look at my brothers, and I steel my spine for the blow.

"I made him, and I can unmake him. You're a grown woman now. If you want to be collateral damage, that's your choice."

"You didn't make him. He made himself. You keep trying to destroy him, and he continues on despite you. Just like your sons."

"At least my *sons* contribute something meaningful to this world."

"In spite of you." I turn then, before I can let him see my face falter or break. He's barely spoken to me since I took Tobias's side in the big standoff. This will probably be the last time we talk for a long time. Maybe ever—and I'm going to be the one to walk away.

I WATCH HOPELESSLY from my seat in the stadium as they take the field again after halftime. I can tell he's bruised up already when I look at Quentin. They've wrapped his elbow, and he has a gash on his face that they've used butterfly tape on. He's taken an absolute beating because my father has a grudge he wants to settle.

I watch as Easton smashes his helmet against one of the opposing team's players, screaming at him and telling him to go fuck himself for touching his quarterback. The refs break them up and East takes a step back, nodding when the refs tell him to cool down. Then he's dragged back toward the line of scrimmage by two of his teammates. Quentin slaps him on the back, shaking his head and reassuring him that he's fine. I can hear him now, telling East this is just football and sometimes it's rough.

But this is next level. The tension on the field is sky-high, and it's only a matter of time before it boils over and someone does something that they can't take back. Another play sets up and Quentin has his receivers go long while East helps block. Quentin launches the ball, and it flies downfield thirty yards. His receiver catches it and takes off, but out of the corner of my eye, I see another scuffle breaking out.

Quentin's on the ground again, and the refs have thrown a flag, and again I see my brother's number in the midst of the fight. I can see him yelling at another guy from the Blaze. Quentin doesn't get up immediately, rubbing his leg and shaking his head in disgust. My gut churns with worry when the trainers run out onto the field to evaluate him. But it's the next thing that makes my heart slam against my chest. I'm up on my feet and racing toward the edge of the section.

"No. East. No!" Because my brother is racing for the other sideline, ripping his helmet off and spiking it on the ground. A couple of the guys from the Blaze are trying to block him, but he gets to our father anyway. I can't tell what he's saying, but his face says it all. Telling my father the same thing I had at the half.

Refs run over and flags go flying into the air. My father's red face turns to East, and he says something to him. I can't tell what it is, but the next thing East says is crystal clear. "Fuck. You." Whistles blow and Chaos players drag East backwards across the field, but it's too late.

"Unsportsmanlike conduct. Number 87 is ejected from the game."

The tears well up in my eyes as I watch East head for the lockers. I can only imagine the fines and the suspension that's going to follow for him, but my heart warms the slightest bit when half the stadium stands and starts chanting his name.

I'm torn for what to do. Quentin's on the sideline again, being taken into the tent to be evaluated while the backup quarterback runs out onto the field. I want to stay and see if he comes back, but I also want to be there for my brother. I turn to look at Wren and Bea.

"Go. You're the only one of us with a badge with access. Just text me he's okay?" Wren looks at me despondently.

"Okay."

"I'll text you anything about Quentin." Bea gives me a sympathetic look. I give Wren a quick hug and nod at Bea before I take off running through the stadium to get downstairs.

I FIND East in the locker room. His uniform stained from the turf and the paint on the field. He glances up at me, unfazed that I've come down here for him. He tosses his helmet onto its shelf and then sits down on the bench.

"If you came down here to lecture me, I knew what I was doing was stupid even before it happened. But I'm too fucking tired of him to care."

"I know." I sit down on the bench next to him.

"He's doing his level best to murder your guy. You should be up there."

"Wren and Bea have an eye on him. He's in the tent. I wanted to come check on you."

"I didn't just do it for Quentin. It's just years of this shit. Tobias. You. Me. Now Quentin. The way he treats us like we're disposable pawns, and he's the ultimate arbiter of right and wrong. That he can get away with this fucking head-hunting shit. If the league let's him get away with it..." East shakes his head.

"I know. It's fucked up. But you've got to pull it together and ignore him. He feeds off the attention. Off the rage we all feel toward him. Don't let him have it."

East lets out a huff and shakes his head, leaning back.

"He's gonna get Quentin fucking killed. Concussed at the very least. Trying hard to fucking tear an MCL or ACL. He and any players who do his fucking bidding should be suspended but instead, it's going to be me."

"Yeah, I don't think you're skirting a fine. Let's hope not a suspension. Hopefully, management and other players can make some appeals on your behalf, and I'll try to stir shit up on socials in your defense."

"I don't even like Quentin that much. Still warming up to him, but fuck if I'm going to watch our fucking father take him out at the knees because he's got a personal fucking vendetta. I don't think he even cares if they win the game. You think his players would at least fight for that."

"Don't worry about Dad. I'll take care of him."

East's eyes shift to mine. "You sound like Tobias now."

"Oh, he'll wish I was Tobias. If he puts anything more than a few bruises on Quentin, I'll do worse than that."

"Just be careful."

"Oh, I will. But I'm tired of the way he treats people. Especially the people I love."

East gives me a sympathetic look.

"Go back out and watch. Tell my wife I'm an idiot, but everything's fine."

"All right. Let me know if you need anything."

42

Quentin

I WAKE up in the middle of the night, uncomfortable and my whole body aching from the hits I took today. But I have an angel next to me. She fell asleep telling me how much she loved me and how she was going to fix everything however she could.

I kiss her forehead and slide my arm carefully out from underneath her. I don't want to steal any of her sleep away when she looks so peaceful, but after passing out so quickly after the game, I'm wide awake now. I wander out to the living room and settle in on the couch, groaning a little at my lower back.

The beating I took was definitely the worst of my career. I've taken worse one-offs. Had a concussion before, but never anything so consistently brutal. I was pounded into the turf over and over again and slammed with one driving hit after another. I am lucky I can still walk at this point, but I doubt I'll be able to sleep well for a few weeks with every inch of my body aching like this.

I turn on the TV and try to find a comfortable way to sit, one where not too many parts of my body touch each other or another surface, but it's damn near fucking impossible. I flip through channels and give up, opting instead for some on-demand show about unexplored places on earth. I'm lost in it for a while before I hear the soft pad of feet across the floorboards.

"How long have you been up?" Madison asks as she leans over me from behind and kisses the top of my head.

"I don't know. An hour or so. I can't sleep. I keep waking up from laying too long in one position and it throbbing like fucking hell."

"Did you take the pain pills the doctor prescribed?"

"I took some earlier. I don't want to take more than the minimum for the inflammation. They give me fucking hyperrealistic nightmares."

"Do you want ice? Or an ice bath?"

"Then I *will* be wide awake." I give her a sidelong glance.

"Just trying to think of something that would help. I know Tobias swears by them."

"Yeah well, Tobias is insane, and I think he could sleep through a tornado if he needed to."

"I have another idea." I can tell what she means by her tone even if I didn't see the cheeky smirk forming on her lips.

"Fuck. I wish. Any of that would probably fucking kill me. Might be worth it, but I think I'd rather hold off in the hopes I might get more chances than this last one."

"What if I'm on my knees, and I'm careful not to touch you otherwise?" She rounds the couch and gets between me and the coffee table.

The idea is fucking tempting. Having her sweet little mouth

wrapped around my cock would definitely be distracting. The way she touches me is so good that I might even forget the pain for a few minutes at least.

"Getting off might help you get some sleep too," she adds like she can hear my thoughts.

"Fuck..." I groan, running a hand over my face. "I can't return the favor right now. Everything hurts too much and I don't—"

I'm cut off when she takes the tank top off that she has on and the shorts follow a moment later, creating a small pile of light cotton laundry on the couch next to me.

"I can take care of myself for a few nights while you recover. Having you in my mouth gets me close anyway." She gently nudges my knees for me to spread wider, and then nods to my sweats.

I reach for them, my cock already going hard at the sight of her. She's a perfect fucking angel, and I don't deserve her. Not in this life or the next. But the guilt washes over me.

"Madison..."

"You'd be doing me a favor. You took the beating because of me, and I feel guilty for that. The least I can do is give you a few minutes of relief. Doing something I love to do anyway."

"Okay... I'm too weak to say no to you when you're like this." My eyes drift over her body, and I watch as her hands slip over her breasts teasing her nipples and then down between her thighs. She closes her eyes, using her finger to rub her clit a few times. I pull my cock out as I watch her, stroking it to get myself ready for her. A little gasp pops out of her mouth and goes straight to my cock. I groan and her eyes flutter open, taking me in as a smile spreads over her face.

"So good for me," she whispers and the praise makes me so hard I ache for her. Her fingers wrap around me gently, and she starts to stroke them over my cock. "Just tell me if anything hurts. Grab my hair if you want. Whatever makes it feel good for you, okay?"

"Fuck, Madness. Anything you do makes it good."

Her tongue teases along the underside and the warmth of it travels up my cock and through my body. I can feel the tension in my muscles start to ease as her mouth wraps around me, slowly taking me in inch by inch. She works me over in rhythm with her hand, teasing me with her tongue and sucking and licking my cock until I'm fucking lost in it. I slip my fingers through the strands of her hair and gently press them against the back of her head, letting her know she can go harder for me. A little moan of approval comes out of her when I bump the back of her throat, and she sucks harder in the wake of it.

I open my eyes and watch as she uses her free hand to play with her nipple, teasing it with her nails as her hips slowly rock forward as she takes me a little deeper. I can tell she's desperate to be touched, and I hate that I can't do it for her.

"Touch yourself for me." I slip my hand down the side of her face and cup her cheek. Her eyes flutter open, but she frowns and continues. "Madness."

She pulls away and shakes her head. "This is about you."

"Yeah, and I want to see you come. You have one of your toys with you?"

"No."

"Drawer under the side table." I nod and she frowns but reluctantly opens it and pulls out my massage gun. Her brow shoots up as she gives me a sidelong glance.

"Turn it on the lowest setting."

"Sounds like you've done this before." Her lashes lift, and she gives me a suspicious look.

I toss one of the couch pillows down between her legs and smirk. "No. Just fantasized a lot about using it on you. If you put it in between, I think it'll help you where I can't."

"I'm really fine. I can wait."

"And I really love the way you suck me off when you're close to coming yourself. So you *are* doing it for me."

She relents, turning it on to a low hum and sliding it between her legs, wedging it against the pillow as she leans forward. I watch her lashes flutter and a small curse come out of her.

"Oh god. That is good. I don't... I'm going to come. *Soon*."

"Good. Finish us both off, Madness."

She leans forward and takes me in her mouth again, and she's rougher and sloppier in the way she sucks me this time. It's exactly what I need.

"Fuck, your mouth is so fucking sweet and perfect. So, so fucking good. Gonna fucking come..." I groan and my vision goes black as I feel the fucking wave of it hit me hard. It radiates through my body, and I forget myself for a moment. Too fucking lost in how good it feels to think straight. My eyes open when I realize she's been swallowing me down, a devious little grin on her face as she swipes at the corner of her mouth. "That's my good girl. You come with me?"

She nods and hands the pillow back up to me. I can't help but think how gorgeous she is. Her lips puffy and her cheeks pink. I just want to have her like this always—sated and happy.

"Feel any better?" she asks as I hear her click the massage gun off.

"What pain?" I give her a lazy smile.

"I'll get you a washcloth." She stands, bending down to kiss me. I'm half tempted to pull her into my lap, but I know she'd yell at me for risking more pain when she's worked so hard to give me some relief.

"Thank you."

She comes back a few moments later, and we both get cleaned up and she puts her clothes back on, settling next to me on the couch.

"I'm sorry for what happened today. I know it's my fault." She traces a soft line down my leg.

"It's not your fault. You didn't do anything. I did. And he can do his fucking worst. He won't drive me away this time. You know that, right?"

"I know but I'm not sure it's worth all this."

"Madness, I'll do this every week if it means I get to keep you. I don't think you realize how much I love you. How empty the years without you felt, especially now... when somehow, you're even more than I remember." I run my fingers over the soft skin of her thigh, and she places her hand on top of mine.

"I love you, Quentin. I'm just scared, I guess. You're the only man I've ever really loved, and I lost you once and I'm scared to lose you again. That this will all be too much for you. Me and my crazy family. All this drama. It's a lot. You could have something simpler somewhere else. I know right now it's new again, but long term..."

"I told you, Madness. You and me *always*."

43

Madison

THE NEXT DAY after we wake up late, have breakfast, and take a long morning shower where I can thoroughly catalog all the bruises my father put on him, I'm set on revenge. No contact isn't enough for me anymore. I want to punish him. Annihilate him. Destroy the man from the inside out, so he can never hurt another person I love. Which is how we end up at Easton's house with Tobias on a video call listening to me rant about all the ways I hate our father.

"The league will investigate the headhunting. They'll be fined and punished." Tobias tries to reassure me.

"Will they? It seems like the refs are in on it. Like the league is in on it. Or at the very least he thinks he has enough power that they won't try to stop him."

"I mean, they'll absolutely fine him. They'll fine East too."

"And East's fine will probably be worse."

"So be it." East shakes his head.

"And what's it going to be anyway... a hundred, maybe two hundred thousand dollars? It'll barely be enough to get his attention. I want him to hurt for this."

"Just stay away from him. Not talking to him is the best thing I've ever done." Tobias sounds nonchalant on the other end.

"Did you fucking see what they did to him? He could have fucking died, Tobias. They could have snapped his neck. Dad would have killed him on that field without a second thought. Used his own fucking players to do it."

"I saw. I'm pissed off too, but he does have a lot of power, Mads. A lot of people on his side who we'll have to fight uphill against to have him see any kind of accountability."

"What if we make a statement? The three of us condemning his behavior?" East spitballs.

"He'll have his PR people spin that so fast." Tobias shakes his head.

"He's right. He'll make it about us being petulant, ungrateful children. It'll go one cycle in the media, and we'll be lucky if people remember it right. They could just remember 'Westfield bad' and not anything more nuanced than that." I sigh in frustration.

"I think we could also just let it go. I mean you three do what you feel you need to. I'll support you however I can, but I don't need you to take a stand for me." Quentin rubs a circle on my lower back, and I offer up a half smile.

"It's about more than that. He has to be stopped. I think he might even have told his own offensive line to play like shit yesterday. I think he wanted to threaten A.J. too."

"I mean our defense has been on fire this year. Cooper and the other pass rushers have just been fast as fuck." East throws his hands wide.

"Yes, but they got to the championship game last year in

part because of their O-line. A.J.'s the kind of quarterback who needs an extra second. They were giving him none yesterday," I counter.

"Okay, we're getting off topic. Let's stay on the subject. I haven't watched the game from yesterday, obviously. I'll try to find some tape. But you guys think he wasn't just headhunting but that the refs were blatantly ignoring it?"

"They were ignoring it or they fucking can't see. It's one or the other," East growls.

"I know at least one of the times, the ref was standing right by me when I took a late hit. Not a little late, a full two seconds late. The stadium booed when they saw the replay, and nothing. No flag."

"They really need to make no-calls challengeable," I huff.

"Do you know what the game would look like if they did that?" East raises a brow at me. "Everyone would have a grievance."

"Okay. Okay. So we get the tape, and we stitch together the evidence and send it to the commissioner." Tobias starts to formulate a plan.

"And we drop it online. I think we give it to the fans. Let them blow it up. Have them tagging the commissioner and anyone else who will listen. Stir the pot as fast as we can," I suggest.

"It still might take more than that. Especially with the refs. To prove they purposefully looked the other way..."

"Someone will have to go through a lot more tape. This would have to be a pattern for anyone to take it seriously."

"Bea and I can watch the tape."

"That's going to take dozens of hours," East notes.

"Well, it takes what it takes."

"And your job in the meantime?" Wren pipes in.

"It can be the first thing you hire us to do." I look to Quentin and he nods.

"Okay. So that's for starters. I'm going to talk with A.J. too."

"About what?" Tobias asks.

"To see if he thinks anything untoward was going on yesterday too. If any of his guys might corroborate."

"That's a big ask, and an awkward position to put him in."

"He owes me a favor."

"He wouldn't even be in that position if it wasn't for me." Quentin looks remorseful.

"It's water under the bridge. He's a friend. And he's an honest person. He'll tell me if he thinks there's something rotten going on."

"Let's hope so." Tobias sounds unconvinced.

"It's better than nothing, Tobias. We have to start some-where." I can hear the conviction in East's tone. He was furious yesterday and the anger has stayed with him. I'm not sure if he already felt protective over Quentin or if it's just that he's as tired of our father's bullshit as I am at this point. It's probably a bit of both.

"You're right. I just could have lived without having to hear his name or talk about him again. I was enjoying my Coach-Westfield media blackout."

"It's just temporary. Hopefully, with a good ending that lets us all go back to what we actually want to be able to do with our time." I try to put a positive spin on our situation.

"Let's hope."

44

M adison

"SHOULDN'T the realtor meet us here? There's no lock box." I frown a little and shift on my feet as we stand outside a gorgeous older home Quentin has brought me to see. It's massive but it still has so much character: a wraparound porch with balustrades, a massive tower on one side, so much detailing with spandrels and carved panels, beautifully gabled roof lines, and decorative shingles. It's hard not to stare at every little detail that went into the place.

"Just went on the market. They let me have the key. It's not exactly like I can hide from the consequences. I think they know who I am."

"I guess. It just makes me nervous."

"It's fine. I promise," he reassures me.

"It's a nice porch out here though. I like it. You could put some pumpkins and mums out here for the fall. A few spider webs and a wreath for Halloween. Oh, and we could put a couple of rocking chairs out here. What do you think?"

"I think you're already decorating the place." He grins.

"Maybe a little bit. But it's so cute." I smile at the painted door and the stained-glass window on the front of it.

Quentin ushers me inside and then flips on the lights for us. I'm stunned when I see the immensity of it. A massive staircase at the end of the entryway and rooms and hallways that dart off from the main entrance. I walk into the side office, running my fingers over the bookcases and peek back out at the view through the window. A view of the porch and the lawn out front—not that there's much of one as it's full of flowers and hedges.

Then I walk down the hallway to the kitchen. It's been completely redone and it's like someone had a handbook to every single thing I like—from the colors of the cabinets to the counters. Everything about it's perfect. I see a door at the far end and when I open it, there's a massive pantry. It has an extra fridge, a second dishwasher, a fancy ice maker, and a small prep sink too. My jaw drops, and I turn around and look at Quentin.

"Okay but seriously, what are the odds? It's like all the perfect things!"

"Yeah? You should see upstairs."

"What's upstairs?"

"A loft and a media room, a few smaller bedrooms, and bathrooms. But the master bed and bath are pretty nice."

I run up the steps, letting my fingers skate over the banister on the way up. This place feels like home already, and I think I might be ready to beg Quentin to put an offer on it just so that I can stay here sometimes. I definitely can't afford it. Not in this neighborhood or at this size with all these perfect finishes. There's another stained-glass window at the top of the stairs, one that has a scene that could be straight out of an Austen novel. A blue-green sea of grass that ends in a cliff that dives off into sparkling azure waters.

"Take a left up there." Quentin makes his way up the stairs behind me, and we walk through the rest of the bedrooms. They're all adorable in their own way. Quirky with the way the gabled roof and the architecture create the interior, but beautiful all the same.

"I love these so much. There's just so much character in this place. But the way they've updated it all... It's like they cared about keeping it authentic as much as possible. Not just tearing everything apart. Whoever their contractor was, we'll have to find out."

"This way. The master's down here." He urges me on, a smile on his face as I follow him.

When the door opens, I gasp at the sight of it. The room is huge, and a glass fireplace sits in the center of it, dividing it into the space with the bed and a sitting area on the other side. I start to walk that way but Quentin wraps his hand around my wrist and gently tugs me back toward him.

"First, look at the bathroom."

I raise a brow at his excitement for the bathroom when there's an obviously gorgeous seating area surrounded by windows right in front of me, but I follow him anyway. The bathroom is exactly like the kitchen. Every detail is the way I would want it. A massive two-person shower that lines the wall, a tub tucked in front of a window that overlooks the back of the house, and his and hers sinks and vanities. Two huge doors go off to the sides of the room and Quentin turns the light on to illuminate his and hers closets. Complete with custom shelving.

"Okay. This is honestly a little eerie. Whoever picked all this had good taste. But I need to see the sitting area." I walk back toward the fireplace and Quentin flicks a switch that lights the fire, blue flames coming up from the black crystals at the bottom of it.

When I walk around to the other side though, I come up short. There's a large plaid blanket on the floor along with a bottle of champagne and two glasses.

"Um, I feel like we maybe aren't supposed to be in here. Are you sure the realtor said it was all right?" I turn back to look at Quentin, but he's disappeared. At least until I look down and see him on one knee.

"What... What are you doing?" My voice is shaky, and I take half a step back trying to process what I'm seeing.

He doesn't answer and just pulls a box out of his pocket, opens it, and then holds it out for me to take. I stare at him blankly for a moment, trying to make sense of it before I take it from him. It's a gorgeous ring. Exactly what I would have picked. Simple. Elegant. Just a plain teardrop diamond on a solid gold band.

"There's an inscription inside. If you hold it near the fire, there should be enough light that you'll be able to read it." He says it with the kind of confidence that sounds like he knew it would be like this.

I pull the ring out and move it, so I can see the inscription. I turn it slowly and read the words to myself silently. My heart pounds in my chest as I do it.

*If I loved you less, I might be able to talk about it
more.*

The tears come. Fast and furious, streaming down my cheeks before I even realize I'm crying. The quote is one of my favorites from Austen. When I look up at Quentin, he's crying too. Not as wild as I am, but the tears are there in the corners of his eyes threatening to spill over.

"You know who I am," he says softly, echoing the rest of the words. "You understand me."

"Yes. Yes. A million times, yes." I slip the ring on and then fall to my knees and wrap my arms around him.

"I love you," he whispers. "More than I can take. Being away from you has felt like torture. Like my heart was outside my chest. I want you forever, Madness."

"I want you forever too. And the ring, Quentin. I love it so much. You know me so well."

He kisses me softly, and I melt into him. When we finally break from it he studies my face, smiling.

"What do you think about our house?"

"*Our* house?" I swipe at my tears and look around.

"Our house. I bought it when I first moved here, but I couldn't renovate it until I knew for sure you still liked the things you used to. If you still wanted the cozy old house with all the character or not."

"Is that why you took me to all those heinous ones?"

He nods and I laugh. "So clever. I can't keep up with you. But how did you know I'd say yes... That we'd fix things?"

"I always knew I wanted you back. The second you tore into me that first day like you wanted to kill me, I knew you still had feelings for me. Then it was just a matter of showing you I could finally be the guy you need. I can be a patient man when I need to be."

"But you knew or at least you thought I was in a relationship when you bought this?"

"I told you. I didn't care. It just meant the timeline was going to be a little longer."

"You're... something." I smile through my tears.

"I'm in love with you, Madness. Always have been. Maybe to the point of it being an unreasonable amount. But I don't care as long as it means my heart is back in my body and that ring is on your finger."

I hug him again, so tight, to remind myself that this is real. That I have him back. That he just proposed to me in our home. After all the years without him, how bleak everything seemed, how often I felt alone—I feel like I have to hold on tight, ground myself, to believe in it. I don't want anything to get in the way of us a second time.

"What if I said I don't want to wait to get married?"

"I'd say we get married the second you say you want to and not a moment later."

"So agreeable."

"Easy when you offer me things I want anyway."

"With the season it'll be hard, but I can look into it and see how long it will take. If there's a waiting period or not to get the license."

"Look it up tonight. Then tell me when you want to do it. If I have to skip out early on a practice and tell them I have an appointment, I will."

"I mentioned that I love you, right?"

"Once or twice. I'll never get tired of hearing it though."

He kisses me softly and I melt into him. So thankful that I finally have him—finally have *us*—again.

 uentin

LUCKILY CINCINNATI IS a lot like Vegas, and no one here believes in waiting periods for true love either. The only trouble was getting an appointment at the courthouse. But two days later, I'm standing outside a courtroom in a suit staring at the most beautiful woman I've ever seen, wearing a gorgeous white dress she picked up from a local shop. My uncle ended practice early, so he could be here with me, grumbling about how it's one of the better decisions I've ever made, but that I should have tried to make it happen in the off-season.

Easton, Wren, and Bea are all standing with Madison, taking pictures of her and with her while we wait. Cooper came over with Bea, telling me someone other than East from the team needed to be at my side, and he decided to self-appoint.

Wren and Bea between them manage to have Scarlett, Tobias, Xander, Harper, Joss, and Colt all at the ready for a video conference call once the ceremony starts. The guys are planning to take a break from their practice and the girls are all over at the museum Scarlett oversees. All of them trying to support Madison in the wake of losing her parents in one fell swoop when she and her brothers decided to officially file complaints against her father with the league alongside the Chaos, my uncle, and me.

"Undergrove and Westfield!" They call our names, and I feel the butterflies in my stomach. I glance over at Madison, and she holds her hand out for mine, smiling.

"Ready to do this?"

"I've always been ready." I squeeze her hand, and we head inside, our family and friends trailing behind.

The ceremony itself goes by in a blur. I'm repeating whatever they tell me to, exchanging the rings that we quickly bought at a local jewelry store while promising to get better ones later, just staring at Madison and how utterly beautiful she is. Thinking that I don't deserve her and trying to tell myself that this is all real, and I'm finally getting the girl—*my* girl.

"You may kiss the bride."

The words knock me back into reality, and she leans in at the same time I do. I try to be tentative and careful—respectful of the fact that we're in public, but the second her lips touch mine, I wrap my arms around her, one tight around her waist and the other threading through her hair as she turns from a bride to my wife.

I hear the low whistles from our friends, and she starts to shake in my arms, laughing as I kiss her senseless, and our friends flash their phones as they document the moment. When we finally pull away, her blue eyes stare up into mine. I've never in my entire life felt the way I do now. Like everything finally matters and is right in the world. The thought consumes me. Overwhelms me until the tears hit, and I have to kiss her one more time, just to convince myself it's real.

"I love you. Forever," she whispers against my lips.

"I love you, forever," I answer her, and then we thread our fingers together, turning to the small group of support we have, and walk out of the courthouse.

When we get outside, Madison holds up the small bouquet of roses she put together.

"Should I throw them?" She grins.

"I mean... only one person who could really catch them here." Wren looks to Bea.

"Uh... I will happily hold them for you. Take them to the preservation place and have them all ready to go. But maybe let's skip the throwing?" Bea quickly covers, ever the pragmatist.

"Yes. Just hold them for me." Madison and Bea exchange looks before she holds them out for her, and Bea takes them. I don't miss the dodge of Cooper's eyes between them and down at the flowers before he stares at Bea.

"All right. First some more pictures around the city and then to West Field for food and drinks!" Wren orders the group, and we all fall into line as she leads us toward the driver where he's waiting to let us pile into the car.

SEVERAL MORE GROUPS of players and friends come to meet us at West Field as the night goes on, congratulating us and celebrating with a toast. We have our fill of food, watching most of the Thursday night game on the screens and have way more to drink than we should have.

Easton starts passing out late night menus as Wren tells the bartender to get another round of water ready. We'd made a midseason exception to have a couple of drinks tonight but we needed food and water to balance that out.

"Um, the whole nine inches?" Madison reads off the menu and looks up at Wren. "Do I want to ask what that is?"

"It's fucking amazing is what that is."

"Your brother's invention. And title, actually." Wren gives Madison a wry smile as she raises a brow at the back of her husband's head.

"And you let him get away with it?"

"If I don't give into him sometimes..." Wren shrugs in response but her bemused expression shows how much she adores him.

"So what is it?"

"Footlong. Cincinnati chili. Cheddar cheese. And last but not least, the secret ingredient. With a side of fried pickles."

"My stomach hurts just hearing you say that. Do I want to ask what the special ingredient is?"

"Cream cheese."

"*Cream* cheese?" Madison sounds aghast.

"They put it in the dip. I decided to put it on the hotdog." Easton's self-satisfied smile widens.

"Oh my god. I just realized why you gave it this title." Wren snatches the menu and smacks Easton over the head.

"Wait until you hear the title I've got for that new chocolate cake you had the chef make." Easton grins at his wife.

"I think I might need to apologize for bringing you into this family." Madison turns to me with a sheepish grin.

"I love them. Not quite as much as I love you though." I kiss her forehead and she leans into me.

"Another round for you and Bea?" Wren nods to Madison and holds up two drinks.

"Yes. I need to give a toast!" Bea leans over and grabs the drinks.

"Okay but last one, or I'm gonna fall asleep before I even get home."

"Can't have that on the wedding night." Cooper grins at me.

BUT TRUE TO THE WARNING, when I carry Madison over the threshold she's half-asleep in my arms as she clings to me.

"I just need a quick shower, and it'll wake me right up." She yawns.

"It's fine if you're tired. It was a long day."

"Longer for you. You had practice and you're awake."

"Still…"

"It's our wedding night."

"The first of a lot of nights we're married, Madness. We've got the rest of our lives to make up for the lost time. I'll be fine."

"Nope. Showering. Perking up. You just spend your time deciding how you want me. Or you can shower with me." She gives me a devious little grin that breaks into a yawn.

"You sure you're not gonna fall asleep in the shower?"

"Positive. I'm just gonna lay down for a minute while you turn the hot water on."

"All right." I set her down on the bed, and she lays back against the pillows, giving me an adorable grin before she curls up.

I walk into the bathroom and flip on the lights, turning on the hot water and getting the towels ready before I strip out of my own clothes. It only takes me a couple of minutes, but by the time I get back out to the bedroom, she's fast asleep, breathing deep and lost in her dreams. I don't have the heart to wake her, so I just take a quick shower and head to bed.

I'm half-awake when I feel soft hands trailing over my chest and lips making their way up my throat. I feel the weight of someone on top of me and the soft tickle of her hair over my shoulder as she nips at my earlobe.

"The sun hasn't come up yet sleepyhead. We could still technically have sex on our wedding night," Madison whispers at my ear.

"Yeah?" I whisper back, opening my eyes slowly as my hands drift over her hips. I realize she's already naked and on top of me.

"Yeah," she sighs softly as she rolls her hips and brushes over my dick. I'm already going hard from the way she's touching me and when she leans down to kiss me again her nipples brush over my chest, and I wrap my hands around her ass.

"I think I like this being married thing already. Do I get to wake up like this every morning?"

"Hmm." Her eyes are closed as she concentrates, and she rolls her hips again "At least on the mornings you've been a good boy for me." She half-opens her eyes to give me a playful smile.

"I think I can handle that." I bring my hand up her side and then trail back down the center of her chest and over her stomach, lower and lower until the pad of my thumb circles over her clit. "That a good start?"

"Yes. So good..." She bites her lower lip, and her eyes shutter again as she concentrates on the sensation.

"What else do you need?"

"You inside of me." She lifts her hips again, and I grab my cock, teasing her with the tip until she lines herself up. Another soft sigh escapes her lips as she comes down on me slowly. "You feel so perfect, Quentin."

It's the kind of genuine praise from her that makes me so grateful she's mine. I keep the pressure on her clit as she starts to ride me, and her soft moans and the way she picks up her pace start to take me to the edge of my orgasm.

"I need you to come all over my cock. Show me how it belongs to you now. How much you need me to take care of this sweet little cunt every morning."

It's all the encouragement she needs, and she starts to ride me faster. She leans down to kiss me, and I wrap my hand around her throat. Her eyes open, and I see the fire in them as she starts to ride me harder, gasping as I counter her strokes. There's a little upturn at the corner of her mouth, and I'm just waiting for her to make a quip about me not being a very good boy. So I tighten my grip instead, stroking one finger down her throat and the other over her clit before I speak.

"I know, Madness. I know. But you come so much harder getting the good girl fucked out of you instead."

Those words have her breaking on the next wave, and she comes hard, whimpering as I fuck her through it and drag a blinding orgasm from me in the process. We're both nearly out of breath when she tumbles down next to me onto the pillows. She stretches one bent leg over me and curls up on her side.

"That'll cost you, you know," she teases, her fingers tracing over my jaw.

"Worth it." I smile back at her, and the little grin that appears makes heart swell in my chest.

"True," she whispers, leaning forward and kissing my cheek before she rests her head against my shoulder. I wrap an arm around her as the sun starts to peek through the windows and we finally start our first day married.

It might be ten years late. But it's better late than never.

M adison

WHEN QUENTIN OPENS the door a few nights later, my father is standing there looking flushed and pissed as fuck. Like he just walked off a plane and climbed the steps up to this apartment. Which he might have done judging by the rage that's rolling off him.

"What do you want?" Quentin moves to block the door with his body.

"Where is she?"

"Where is who?"

"Don't be a smartass, you fucking prick. My daughter."

"You don't have a daughter anymore. I suggest leaving before you embarrass yourself."

I feel my heart race in my chest. I can't believe he's here. I thought I'd be safe for the season at least. He'd be too busy with the team, too needed in Chicago, and too chronically on the road to even think of making a trip down here. I blocked his and Mom's numbers proactively and on every social media app I could think of. My stomach somersaults, and I take a step backward in the apartment. It's a mistake because he spots the movement.

"I suggest you come to this fucking door right now," my father bellows.

"We have neighbors," Quentin warns.

"Like I give a fuck about this shithole and your neighbors. All this money and you still can't fucking afford a decent place to live. Still spending it all on booze and drugs?"

"Do not talk to him that way!" I raise my voice just enough to be sure he can hear me.

"Then come to the fucking door."

"I don't want to speak to you. We have nothing to say. You had your chance. You picked door number two."

"Madison fucking Westfield... Get your ungrateful fucking ass to this door."

"That's not my name."

"Don't be a smartass. You're too old for that shit."

"Don't you fucking talk to my wife that way. You lower your fucking voice, and you talk to her civilly or you won't talk to her at all."

"Your wife," he scoffs. "As delusional as you ever were."

"No, Dad. That would be you." I walk up behind Quentin and hold up my hand, the engagement ring and the wedding band flashing in the light.

He stares at them for several seconds before his eyes shift to me in horror. "Jesus Christ, Madison. I thought after everything you'd have grown the fuck up and made better choices. I didn't love A.J. for you, but he was a hell of a lot better than trash like this."

"My husband is the best man I've ever known—the love of my life. I never stopped loving him. You just made me think I was wrong because you thought you knew better. You thought you could control everyone and everything. That's all Tobias, East, and I are to you. Puppets to be controlled. Minions to make you look better. Well, I'm done with it. They might be stuck with your name, but I'm not. I'm done with you."

"You don't know what you're saying. What you're bringing on yourself. If you think I'll just sit back while you try to destroy my career and everything I've built with your unfounded bullshit accusations, all because your boy here can't stay on his feet on the field..." He laughs, it's sardonic as hell. Creepy even. "Well, you're right. You're not my daughter anymore. Never were a very good one."

It stings like he wants it to, a bullseye to my already sore heart, but I'm not about to let on.

"You were never a good father. So I guess we're even there."

"I did everything for you. Paid for everything. You had everything you wanted. But that wasn't good enough. You had to go and instigate your fucking brothers against me. All for what? So you could slut around with trash like him?"

I see Quentin's fist ball up, and I grab his wrist just in time.

"Don't!" I shout, disrupting his one-track mind. Quentin's eyes glitter with rage but they turn to me. "He's a washed-up old man with nothing left. He knows the end is near. And what was it you always said, Dad? Hit dogs holler?"

My dad shakes his head in response, a clicking sound from his cheek as he pulls his lips to the side and then meets my eyes.

"I always did think it was too bad that it was East instead of you who was born to that bitch in Vegas. Could have left you there with her and the rest of the trash in that city. You didn't deserve everything I gave you. Such a selfish bitch."

I squeeze Quentin's wrist even tighter because I know he's baiting him. Begging Quentin to throw a punch. It's exactly what he wants. Thankfully Quentin listens to my silent plea.

"I *hate* you," I say it with the kind of finality I know it has. That any hope for reconciliation, *if* there ever was any, between us is gone. I can see that understanding reflected in his face as he looks at me one last time.

"You'll hate me more when I'm done destroying you both." He turns his back and walks down the hall, taking the steps instead of waiting for the elevator. Quentin shuts the door behind him and turns to me, concern etched all over his face.

All the adrenaline surging in my body comes to a halt, and I suddenly feel so heavy—like I have a lead weight on my chest all of a sudden, and I'm a thousand feet under water. It's only half a second before the tears come, and I collapse into Quentin's arms.

"Jesus Christ, Madison. I'm so sorry." He wraps his arms tight around me, and I bury my face in his chest.

"It's fine. It's who he is. It's who he's always been. I was just too blind to see it. I wanted him to be better than he was. I thought he could be. I should have known better," I mumble into the cotton of his shirt.

"You didn't deserve that. All that shit he said—it's bullshit. You're right. He's guilty and he's fucked. He knows it and he's trying to make everyone as miserable as he is. He knows you're better without him, and he hates it. But that's on him. Not you. You know that?"

"I know. I know." I hug Quentin tight. "But it still hurts so much to hear him say it."

"I know it does. But you don't ever have to see him again. Ever. Fuck, I might kill him if I see him again, honestly."

"He's not worth it, Quentin. He wants you to react. Was probably praying you'd hit him because it'd make everything easier for him. You can't let him have that." I pull back, searching Quentin's eyes to make sure he's hearing me. "Promise me."

"I know. I promise. But I can fantasize about it." He grins at me.

"That's true." I smile through my tears.

"I'm telling Tobias and Easton about this. Whatever the plan is, we're fucking upping it tenfold after that."

"He'll just feed off it. It's what narcissists like him do."

"Well... we'll figure out something. I'm not letting that go unanswered though. He doesn't talk to you like that."

"I love you," I whisper before he hugs me tight again.

"I love you too."

We stand like that for several minutes, and I can't help but think how I'm the luckiest person on earth. To have this man who would fight for me to hell and back and take my side every single time. The kind of love where everything else in the world could be wrong, but I know that he'll keep us safe. I'm not quite ready to let him go, but I'm also ready to collapse in a small heap on the floor.

"Ugh. That was exhausting. Now I feel like I have zero energy. All of it's been sucked into his black hole of bullshit."

"Want to watch a Jane Austen movie in bed until you fall asleep?" He kisses my forehead.

"You are the most perfect man in the world, you know that?"

"I don't know about that, but I do try to be perfect for you at least."

I kiss him softly and wipe away my tears.

"Yes. Let me just get in some PJs."

"Want any snacks?"

"Maybe a little ice cream?"

He grins at me. "You got it, boss."

Quentin

THE NEXT DAY I'm at Easton's after practice while Madison finishes up some work with the Chaos PR team. She's been working extra hours trying to get everything ready for the handoff now that we're married.

"He came here too." Easton shakes his head. "Told him to fuck off with his shit when I have a pregnant wife in the house. She doesn't need the stress."

"Where is she now?"

"Checking in on things at the restaurant. Won't be managed and doesn't want to sit down. I've at least convinced her that she can check in and doesn't need to work a full shift. Between that and visits with Gramps, she's always on her feet. Wish I could get her to settle down more."

"I imagine it'll be that way with your sister."

"Something you need to tell me?" Easton raises a brow.

"No. She's got a few things she wants to do with Bea before we think about kids. Plus, I figure I'll let you test it out first. You can tell me how it goes."

"I'm already terrified. Excited but terrified. All these baby prep books and videos and classes. I'm just fucking praying we can keep her alive."

"I'm sure you'll do fine. Cooper does it by himself part-time. Maybe he's got tips."

"Maybe." Easton makes a face like he's still thinking about the prospect of fatherhood before he shakes his head and looks at me again. "Anyway... I'm sorry you had to deal with my father. He's fucking unhinged at this point, and there's really no reasoning with him. Madison filled me in earlier today on what happened, and I'm just glad you were there for her. I know I gave you a hard time at first but..."

"It's fine. You had your reasons. I don't blame you. If I had a sister I'd probably feel the same. Honestly, even just with my cousin, Winter, I'd be furious. She's a sweet person just like Madison underneath the hard edge they both have, and I get why you're so protective of her. Just know I'd rather die than let anything ever hurt her again."

Easton nods and then lets out a sigh. "Given you're part of the family now and I know for a fact you can keep a secret... I should tell you something I know. But I need it to stay between the four of us; you, me, Madison, and Wren. I haven't even told Tobias because I don't know Scarlett well enough yet to know how this could spread."

"Okay..." I frown, worried what could be happening now and bracing for more bad news.

"A good friend of mine from college is the offensive coordinator for the Blaze. Liam Montgomery?" I nod when I recognize the name. "He started off as the quarterback coach but the way my dad and the GM like to blow through staff, he got a promotion opportunity younger than most. He deserves it though. The way he thinks about the game, he binge watches game tape and studies and restudies every move out there. Obsesses over getting every detail right. He was a phenomenal quarterback. If he hadn't gotten hurt would have been the best out there. Probably the best in generations..."

"Impressive." I'm curious where this is headed other than East reminding me I'm not his favorite quarterback. Though I'm pretty sure I'll be changing that by the end of the season.

"He has information on my dad. He was uncomfortable telling me before, obviously—it's my dad. But the stuff he has on him, if the league actually gives this whole incident a real investigation—digs deep instead of brushing it off like they sometimes do—it'll sink his career for good." East's got a somber look on his face.

"What kind of stuff?"

"Manipulation of some of his players. Off-the-books bonuses. Kickbacks to refs. Threatening coaches. Liam thinks a couple of the other coaches will come forward too. A whole pattern of behavior that the league will hate. They'll want to bury it. He's a legend, and they've protected him for so long already... But I don't think they can ignore all of us."

"Well, I'm glad to hear it. But I know that will be hard on all of you."

"He went too far this time. He's been going too far for years. God knows what else he's done that we don't know about. But I'm not about to sit by and watch it continue."

"Understandable."

"So we'll just have to brace for impact. I'm sure there will be a media storm."

"Yeah. I'm sure it's going to get ugly. Madison will want to manage it, and it's going to be too much for her."

"I'm hoping she'll read Bea in on it, and between the two of them, we can all get out of this without too much of a headache."

"I'm sure Bea will want to bear the brunt of it to protect Madison."

"And my sister will insist on throwing herself in front of the bus anyway."

I shake my head because he's not wrong. "Well, I'll put the husband-pressure on her. You put the brother-pressure on her and, hopefully, we can convince her to let Bea handle it."

I nod and we sit in silence for a moment.

"I'm sorry."

"For?"

"Your dad. Mine was an asshole too. Fucking sucks yours couldn't do better by you all."

"Well, gives me that much more motivation to do better myself on that front."

"Agreed."

Because while I'm more than happy to be patient while Madison conquers the PR world with Bea, I also can't wait for the day I get to be as happily terrified as East is over being a dad.

EPILOGUE

M adison

PENNY BURSTS through the door with our coffee orders in one hand and a stack of paperwork in the other. She's the new assistant Bea and I hired when we had an avalanche of new clients come in within the first couple of weeks of our opening. Between our clients and our construction manager, we have more meetings than we have free time. Penny's been keeping us fed and caffeinated, not to mention keeping us on task when we start to get distracted by the myriad of drama and scandals that come across our desks. Our reputations as fixers have attracted some incredibly important client accounts in just a short time, and Penny has been our lifesaver—already proving to be indispensable around here. She's the oldest daughter of the Chaos's long snapper too, so she's already well connected and knowledgeable about the football world, which has made her an amazing asset.

"I got that contract signed while I was out. Wyatt was already downtown, so I texted to see if he could meet me at the coffee shop to sign it."

"Look at you keeping the clients in line already." Bea smiles at her.

"Gunning for that promotion when you all become so popular you need a third partner." She grins as she sets our coffees down on our desks.

I grab one and take a long sip. Not much tastes better than vanilla caramel coffee with extra espresso in the afternoon after a long day. And it has definitely been one of those because my father—there needs to be a replacement word for a man who was your father but now might as well be a complete stranger —was finally getting some of his comeuppance.

The league has suspended him pending investigation, and his offensive coordinator, Coach Liam Montgomery, has taken over the team during his leave. The Blaze is doing better than ever, and from everything A.J. has said, that's in large part due to my father's absence. I can only imagine how much salt that's pouring in the wound, and while I try very hard not to be a vengeful person, I'm absolutely a fan of seeing justice being meted out. Now, I just have to hold my breath and hope that they find him guilty and make his continued employment in the league untenable.

"Another article discussing predictions for the league's findings," Bea announces as she scrolls it on her phone. She's been helping me filter the news at the insistence of my family and while I protested at first, I've been kind of happy to be able to take a step back from it. Especially since I put myself in therapy again after recommending it for so many of my players and finally, I feel like I'm coming to terms with a lot of the things that have been heaped on me by my parents over the years.

"And?"

"They think he'll be found guilty. 'Sources say Coach Westfield has a long list of offenses and witnesses that are likely to put a swift end to a once storied career.'" Bea looks up, half-concern and half-relief on her face for me.

"Good." I take another sip of my coffee. It's bittersweet that my brothers and I put this all in motion, that telling our story to the league and some of our closest friends on the Blaze meant that they finally felt confident enough to come forward with their own stories. I hate the fact that A.J. and Liam had held back so much to try to protect us. Just another thing my father took from us that I'm not sure I can ever completely undo.

My phone dings with a text and snaps me out of my melancholy when I see the name that flashes over the screen.

HUBS:

> I'm at the grocery. I got you ice cream already and some of that new protein powder you wanted. Thoughts on dinner?

> What kind of ice cream?

> Cookie Dough.

I grin at my phone and the fact he knows me so well.

> Perfect. Dinner... I don't know, you don't want to go out?

> We can go out if you want. I just thought something easy at home. We can watch an episode of something or a movie?

> We're turning into an old married couple.

> So my plan is working.

I can't help the laugh that tumbles out and both Bea and Penny look up at me.

"Something funny?" Bea raises a brow and glances down at my phone.

"Just Quen being himself."

"You two are adorable." Penny grins at me.

"They are that. We have to do some planning soon, for the big wedding party you know. I've gotten more than a few questions about when that's happening. People who didn't get to come to the courthouse want their chance to celebrate." Bea's eyes narrow a little.

"Like me!" Penny pipes in, and I smile at her.

"You're top of the list. And yes, we do. I was hoping for this whole thing to be over first, but I think I need to stop waiting and just enjoy things while I can. And getting to pick the cake and first dance and all of that does sound kind of fun."

"I wholeheartedly agree with that assessment."

"Mmm. Same. You two are my relationship goals." Penny grins at me.

Another ding from my phone and I look down. It's a picture of a grocery cart with several dinner options spread out in it along with some flowers in the corner partially cropped out.

> Flowers for your mistress again? We've talked about this.

HUBS:

> Damn. I thought I managed to cut those out. I'm sorry. I know you told me I had to quit her, but when she wakes me up in the middle of the night... I can't say no.

I laugh again and Bea shakes her head and smiles as she resumes her research. I send him a little teasing emoji and then type my response.

They're beautiful. I'll pretend to be surprised when I see them in person. And let's do the Thai.

Got it. See you at home, Madness. Love you.

I grin as I slip my phone back into my purse. I never knew I could be this happy again, but between my husband, our new PR firm, and the resort plans Bea and I have in the works with our construction manager, I think I might finally be getting the fairytale ending Quentin used to tease me about. One for both of us.

GLOSSARY

OTAs: Organized Team Activities. These are practices that occur in the offseason. They are optional and not all players attend. It's a chance for players to stay in shape and for new/rookie players to meet other players from the team or for players on the bubble to try to secure a position on the team or practice squad.

West Coast Offense: An offense that focuses more on the passing game than the running game which creates opportunities for big plays by receivers. In the non-fiction world it was developed in Cincinnati but made famous in San Francisco hence "West Coast".

Canton: Canton, Ohio is home to the Pro Football Hall of Fame

ALSO BY MAGGIE RAWDON

Plays & Penalties Series

Pregame - Prequel Short Story

Play Fake - Waylon & Mackenzie

Delay of Game - Liam & Olivia

Personal Foul - Easton & Wren

Reverse Pass - Ben & Violet

Seattle Phantom Football Series

Defensive End - Prequel Short Story

Pick Six - Alexander & Harper

Overtime - Colton & Joss

Wild Card - Tobias & Scarlett

Queen City Chaos Series

Before the Chaos - Prequel Novella

Why Choose & Dark Romance

Lords of Misrule

Thick as Thieves

ACKNOWLEDGMENTS

To you, the reader, thank you so much for taking a chance on this book and on me! Your support means the world.

To Kat, thank you for your constant help, support, and patience. I'm so grateful for you. There's no way I'd ever get a book out without you and your team!

To Autumn, for all of your support and your tireless work to help promote and support my work. So thankful for you!

To Vanessa, thank you for catching all my mistakes, being my sounding board, and helping me climb the mountain of admin work that seems to grow every time I try to tackle it.

To Emma and Shannon, thank you for your humor, encouragement, and constant support.

To Thorunn, thank you for always chatting football and fiction with me and keeping me sane through the hard writing days.

To Jenn and Ashley, thank you for taking time out of your day to give me your thoughts on Quentin and Madison's story. So grateful for your feedback and support.

To Mackenzie, for your constant support and your help finding all the best moments in this one.

To my Promo Team, thank you so much for all the support you give my characters, books, and me. I wouldn't be able to do this without you and I'm so incredibly grateful! Extra special thanks for when I was doing everything down to the wire and you had to wait patiently through that ending in *Before the Chaos*.

ABOUT THE AUTHOR

Maggie Rawdon is a sports romance author living in the Midwest. She writes athletes with the kind of filthy mouths who will make you blush and swoon and the smart independent women who make them fall first. She has a weakness for writing frenemies whose fighting feels more like flirting and found families.

She loves real sports as much as the fictional kind and spends football season writing in front of the TV with her pups at her side. When she's not on editorial deadline you can find her bingeing epic historical dramas or fantasy series in between weekend hikes.

Join her newsletter here for sneak peeks and bonus content:
https://geni.us/MRBNews
Join her readers' group on FB here:
https://www.facebook.com/groups/rawdonsromanticrebels